NUMBER 103

Edited by

John P. Gunnison

• **Cromba Has A Thousand Spears by John Peter Drummond...........pg 4**
• **Golden Claws of Raa by John Peter Drummond.........................pg 58**

 Additional copies, as well as library or wholesale discounts, are available through Adventure House, 914 Laredo Road, Silver Spring, MD 20901 or through Diamond Book Distribution Company and Diamond Comic Distribution Company.

Subscription Rate - $45.00 - 6 Issues - Advertising Rates - Full Page - $75.00.

Printed in the United States of America

ISBN: 1-59798-177-X
ISBN-13: 978-1-59798-177-4

First Adventure House Edition November 2008

Fiction House was a busy publisher. Not only did they publish a fairly extensive line of popular pulp magazines, but also a burgeoning line of comics. So I guess we can forgive their little peccadillos that plagued not only their editorial staff, but other companies as well. Where am I going with this? Well Fiction House was fairly well known for their mis-numbering spines and contents pages with incorrect volume and number data. But for a pulp publisher, a mistake of a story title was made only once in a blue moon. If one looked on the cover...right there for the world to see ZOMBA Has A Thousand Spears...yet low and behold on the contents page CROMBA Has A Thousand Spears. Does that mean our hero Ki-Gor had to go up against two people with an aggregate of two thousand spears? Just for the heck-of-it...I've decided to keep the goof and leave the title as ZOMBA and the interior as CROMBA. Go figure.

"Zomba Has A Thousand Spears"
by John Peter Drummond

When assegais-wise Masai warriors quailed before the twin-fanged beasts of the Black Vengeance Monster, Ki-Gor knew that captive Helene was doomed to die . . . Unless his lion-thewed strength alone could crush those snarling devil-dogs!

PLUS

"The Golden Claws of Raa"
by John Peter Drummond

Sam Slater, cobra-eyed merchant of warrior-flesh; Mog, the gorilla with human blood on his dagger-like teeth—and Raa, white queen of the ape legions . . . these were Ki-Gor's enemies in a battle that only the voodoo of Fate could decide!

Happy Reading

John P. Gunnison
gunnison@adventurehouse.com

Ki-Gor unsheathed his dagger as Thor's blade swung down!

CROMBA HAS A THOUSAND SPEARS

By JOHN PETER DRUMMOND

When assegais-wise Masai warriors quailed before the twin-fanged beasts of the Black Vengeance Monster, Ki-Gor knew that captive Helene was doomed to die . . . unless his lion-thewed strength alone could crush those snarling devil-dogs!

KI-GOR moved along the shadowed path at a silent, tireless trot. His face was troubled. N'Geeso, the pygmy chieftain, agreed with him that the only wise course was to make an immediate trip to the Masai lands.

Perhaps they were becoming upset over nothing, but they both sensed something ominous in the continuing silence of the Masai drums. Over a period of three days the pygmy drummers had called to Tembu George, telling him of the two Masai warriors found slain near Ki-Gor's camp. It was in no way like him not once to answer or acknowledge their message.

Ki-Gor's mind flicked to the two dead natives whose bodies had been found on alternate days. There was a strangeness about their manner of dying which puzzled him. It was strange also that they not only came unannounced into the pygmy area, but that they failed to travel together.

His pace slowed as the murmurous

splash and fall of water reached his ears. It was the sound of the clear, cool stream beside which he and Helene made their permanent home. He realized now he had made a mistake in not telling Helene his worries at the very first. As it was, he had to spring the idea of the trip on her suddenly, and it hadn't been a hand of days since he had solemnly assured her he would not stir from his homefire for a moon.

A thin white ribbon of smoke rose from the fire. Through breaks in the great shade trees, golden columns of sunlight thrust down to the earth, and at the upper end of the camp the singing water rushed over the falls in a shimmering burst.

Ki-Gor's glance searched the camp for his red-haired mate. Failing to find her, he had stopped uncertainly when, from the corner of his eye, he caught a flickering movement across the pool. He turned in time to see the white flash of a body knife into the pool.

He smiled, abruptly reassured, and swiftly reached the water's edge. He leaned forward, staring into the depths where brilliant-hued fish cut nervous patterns against the clean gravel of the bottom. Carried by the momentum of the dive, he watched the slim form arcing down through the water in a swirl of bubbles.

The bubbles and the dance of the sun through the water briefly cloaked the gliding feminine figure from Ki-Gor's gaze. She angled toward the bank on which he stood, swimming along the bottom with quick, graceful strokes. He saw her then with sudden clarity as she swept close beneath him, playfully twisting half-over on her back in an effort to touch a startled *nuhuana* fish.

He saw her hair streaming dark against the fairness of her body, saw the full, taut beauty of her breasts, the supple lines of her soft-curved hips and long, beautiful legs. Ki-Gor stared, a queer, almost foolish look possessing his face. Then he gave a low, astonished cry and started back from the stream so hastily he nearly stumbled.

The woman in the water wasn't Helene!

He had never seen the woman before. There were few enough white residents in this remote section of the Congo and all of them were men. Where had she come from? What was she doing frolicking unclothed about his camp?

Ki-Gor was utterly confused for a moment. Then as he thought of Helene, he threw a guilty look over his shoulder, half-expecting to see her staring reproachfully at him.

But when he found the camp still deserted, he began to wish fervently that his wife would appear.

Except for Helene, Ki-Gor knew little of women. His life in the jungle had given him no opportunity for association with them. He had no notion of his own attractiveness for women.

The swimmer's hard breathing had stopped now, and Ki-Gor was uneasily aware of how quiet she had become—too quiet. Involuntarily, he turned to look for her.

She was facing him, slowly and silently treading water, inspecting him from head to toe with her large, dark eyes. She appeared completely unperturbed.

"I've waited long for you, Ki-Gor," she said in a husky voice, and the faint pout of her full lower lip seemed to accuse him of deliberately keeping her waiting.

He blinked. "For me?"

"Yes," she said. Then unexpectedly, she added, "You're very nice, Ki-Gor, much nicer than I expected." Her glance slid like the touch of fingers from his blond mane over his firm-jawed face and down his powerful, bronzed body.

FOR THE FIRST time in his life, Ki-Gor felt uncomfortable because he wore no more than a narrow length of leopard skin fitted tightly around his loins. By all the gods, what manner of woman was this? He retreated a few steps, looking away across the pool, wondering if she didn't realize the water about her was no more concealing than thin air.

"Uh...my wife...you've seen Helene?" the White Lord gulped.

"Oh yes," conceded the girl airily, "I saw her."

Ki-Gor nervously looked about the camp again. "She's here?"

The girl looked down through the

water. "Oh no," she said without interest, "she's gone."

Ki-Gor stiffened in sudden alarm.

"You do know Helene, don't you?" he asked.

"Yes," she said. "Red hair. Blue eyes."

He felt his first small trickle of relief. Thank heavens, this was some friend of Helene's. If she were here by Helene's invitation, then no doubt the girl was all right, despite her strange ways. But where in the world had she come from?

"Wh...when did Helene say she'd be back?" the worried jungle man questioned.

The girl looked straight at him, her raven-dark eyebrows arching in surprise. The expression accentuated the faint upward tilt of her eyes at the outer corners. There was something wild and devilishly pagan about her.

"We didn't talk," she declared. "I have no idea where she went and no interest in when she returns."

Ki-Gor's jaw dropped. "But you said..." he began.

"I said I saw her," the girl said with a hint of exasperation. "But she didn't see me. I watched her most of the morning and even followed her awhile after she left the camp."

The red stain of her mouth quirked belittlingly.

"She's like a child in the jungle," she said. "She never suspected my presence, and a dozen times I was almost close enough to reach out and touch her. Pfaugh! Such a mate for Ki-Gor to have!"

"Look here!" burst out Ki-Gor. "Just who are you and what are you doing here?"

Bewildered though he was, there was a hint of growing anger in Ki-Gor's voice. The girl smiled for him, black lights swimming in eyes suddenly gone wide and engaging. Nothing was left of the vixenish cast which had crept into her expression as she spoke of Helene.

"I'm Neeba," she said softly, "and I came to see you." She swam four graceful strokes to the bank, and supporting herself with one arm on the edge, she held the other out to Ki-Gor. "Help me out," she requested in the most natural manner possible, "so we can talk."

Ki-Gor looked at her against his will. He wavered distractedly, not knowing what to do. But her slim arm remained raised to him, and there was something in her face which made him feel he would appear a greater fool by backing away than by doing her bidding.

He went quickly forward, his glance directed over and beyond her. Her hand, cool from the water, was small and strong as his powerful, calloused fingers closed over it. She made a low, indistinct sound of pleasure at the easy strength with which he swung her from the water.

The very momentum with which he lifted her brought her bare body close against him. He tried to step back, but she made no effort to avoid the contact, even seeming to sway forward more than necessary as the wet softness of her brushed against his muscled bulk.

As swiftly as he could he turned away from the girl and walked with hurried steps toward the campfire.

"Wait!" she cried. "Don't you wish to hear what I have to say?"

Gruffly, he replied, "I'll hear—after you've dressed."

"You don't find me beautiful?" she asked, surprised.

"No!" he snapped, and kept walking.

She was silent a few moments, watching his broad-shouldered back, her brow wrinkled in a puzzled frown as she analyzed what he had said, the tone in which he had said it. Then slowly a smile lighted her face and she gave a husky, understanding laugh.

Standing wide-legged by the fire, Ki-Gor heard her laugh and blood darkened his deeply bronzed features. He heard the light, quick pad of her feet as she ran along the edge of the pool. All was quiet for a minute, and then she approached behind him.

"You can turn now," she bid him in an innocent, little-girl's voice.

He swung to face her, resolved promptly to dispose of whatever queer business she had on her mind. She was smoothing her hastily donned garment with her hands. It was hardly the garb he expected to find on an English-speaking woman.

The rust-colored cloth was loosely woven, fashioned into a kind of singlet, cut low at the shoulders and supported by a single strap. Her shapely legs were left uncovered by the garment's briefness, and the material was drawn tightly about her waist by a belt of copper mesh.

"I'm dressed wrong?" she asked. She fingered the cloth sadly, then abruptly anger touched her. Her lips sheered back from her white teeth and she faced Ki-Gor like a spitting cat.

The girl's rage sobered Ki-Gor. He saw how swiftly her control shattered, knew a second before it happened that she would fly at him.

"I'll teach you!" Her knife flashed free of its sheath and she leaped at Ki-Gor, aiming the glittering length of steel at his throat.

HE DODGED aside with desperate speed, his left hand shooting out to grip her wrist. So fast was she, she almost eluded his fingers. The she-devil is as wild and dangerous as a lioness, Ki-Gor thought, and he shoved her arm up more roughly than he had first intended.

She lunged at him, flailing with her free arm, trying to tear his eyes out with her sharp nails. In self-defense, Ki-Gor had to grasp both her wrists, shove her arms high above her head so that she was held helplessly on tiptoe.

"You crazy little fool," he snapped, "I should shake your teeth out of your head."

He still held her hands so high she could only wriggle futilely. He hadn't troubled to pry the knife from her fingers. She quieted as he spoke, her contorted features relaxing.

They stood no more than six inches apart. The violence of her exertions had left her panting. She had to raise her head to look into his eyes.

"And you didn't mean either that you thought me ugly, clothed or unclothed?" she asked with an odd seriousness.

"No, I didn't mean you were ugly," he said, anxious to be finished of this queer female.

"I am prettier than most white women?" she inquired.

"Yes, yes!" Ki-Gor distractedly agreed, willing to say anything to keep her quieted.

To his relief, she immediately brightened. No sign of her rage remained. He cautiously loosened his grip on her wrists, testing her.

But just as he was about to turn her loose, she frowned again.

"Answer me one more thing, Ki-Gor," she requested. "Would most white men find me—how do you say—welcome?"

"I'm quite sure they would," he hastily assured her.

He turned her wrists loose, thankfully watched her sheath her dagger. He really wouldn't breathe easily again until she left the camp.

"Forgive me, Ki-Gor," she begged with sudden humility. "I misunderstood how you felt about me. I was so hurt and disappointed—and so afraid of what my father would say when I had to go back and face him—that I lost my head. The last thing in the world I actually wanted to do was stab you."

The woman had been talking almost steadily since he first confronted her, but Ki-Gor hadn't been able to piece any sense from her disjointed statements until the frightened way she mentioned her father.

At last, he thought he could see some light somewhere.

His tight-drawn nerves relaxed. She'd run away from home, probably because of some childish quarrel with her father, and she thought to take refuge in his camp. No doubt, she'd been alone in the jungle several days, upset by what she had done, and her nerves were completely unstrung because of her solitary experiences in a dangerous land.

Ki-Gor's features softened. "So that's what all this is about," he declared sympathetically. "You've run away from home." He smiled He scratched his cheek thoughtfully. "Is your father a trader or a plantation owner? You'll have to give me some idea where his place is located."

The girl gave him a baffled look. Then slowly she shook her head.

"I didn't run away from anywhere," she said. "Oh, no! It was my father who sent me to your camp." She hesitated, a slight embarrassment touching her. Her cheeks colored. "He said it was high time for me to get married and he said you'd make the best husband for me."

II

KI-GOR was too thunderstruck by the girl's words to speak.

"You see now why I was so upset when I thought you didn't like me," she continued brightly. "Why I just couldn't go back and tell him you wouldn't have me. Besides," she said, as though admitting him to a secret, "after seeing you, I *like* the idea of marriage."

Ki-Gor's throat worked spasmodically as he sought to make his voice function. "Of all the crazy things I ever heard," he exploded, "this is the craziest! What on earth kind of father do you have," he sputtered incoherently. "He must know that I'm married and, when did white men start sending their daughters around through the jungle as gifts?"

She listened calmly while he stormed. She fluffed her long, black hair over her shoulders to hasten its drying.

"Of course, we knew you had a wife," she said, "but what is that to get excited about? The native chieftains and their foremost warriors and hunters take many wives. Certainly, you are greater than any of them."

She eyed him approvingly, continuing to caress her hair with her hands.

"I don't object to your having another wife, so why should you be so concerned?" she pointed out matter-of-factly.

"Of all the. . . !" choked Ki-Gor, but he was too stunned to express himself adequately.

"It's not as if you were recently wed to Helene," she said. "Had that been the case, naturally I wouldn't have come to you. But as my father says, you've had more than enough time to be ready to welcome a second wife, and he also explained that in the way of first wives, Helene will sulk a little at first, but in time will accustom herself to the idea."

The White Lord gave an incoherent growl of anger. "Let's go see this father of yours," he barked. "There are a few things he's going to be set straight on. Let's start right now!"

She lowered her eyes, a half-smile playing shyly about her lips.

"He said we weren't to visit him," she said huskily, "until we could bring him a grandson."

"What!" roared Ki-Gor.

"We mustn't anger him," she warned, "by going against his wishes. But don't worry, I promise you to make good his wish and then he will be so pleased to see us."

Ki-Gor raised his knotted fists, shook them futilely at the sky.

"I swear I'll give that dango the beating of his life," he shouted, "and then send him down to the coast in a cage to be locked up. He's worse than a slave-dealing Arab. And his own daughter!"

He gestured at the girl with savage impatience.

"Take me to him," he commanded.

She backed away a few steps, suddenly watchful.

"I don't know what you're talking about, Ki-Gor," she said quickly, "but don't be a fool. No man opposes Thor. Believe me when I say you'll be signing your own death sentence if you don't marry me."

So that's his name, thought Ki-Gor. It was a strange name for a white man, and one which he'd never heard anywhere in the Congo.

"I like you, Ki-Gor, and I don't want you to die," the girl added pleadingly. "Why must you act so strangely? You said yourself you found me attractive. Marry me, then, and seek no trouble from Thor."

The girl's frightened air somewhat sobered Ki-Gor. Why should she be so terrified? She acted as though her father were some grim and awful diety.

"Don't be afraid," he told her. I mean you no harm. I can't say I understand this mess, but you appear to be more the victim than anyone concerned. Now take me to Thor and I'll get to the bottom of all this. It'll be to your advantage, I promise you."

Ki-Gor had dropped his spear beside the pool when he helped the girl from the water.

He started toward the weapon now. He heard Neeba's sudden gasp.

"Just stop where you are, Ki-Gor!" a flat, cold voice behind him commanded.

It wasn't Neeba's voice. Someone else had crept into the clearing. He halted, began slowly and cautiously to turn so he might see the newcomer. There would be time enough to deal with any threat, without taking unnecessary chances. Could it be that Thor himself had come to confront him?

"No tricks, now," the toneless voice warned. "You're not dealing with the simple little Neeba. There's nothing I'd like better than to put this spear through you."

"You!' cried Neeba. "Why'd you have to come back? I told you I could handle this."

The unseen person gave an ugly, disparaging laugh. "I've seen how well you've been handling it, my dear. I've been watching your antics from the edge of the jungle."

Then Ki-Gor was turned far enough to see the newcomer. His eyes widened. Could his vision be playing him tricks?

A second girl, the exact physical counterpart of Neeba stood in the clearing. In face, form and dress the two were identical twins, but it took only a glance to tell Ki-Gor that in other than looks they were little similar.

WHERE Neeba was like a healthy young animal, hot-blooded, uninhibited, fiercely alive, the newcomer displayed a sneering coldness. There was no dance of fire in her eyes, only a dark, flinty hardness. In contrast to Neeba's easy litheness, she held herself with a tense rigidity.

"Don't stare so stupidly," she snapped at the White Lord. "Yes, I'm Neeba's sister, though after seeing her performance I take small pride in admitting it."

Neeba's face was pale with emotion. "You're a dirty sneak, Vani! Thor told you to let me alone. He preferred this done my way, and he said to give me a chance."

Vani, her eyes glued to Ki-Gor, kept her slim, barbed-pointed spear raised shoulder high for an instant thrust. Her concern was for him, not her sister. Negligently, from the corner of her mouth, she threw her answer at Neeba.

"I finished my job, so I came back. It's lucky I did." She sniffed. "Thor must be failing in his mind to think that this bull ape would want you for a wife. There's only one way to handle this fellow, and that's what I propose to do."

"No!" shouted Neeba. "Don't you dare! You're deliberately trying to ruin everything for me."

Ki-Gor was puzzled. The enmity between the sisters was too bitter to have been inspired by this current misunderstanding alone.

"If I might say a word," he told them with weary patience, "I think I can remove any cause for your quarrel. This whole thing is utterly ridiculous. I don't propose to marry Neeba under any circumstances. Now you, Vani, put that spear away before somebody gets hurt, because you're even crazier than your sister if you think I can be forced to take a second wife."

Vani's features twisted with an ironic smile.

"You quite misunderstand me," she said hoarsely. "I'm not interested in forcing you to marry anyone." She paused for a moment, while the smile grew crueler. "I mean to kill you! That's all I'm interested in doing."

Ki-Gor had heard threats uttered against his life by more than one enemy. Those men had hated him, and though they had voiced their threats in different ways, their flaming hatred had been apparent in every word, every gesture. But the flat, passionless tones of Vani somehow carried a greater deadliness than any of the others.

"Let him alone, Vani," broke in Neeba. "He'll have me, I tell you, if you'll give him a chance."

Vani made no reply. Instead, her eyes abruptly narrowed and she pivoted slightly, swinging her spear up and back. The line of her body, the rigid set of her lips revealed that she was about to send the spear hurtling into the White Lord.

For once, the chain lightning reactions of the jungle man were slowed. It was all too unreal, too impossible. It just couldn't be that a girl he had never set eyes on before would kill him in cold blood. He had his knife at his belt, and against a man, he would have gambled on his ability to unsheath and throw it before the spear could bring him down. But the White Lord couldn't shed a woman's blood. Surely, Vani was only trying to bluff him.

Had it not been for Neeba, Ki-Gor would have died where he stood, died without ever piercing the story of terror and mystery which lay behind these two whom he so mistakenly tried to judge by the standards of ordinary women.

But Neeba had no delusions about her sister's intent. When instead of answering her, Vani deliberately tensed for a spear thrust, uncontrolled rage splintered Neeba's features. Like a striking leopard, she literally catapulted through the air to smash against her twin.

"You bloody dango!" she shrieked as the surprised Vani reeled back to sprawl flat in the grass. "I told you to let him alone." Neeba wrenched the spear from her grasp.

Vani glowered up at the trembling girl. Her eyes were pools of evil and her voice a whisper of hate.

"I'll kill you, too," she swore. "I'll kill you for this!"

Neeba spoke between gritted teeth. "Try it," she urged nastily. "You know what Thor would do to you. He's warned you about harming me. You can't fool him, you know."

For the first time Vani's glacial calm was shattered. "Curse Thor," she shrieked, "I'm not afraid of him. You'll see, one day I'll slit his belly open, just as I will yours." But it was obvious the name "Thor" acted on her with magic effect.

Vani picked herself up and started backing toward the jungle, her glance going rapidly from her sister to Ki-Gor. She stabbed a clawed hand at Neeba.

"You'll see," she muttered. Then she turned and sped into the forest.

Neeba shook the spear at the place where her twin disappeared. Her eyes were still murky with anger when she faced Ki-Gor.

"I've got to go after her," she said thoughtfully. "Promise me you'll stay away from your camp for two days. By then I'll be able to make her leave, but in the meantime please hide out. I won't have a chance to save you if you don't."

Ki-Gor gave a bitter laugh. "So now I'm to hide out, am I? You haven't caused enough trouble, so now I'm to be run off from my own camp because of a silly girl's tantrum."

"Please," she begged. "You don't understand how serious this is."

"I understand that I've taken more than any other man would swallow," he cried. "Forget about this Vani. Thor's the one I'm interested in! You're going to take me to him... Right now."

She glanced nervously after her departed sister, plainly eager to start after her.

"I'll come back," she promised, "as soon as I get rid of her. I'll make all this trouble up to you, Ki-Gor. You'll never be sorry."

Ki-Gor took a quick step toward her. "I said we were going to see Thor now!" he thundered, meaning to grab her arm.

She fell swiftly back before him, bringing the spear into position for use. The wild, dangerous look came over her again.

"I don't want to hurt you," she warned, "but I'll do it if you try to interfere. I won't kill you, but I'll fix you so you can't follow me. Don't make me do it, Ki-Gor. I'm trying to save your life!"

KI-GOR knew by now that either of the twins was capable of any insane action. He could tell by the easy way she held the light spear that she knew how to use it. Why provoke her? The wisest course would be to let her start after her sister and then follow her. By following that course he would find Thor just as quickly and he would be spared the maddening company of the girl in the meantime.

"All right," he growled, "we'll do it your way."

He turned away and started toward the pool. Inside him his blood boiled as he thought of what he would say and do when he confronted Thor. Any white man so low that he would deliberately allow his girls to go native needed some drastic educating.

"Thank you, Ki-Gor," Neeba's warm

voice followed him. "I couldn't bear to think of you hurt. I'll come back to you, my Ki-Gor, as soon as I can."

Ki-Gor winced at her tone. What had he ever done to deserve this? He heard her run lightly across the clearing, disappear into the jungle with the faintest rustle of leaves. He didn't turn around or evidence any interest in her departure. She was quite capable of waiting just within the cover of brush to see whether he meant to follow her.

He stopped at the edge of the pool, stood with folded arms, staring off into space. His head was still spinning with the events of the past half-hour. With desperate impatience, he waited for a safe interval of time to pass before following Neeba's spoor.

Then just when he concluded that no matter how suspicious she was, she'd be gone, he heard quick footsteps entering the camp behind him. This time his irritation knew no bounds. He spun, a threatening frown on his face.

"By all the gods, I've had enough," he blurted.

Then his voice faltered and he reddened. His astonished wife stood watching him.

"What did you say?' she asked.

"Oh...I...uh...I," he stumbled.

"What's the matter with you, Ki-Gor?" she asked, eyeing him closely.

He had wished desperately for Helene when he first encountered Neeba, but in the confused period after Vani appeared he hadn't had time to think about her again. All in a rush, it occurred to him that the story he had to relate might sound a little odd to a wife's ears. Great jumping crocodiles, how could a man explain to his wife that two white women, as alike as peas, had appeared suddenly out of the jungle, one trying to marry him and the other trying to kill him!

What would Helene think? Why, it didn't even sound reasonable to him. He was stupid as a water buffalo not to have given some thought to what he would say.

Helene was inspecting him as only a wife can. "Surely, Ki-Gor, after all these years, you haven't finally let N'Geeso talk you into drinking some of that poisonous stuff he calls beer."

"I'm all right," he said lamely. "I—I was thinking of something else."

Ki-Gor couldn't help comparing Helene to the twins. How fresh and clean was his young wife's beauty. He savored her frank blue eyes, her finely modeled face, her slim, long-limbed body with renewed appreciation. Neeba's sulky, earthy beauty and Vani's cold physical perfection seemed dark and somehow evil when contrasted with Helene's warm, golden charms.

"That's a relief," she said, a twinkle appearing in her eyes. "For a moment, I thought you were throwing me out." She walked slowly past the dying fire and approached him. "I've often wondered how these native women must feel when their lords gruffly announce one day that they are tired of them and are taking a new wife. The way you barked at me I thought the time had come for me to learn."

He swallowed. "The very idea," he said, a bit more indignantly than the occasion demanded. Then he immediately checked himself, regretting that he hadn't laughed and lightly related the story. It had been a perfect opening, but he had muffed it and the telling would be doubly hard.

"Oh, don't look so serious, honey," Helene smiled. "Don't you know when I'm joking." She patted his cheek and raising herself on tiptoe, kissed him. "You're probably hungry. I didn't mean to be gone so long."

Well, he might as well get it over with, thought Ki-Gor. "Uh, Helene, there was something I wanted to tell you about. Sort of an odd thing."

"That reminds me," she interrupted him. "I met two mighty excited pygmy kids on the trail. They said they thought they had found a body down near the river. They had been too frightened to go near enough to be sure and ordinarily I would have put it down to the imagination of would-be young hunters, but because of those two poor Masai you found, I thought maybe you should investigate."

She knelt by the pool, washed her hands and face in the cold water.

"It's probably the remains of some animal,' Ki-Gor agreed.

"Just to be on the safe side, though," Helene said, "you go take a look. I'll stay and get lunch started."

Ki-Gor welcomed Helene's urging with a guilty sense of relief. The place the boys described was only about ten minutes distance from the camp. He'd tell Helene about the sisters when he got back, and there would still be plenty of time for him to follow Neeba.

He picked up his spear and started off, but he suddenly halted. What if those wild twins returned while he was gone? There was no telling what they might do to Helene.

"I'm not hungry yet," he lied. "Come along and keep me company. When we're ready to eat, we can spear a few fish and cook them there on the river bank."

His suggestion pleased Helene, and she promptly agreed to go. He somehow couldn't find a convenient moment to tell her about the two strange women. When they reached the winding river path, Ki-Gor kept a few steps ahead of Helene, pretending to give close attention to the search. Actually, he wanted to avoid those knowing blue eyes of hers. He often felt she could read his mind.

But the scent which suddenly struck his animal-keen nostrils brought his full attention back to the matter at hand. It was the scent of fresh blood—human. A few more steps and he saw it.

Ki-Gor stopped quickly. He raised his arm, pressing Helene back, seeking to shield her from the gruesome spectacle. He was too late to spare her the sight of the feeding jackal.

III

THE JACKAL'S HEAD shot up as it sensed the presence of man-things. The ugly creature bristled, snarled its hate. With a low curse, Ki-Gor moved sideways, finding room to raise his spear. Instantly, the jackal's bluster dissolved into cowardice.

As it spun to flee, Ki-Gor's racing spear found it, tumbled it kicking into the underbrush. "The boys were right," Ki-Gor said grimly.

"It's—it's horrible," gasped Helene. "He's been torn to bits!"

"There's no need for you to watch," the White Lord said, taking her by the shoulders and turning her away.

His own face reflected the unpleasantness of the job he must do. He recovered his spear from the dead jackal. Carefully, he studied the ground about the torn corpse, noted the red smears on the trees where the black had tried to climb to safety.

He forced himself to roll the dismembered head from beneath a bush with his spear-point and studied in white-lipped silence the distorted features.

"Another Masai," he reported hoarsely to Helene. "The warrior, Tambi, one of Tembu George's bravest men."

Helene's only answer was a sickened intake of breath. The silence was unbroken for long minutes except by the steady bite of Ki-Gor's spear-point into the turf. When he had scooped a depression in the earth, he laid the broken body into its grave, covered it with a mound of heavy rocks.

"It is no end for a warrior," he stated bitterly as he raised from his task. "Come!" he said to Helene and he led her past the rude grave.

Two hours later they paused far down the river. They had no stomach for the picnic they had planned, but Helene gathered some fruit and forced the White Lord to eat a little. His somber mood remained unbroken.

"This is the third one," she said at last. "What does it mean? What is it that would prey on the only three Masai within a hundred miles and yet would leave the pygmies unmolested?"

Ki-Gor sat cross-legged on the grassy river bank. He looked down at his hands. "I don't know, Helene," he answered low-voiced.

She reached a hand to his chin, turned his face toward her.

"Tell me the truth," she demanded earnestly. "There's something wrong about all this. I've seen how heavily it has borne on your mind."

His grey eyes tried to avoid her glance, but she wasn't to be put off.

"Yes, there's something wrong," he finally admitted, "but exactly what it is, I don't know. We were late in finding the other two bodies and most of the signs had been obliterated by the scavengers. This time the spoor was fresh, so fresh it makes my heart ache that I didn't take this trail home when I returned from the pygmy kraal a short while ago. Perhaps I would have met Tambi. Perhaps I could have saved him."

Helene caressed his arm with her cool fingers.

"Now, Ki-Gor, don't try to take any blame on yourself," she said. "You had no way of knowing he was coming. As close a watch as the pygmies keep on the trails, they didn't even know he was within their lands."

The White Lord restlessly fingered his spear, trying the keenness of its edges on the reeds at the water's edge.

"Those tracks about Tambi," he broke out, "they're like those of a dingo pack in some ways, yet they're too large, and so deep that they indicate a heavier animal. It puzzles me," he confessed. "I've never seen dingos with jaws powerful enough to rip a man to shreds in that fashion."

He got up, too restless to remain still any longer. The play of sunlight through the trees dappled his powerful, bronzed body. His jutting chin was hard-set as granite.

"And when the wild dog packs kill," he went on, "they kill for food. Though Tambi was torn to pieces, his flesh was uneaten."

"But sometimes animals run amok, don't they?" asked Helene, "and kill for the sheer lust of killing?"

"Yes," he granted, "but not in this case. Not a single pygmy has been slain. If it were bloodlust driving the pack, the killers wouldn't have wasted their time searching out three lone Masai among hundreds of pygmies."

His words drew Helene to her feet. Concern was suddenly written deeper on her face.

"You talk as if these were deliberate murders," she said apprehensively. "Men are the only ones who murder like that. You said yourself that animals had done the killing in these cases."

His glance turned from the river, probed over the shadowed green tangle of undergrowth which swallowed up the trail. He loomed huge beside Helene's slim, golden beauty.

"I don't know the answers yet," he said. A resolute tone entered his voice. "I could be wrong. I hope I am." His eyes were bleak and cold "But it's my guess that these three Masai were runners, trying to reach my camp with a message. Someone didn't want them to reach me."

HE TIGHTENED the cords securing his bow and quiver of arrows on his broad back. He suggested to Helene that they move on. She noted that he led her toward the pygmy kraal.

"Tambi and the others were among Tembu George's top warriors," she said after considerable thought. "He doesn't use men like that as runners."

Ki-Gor walked beside her with the weightless, soft-padding stride of a wild creature, ever poised and watchful.

"You send your best and bravest men where the danger is greatest. That's one of the difficult things of being a chieftain," he explained. "It looks to me like Tembu George was forced to gamble three of his most valuable warriors on the chance that one of them might get through. Otherwise, why wouldn't three men from the same kraal travel together instead of different days by different routes? No, I don't like it at all."

Helene threw a startled look at her husband. By no stretch of her imagination had she envisioned anything as serious as Ki-Gor pictured.

"Oh, surely it couldn't be anything as serious as that," she said in an attempt to ease his mind. "Before we get too worried, let's have the pygmies make drum talk with the Masai. By nightfall we should have their answer relayed back and we'll know exactly where we stand."

The idea had come suddenly to her, and voicing it, she felt it was an obvious solution.

Ki-Gor shattered her composure with his low-spoken answer. "N'Geeso and I have already tried that, Helene, and always the reply comes back from the relay drummers that the Masai drums will not speak."

"Oh, no!" exclaimed Helene. She realized immediately why Ki-Gor seemed so upset. She had seen the burned-out dead-strewn villages left in the wake of slave raiders or pillaging tribesmen.

Because Ki-Gor often used the war-like Masai to police the jungle and drive out the trouble-makers and slavers, the tribe had more than its share of bitter enemies. A combination of tribes could have made a swift strike, catching the Masai off-guard. And if Tembu George and his people were in trouble, it was inevitable that Ki-Gor would share their peril.

For a brief instant, she thought of the promise she had gone to such pains to wheedle from Ki-Gor, the promise that for a moon he would stay quietly with her at Silver River. Now there would be no pleasant, carefree days.

In his role of jungle protector, he was too often in danger for a wife to ever know real peace of mind. In the grim, dog-eat-dog life of the forest, he was the final resort of countless black tribes when tragedy threatened to engulf them.

Her face was composed, giving no hint of her thoughts. "You must go to the Masai kraal at once, Ki-Gor," she said.

Ki-Gor stopped in the trail. "You really think so?" he asked.

"Of course," she assured him, "it's the only thing to do." She smiled up at him. "We'll let the promise go."

A noise, rather like a disgusted snort drew the jungle couple's attention to a branch over their heads. A sour, red-faced baboon stared down at them like a gouty old English lord of Victorian vintage mortified by the goings-on of rabble outside his club window. That was the comparison that went through Helene's head.

But the White Lord saw the animal's button-hard black eyes and their cold, shallow gleam made him start with remembrance. It was of Vani he was reminded. By all the gods, of course, he couldn't leave Helene at the camp if there was the slightest chance of that queer woman or Neeba either, returning. She must come with him.

He would have to forget the twins temporarily. He could look into that matter when he returned from the Masai kraal. In a way, he was relieved to be able to leave behind the matter of Thor and his daughters.

"You will come with me," he said quietly.

The baboon gave another snuffle, turned away from them with slow dignity and moved off, revealing a posterior as vividly scarlet as his face. Ki-Gor and Helene watched with amusement as the baboon leaped for a liana, caught it, and swung, chattering, squeaking and chirping, into the trees. Then, they started on the trail.

IV

ONLY ONE day's trek separated them from the Masai kraal when Ki-Gor, Helene and N'Geeso halted in early afternoon beside a small spring. Two days before they had reached the furthermost point possible by river, and after beaching the canoe, proceeded on foot.

"Why do you want to stop now?" Helene asked her husband.

Actually, she was bone-tired and her whole body cried out for rest. Perfectly conditioned as she was, it was a gruelling task to keep pace with the steel-muscled White Lord and the short-legged pygmy, N'Geeso. They had tried to regulate their speed to accommodate her, but worry about Tembu George unconsciously kept flogging them faster. Fearful they might be stopping on her account and consider her a burden, she was quick now to protest this unnecessary halt so Ki-Gor wouldn't guess her true weariness.

"We've come far and fast," Ki-Gor said, "but now it's time to go slow. We're not more than a day from the Masai kraal. Before getting any closer, I want to do some scouting."

Helene saw the thoughtful pucker of approval on N'Geeso's wise little face. Both men, she realized, were thoroughly convinced they were going to encounter trouble. They had endured so many dangers that they seemed to have an intuition which warned them of impending peril.

"N'Geeso will build a tree house for Helene," the pygmy told Ki-Gor. "All will be well while you're gone." With such simple, quiet-spoken words did he pledge his life in Helene's protection.

Ki-Gor made a gruff noise in his throat. "I have no cares about the two of you," he said, looking away. He was silent a moment. "I don't know how long I'll be gone, perhaps a day, perhaps two."

Then she knew the White Lord meant to travel alone to the kraal. Moving along the tree-routes with that incredible swiftness which even the apes couldn't match, he would be able to reach the village around dusk.

"Darling, take care of yourself," she said, for she was a wife, not a warrior who must always mask his feelings.

Ki-Gor took another look about the

clearing to fasten it in his mind. Then he put his right hand behind her head, shook it gently as he drew her near to him.

"I'm nearly grown," he laughed. "You're to sleep, not worry."

He turned away, his white, strong teeth still showing in a smile. He couldn't travel with the long spear in the trees so he tossed it suddenly, broadside, at N'Geeso. It was an old warrior's trick, but though N'Geeso had no warning, like a striking snake his right hand shot up and snared the shaft coming at him.

"Don't, Ki-Gor!" Helene cried in alarm. "Some day he's going to miss."

"Never fear," cried N'Geeso for Ki-Gor's benefit. "That One couldn't catch an old woman off-guard, he is so slow."

With a parting chuckle, Ki-Gor raced forward a few steps, caught a dangling length of liana, swung with monkey-like agility into the trees. Within moments, he was gone, speeding along branches, swinging out over open spaces on a slender vine or diving like a bullet from one swaying branch to another.

With an animal's unerring sense of direction, he drove a straight path toward his objective, slicing hours off the difficult trip it would have been on the ground. Yet great as was the shortcut the tree-routes made possible, the afternoon had slipped away by the time the increasing number of well-trodden paths beneath him told of the kraal's nearness.

Ki-Gor was forced to move slowly now, even though he had climbed into the upper branches in order to utilize the last reddish rays of light. The jungle below was already cloaked in gloom. Ordinarily, he would have descended to the path at such an hour, but the utterly deserted trails and the strange quietness everywhere made him wary. He ran no risk of discovery in the leafy heights.

The grey world about him deepened into black as he felt carefully out on a limb overlooking the Masai kraal.

His first reaction was one of relief. The kraal was bright with fires and the tribesmen were very much in evidence. Then as more details of the scene registered on him, his face in the darkness grew grave.

No wonder the kraal stood out in such clear relief. Outside the walls the village was closed in by a solid circle of fire, burning logs stacked one on another in a continuous line, while within the kraal itself more than a score of campfires blazed. And in the bright light Ki-Gor could see where the walls were newly patched with fresh green logs in many places, where there were unexplained gaps in the usually neat and regular rows of huts.

But it was the Masai themselves who alarmed him most. Hardly a sound rose from the usually noisy tribesmen. They stood about in close, uneasy groups, but there was no conversation. They were like dumb animals huddled for warmth. Common to almost every black was an attitude of listening.

The Masai were afraid! Despite the spears, the bows, the cruel swords they held with such taut fingers, the mark of fear was on them.

Fear was etched in their eyes.

These were the warriors who laughed in battle, who always invited danger. These were the men said to be harder than the steel of their weapons. In other days before the White Lord came to control them, the Congo had trembled at their very name for they had lived only for war and conquest. Tembu George was foremost now in Ki-Gor's thoughts. He searched the kraal for the great-thewed giant who led the Masai.

Though it should have been easy, he couldn't seem to pick the Masai chieftain out of the crowd. Misgivings stirred anew in him, but he told himself that Tembu George no doubt was in the council hut with his headmen laying plans to meet whatever emergency it was that threatened his people.

A glance told Ki-Gor that all trees whose branches had overhung the walls had been cut down. He couldn't run out on a bough and drop down within the kraal as he had done so many times in the past. And the tree he was in, though it provided a clear view of the kraal, was even outside the circle of fire.

HE CLIMBED toward the ground, deciding it would be best to show himself in the firelight and give the blacks plenty of time to recognize him. As edgy as they were, they might be prone to shoot before asking any questions if he suddenly appeared too near the stockade.

He kept within the jungle's dark edge until he was opposite the gate. Then he stepped into the light, raised his spear high and cried in a booming voice, "Ho! A friend comes!"

There was a pause in which he imagined a deeper, more electric quiet fell over the kraal.

"Is Ki-Gor no longer welcome with the Masai?" he cried with a touch of exasperation when the awkward silence continued unbroken.

His words apparently lashed a few blacks into life for he heard the scurrying of feet, muffled voices. Then the gate was shoved open just wide enough for a warrior to slip through. It was the bull-chested Nibaiya, one of Tembu George's lieutenants. He held a long pole in his hands.

He raced forward without a word, jabbed open a small lane through the burning logs. Ki-Gor saw that the man was trembling in his haste, his eyes wide and staring with tension.

"Quickly, O White Lord," he gasped, "get inside the walls!"

What madness lay on Nibaiya? The narrow path through the fire was still thickly carpeted with hot coals, so poorly had he done his job in his rush to be finished. With a frown, Ki-Gor stepped back a few paces, got a running start and leaped over the red-hot strip.

Hardly had he landed when the black went furiously to work raking back the logs he had displaced so the gap would again be closed with fire. Ki-Gor waited for him to finish so he could accompany him back to the gate.

"No, no! Don't wait!" croaked Nibaiya.

Angry words welled up in the White Lord's throat, but he quelled them. He turned, frowning, and stalked toward the gate. But before he reached it, Nibaiya had finished his task and was crowding behind him.

As the heavy barrier slammed shut and the natives threw the great crossbars into place, Nibaiya gave a groan of relief and sagged back against the logs. Beads of sweat glistened on his broad, thick-featured face.

"Where's Tembu George?" snapped Ki-

Gor, resolved to learn without further foolishness the reason for this queer ado. "Maybe his tongue won't be frozen in his head. By all the gods, can a friend be of help to men struck deaf and dumb?"

His questing glance knifed over the kraal. How strange were the faces of the men and women who everywhere had turned to watch him. They seemed torn by warring emotions as though they didn't know whether to be gladdened or frightened by his appearance. Always before they had been delighted to see him, almost smothering him in their rush to bid him welcome.

Nibaiya pushed himself away from the gate, came to Ki-Gor's side. His eyes darted toward the east.

"There's little time, O Ki-Gor," he said hoarsely, "and there's no knowing what the cost of this will be to us"—he hesitated and there was a surly challenge in the look he gave the men about him—"but come, since it's our fault you're here, at least I will explain the terror that is upon us. Then you will better understand why you must not stay with us."

He plunged ahead, his heavy body furrowing a path through the crowd. He continued to glance about him with a kind of defensive belligerancy, as though he knew the warriors disapproved his action. He ripped aside the skin covering the door to a hut and drove inside. The White Lord followed, looking about expectantly, thinking he had been taken to Tembu George.

Except for Nibaiya, the hut was empty.

"Look not for your friend," he cried hollowly. "Look not for the one we called Lord. Night falls over the Masai. Death is around us."

There was a wildness in the black man, a wildness born of sorrow and desperation. Like spiders his hands fingered over his distraught face.

"Tembu George is gone! The black creeping things from the well of death have swallowed him. He went to face them in council, went with a bravery beyond the call of men, and they betrayed him."

Nibaiya was sobbing then, the harsh, tearless sobs of a man who has never known what it is to cry.

"Aye! When he saw all was lost," he rushed on, "he went out alone, as the Old One demanded, to sit in peace council. In his heart was the wish to save his people. But it was only a trick to capture him. We heard his sudden cries of betrayal yonder in the jungle where they talked. Then all was silent. We rushed out to fight and die with him, but he was gone—swallowed up without a trace."

Nibaiya faced him as would a cornered beast. His words flooded out so fast the White Lord could hardly follow his meaning. Realizing the man's state, Ki-Gor went quickly forward, putting his hands on the warrior's brawny shoulders.

"Get a grip on yourself, Nibaiya," he soothed. "I can't understand you. Answer me, is Tembu George dead?"

The touch of the White Lord's hands quieted the warrior.

"Perhaps not dead—but as good as dead."

"Speak plain, man!" demanded Ki-Gor. "What do you mean? And who is the enemy who did this?" His fingers bit into the black's shoulders. "Know you not that Tembu George is my blood-brother? His enemies shall know no rest while I live!"

Nibaiya shook his head slowly from side to side.

"You can do nothing," he said, low-voiced. "By your very presence you condemn others of us to die." He straightened himself. "But even so, I must tell you."

He told how a moon before two white men had come to Tembu George, asking his aid in reopening an old watercourse which had once drained Tiva Lake. The lake was a vast body of water which lay north of the kraal in a rough, densely forested region. It adjoined the lands of two other tribes, and for reasons long since obscured by time, was accepted as a place of evil spirits, a taboo area, by the Masai and their neighbors.

THE TWO WHITES were employed by planters interested in opening up a giant cultivation project two hundred miles away on the N'Tonga River. The ancient watercourse from Tiva Lake had once drained into the N'Tonga, and the two men, who were engineers, had followed the dry bed in the hopes of again starting the waterflow. The planters needed more water in the N'Tonga so riverboats could reach them from the coast.

"They talked to Tembu George," said Nibaiya, "and explained how in the time of our fathers the earth had shaken itself, throwing up a wall of rock which had blocked the river. They said if the Masai would help them, they could dig through the wall and start the waters again. The river, they pointed out, would run through our lands, making game more plentiful, guarding us against drought and giving us an easy path to other sections."

Though Ki-Gor was long accustomed to the round-about speaking customs of black men, he couldn't curb his impatience.

"These white men, then," he anxiously questioned, "they are ones who harmed Tembu George?"

Nibaiya looked past him to the door. "No," he said, "though the cause lay with them." He knotted his fists, shook them as though at the engineers.

For fear of setting the distraught man off on another disjointed tirade, Ki-Gor forced himself to hold his tongue. It was better to bear the torture of waiting, and let the simple man tell his story in his own way.

"Tembu George thought well of what the men suggested," resumed the warrior. "He said to us, 'Let us go and do this good thing.' And when some of the warriors drew back, saying it was an evil place, he shamed them with his laughter. He said juju was only a witch doctor's trick and evil spirits only a dream of a frightened man's mind.

"So we went, some because we believed

Tembu George, others because they did not want the women to think them cowards. We worked hard all day and at night we feasted, for there was game everywhere about us. For a hand of days all went well."

He paused and wiped thick fingers across the wetness of his face. The sharp, sour smell of him lay heavy in the close air of the hut. The smell of fear from any animal, including man, is not pleasant.

"Then one night the guns and personal belongings of the whites disappeared from camp. Suddenly, a day later, all game was gone from the forest. Our hunters went out to seek it—and never returned. We sent out searchers and the forest swallowed them. Then the terror crept close.

"White, ghostly things wavered about the camp in the night. In the day, we saw vague, grey shapes moving in the underbrush. And the wailing blood-cries of those half-seen things pursued us in our dreams.

"Hunger and death stalked us. Warriors were torn to pieces within our hearing, and by the time we reached them, their attackers were gone. We knew the spirits of the lake were offended, but Tembu George was like a madman and refused to let us stop work. He said the job would be finished within a hand of days and all the devils of earth and sky could not stop us."

A bitter, twisted smile crooked Nibaiya's lips. He was seeing again the giant, angry figure of his chieftain.

"And finish we did! With flame and smoke, the white men blew the last wall of rock away and the water leaped into the old river bed. Then Tembu George stood in the swirling current, shook his fists at the jungle and cursed for cowards the sneaking creatures who had tried to block us.

"He led us home, and the fear left us and we rejoiced in his courage—for we had won and we thought we were safe."

The sound that issued from Nibaiya's mouth was a grim mockery of a laugh.

"But the terror followed us. On the third night, the Old One struck without warning as we sat at the evening meal. In a breath, the air was hideous with wierd cries. From the jungle thundered a mass of rhinos, crumpling our walls like dead leaves, smashing a path of destruction

through the kraal.

"Then the slavering grey things came in a racing horde, pouring through the shattered walls."

He put his hands over his eyes to shut out the vision.

"Women, children and warriors were ripped to shreds. Before a score of men could arm themselves, the horde had struck and passed on."

Nibaiya did not mention that his oldest son had ben slain by his side, that his hut had been made a shambles and that he himself had narrowly escaped death before a rhino's charge. The memory of that night was a ghost that would forever walk his mind.

"In the long night, we did what we could, patching and strengthening the walls, building up the circle of fire outside the kraal, readying our weapons." His voice dropped. "But there was no hope in us. Even Tembu George was shaken. What can men do against the dark powers? Those beasts were not of this world. They were things called up from the pit of death and transformed by witchcraft into animal forms. They were things of horror set upon us because we had broken the taboo."

The grimly intent White Lord listened with increasing puzzlement. "Why didn't you call N'Geeso and me to come at once?" he interrupted.

"*They* saw to it that our drum was shattered beyond repair," he said, explaining that the main charge of the rhinos had struck the huge signal drum. "That very night, however, Tembu George did send our two swiftest runners to ask your aid."

NIBAIYA faltered in his tale, his stomach muscles jerking as though he were going to be sick, but he sucked a deep breath into his lungs and went on.

"Those brave ones didn't get far," he rasped. "At dawn we saw their heads stuck on stakes at the jungle's edge. And as we watched, still shaken by their fate, the Old One, tall as a war-spear, with a fierce, streaming brush of white hair and beard, suddenly stood between the stakes.

"He wore a long white robe and his skin was fair as yours. He called awful threats to us in a voice of thunder saying he was the Lord of the Dead, and while he spoke the grey beasts came out of the jungle and swarmed about him."

In a swift, almost incoherent torrent, as though he wanted to rid himself of the story, Nibaiya related how the grim figure had threatened to send the grey horde into the village again unless Tembu George and the two whites came out alone to sit in council with him and learn what must be done to atone for breaking the taboo.

"We had felt his power at the lake," muttered Nibaiya, "and now again at our kraal. We could not stand against him, so our only hope was to bargain with him, keep him pacified until we could reach you. But Tembu George did not trust him, and refusing to risk the lives of others, he went out alone.

"The Old One screamed at him that he would not talk unless the whites came, but when Tembu George said he alone was chieftain of the Masai and could speak for his people, he suddenly agreed and sent his pack away. Then the two of them walked a few steps down the trail, just out of sight of the kraal.

"And the next we knew, Tembu George was roaring he was betrayed. Despite our fear, we rushed out to fight for him. He was gone, disappeared into thin air."

Nibaiya was silent for a full minute, his eyes closed, his breath coming as fast as if he had been running. He did not mention how with Tembu George gone, the tribe had selected him of all the warriors to place its trust in. Ki-Gor guessed the part Nibaiya's natural modesty omitted and his heart went out to this simple, forthright man.

"Then you sent the three men who tried to reach me?" said Ki-Gor softly.

"The five men," gritted Nibaiya. "They were our best, our bravest. Two of them, like Tembu George's runners, never got outside our lands. Their heads were thrown over our walls in the night with a message in picture writing warning us not to try to contact anyone in anyway if we ever wanted to see Tembu George again."

So that was why the Masai acted so queerly when he had appeared. They wanted terribly his advice and aid, but they knew that his presence would condemn their beloved chieftain.

"I understand now your strange welcome," Ki-Gor said sympathetically. "Not for anything would I endanger Tembu George or your people. I came through the trees, so no one knews my presence. I'll slip away, learn more about this Old One, and then N'Geeso and I will work out something without drawing you in."

Nibaiya was looking past Ki-Gor to the door once more. The White Lord turned and followed his fixed stare. In the patch of sky visible through the door, he saw the moon, golden and full.

"It's too late," the warrior said jerkily. "His creatures surround us every night at moonrise. And tonight the Old One comes himself—to get the two white men for hostage."

"What!" exclaimed Ki-Gor, surprised by this new information.

"He said after we turned over the two white men we could talk of freeing Tembu George," Nibaiya revealed.

"And you believed him?" asked Ki-Gor sharply.

The black snarled guiltily, "What matters it what I believe? Perhaps the Old One does lie, but I cannot gamble with Tembu George's life." He half-turned toward Ki-Gor, his voice rising. "Aaaiiee! If I were certain he lied, still I would have to give them up to keep him from setting the rhinos and the grey devils on us again."

Ki-Gor touched his shoulder with a finger. In the yellow torchlight, the White Lord's eyes were narrow splinters of steel, but Nibaiya did not see his face. He merely heard his quiet, controlled voice.

"It seems this Old One badly wants the whites," he declared. "When you give them up, I'd say you give away your only chance to save Tembu George."

THE WARRIOR had expected Ki-Gor to oppose his delivering the whites over to the Old One and was braced for an angry tongue lashing.

"You waste your breath, Ki-Gor!" he snapped. "I know you would save the whites with your quick tongue, but I won't be swayed."

"I said nothing of saving the whites," pointed out Ki-Gor. "I'm interested only in being sure Tembu George is freed when you turn them over to the Old One."

Nibaiya was startled. "You'll not try to stop me?" he asked suspiciously.

"Not at all," Ki-Gor assured him. "The one thing I argue against is the way you propose to make the trade. Don't make him a present of both men. When he comes, give him one of them and say you will turn over the other when Tembu George steps in the gate a free man."

Nibaiya nervously cleared his throat.

"That would be more than fair with anyone else," he granted, "but he'd tear the kraal to shreds if I tried to hold back a man."

Ki-Gor smiled thinly, thumped the black on the chest.

"Think, man!" he urged. "If his promise to release Tembu George was made in good faith, he has no reason to object. If it wasn't made in good faith, why he'll probably murder all of you anyway as soon as he gets his hands on both whites." He forced Nibaiya to look at him. "I'll tell you he doesn't want to risk harming them if he can avoid it. He had to take a chance on the first raid, because it was the only way to terrorize you."

Nibaiya shifted from one foot to another, his face utterly miserable.

"Maybe you're right," he said frankly, "and I might do what you say, if there was a way in the world to fight off another attack." He shook his head in rejection. "It's impossible, though, we just couldn't stand up against those devils again."

"Consider this, my friend," Ki-Gor said. "Why would the Old One go to such trouble if he were absolutely confident of crushing the Masai? Why doesn't he come in and take what he wants?"

"Why . . . why I don't know," the warrior stammered.

"His animals are good for a quick, surprise strike," declared Ki-Gor, "and nothing more Sure, they can do a lot of damage but they can't stand and fight like warriors until a battle's really won. That's why the Old One does so much talking and uses your own chieftain to bluff you."

Nibaiya's features showed he wasn't convinced.

"They're things of the spirit world, those beasts," he muttered.

Ki-Gor didn't scoff. With a deeply serious expression, he said, "Even so, I know a way to send them swiftly back to their own world if they dare attack your kraal."

The black straightened, every line of him attentive.

"Juju?" he questioned eagerly. "You can mix a juju stronger than the Old One's?"

"I can mix a juju which will turn the beasts into nothing more than beasts," muttered Ki-Gor.

"Nay! I cannot believe you," he said in a disgruntled voice. "You preach that the magic-makers are worthless leeches."

"Aaaiiiee!" exclaimed the White Lord. "Haven't I shown the fakers up every time? How would I know their talk of magic was a lie if I did not know what true juju was myself."

Nibaiya screwed up his lips. He was wavering, yet not wholly convinced. His attitude angered the White Lord. Ki-Gor glowered, his great chest swelling as he drew himself up.

"I say to you I can make a spell," he thundered, "which will change every beast who charges the kraal into a flesh and blood creature. And what's more I can arrange a defense which will rip the belly from every one that breaks through the wall."

Nibaiya backed away from him. He was impressed. He ran his tongue over his dry lips.

"If only you could do this thing," he whispered. "If only you could, then would I stand up against the Old One and refuse to give him more than one white man until Tembu George is freed."

The White Lord caught him by the shoulder, urged him through the door into the open air.

"Then our bargain is made," he said decisively. "Let us get to my work."

The black hung back a moment more. "Remember," he faltered, "you stake not only the lives of your friends, but your own life, too, on this juju plan."

"I know," Ki-Gor said with apparent confidence, but in the dim light his face was drawn. "Tell your people I have brought a juju to defeat the grey things. Tell them I, who have never lied to them, say that this is so!"

V

KI-GOR worked them hard. They had no time to think. He calmly took the strong, sure place of leadership which Tembu George had always held, and because he showed no fear or indecision, they did not question the labors which he set for them. He could not rid them of their own gnawing fright, but he could keep them so busy that it could be shoved into the back of their minds for a time.

Great stacks of wood for the fires were piled about the kraal. Dividing the men into four groups, the White Lord set a group to work at each end of the village sharpening the logs on one end and bracing them slantwise in the ground. The work went fast under Ki-Gor's relentless driving and soon facing the inside of each of the four walls were close-set rows of huge, wooden lances.

Behind the slanted posts, a vast assortment of weapons made for cutting or stabbing were implanted in the ground so that a barbed garden, yards wide, bristled in a continuous square.

Finally, Ki-Gor stationed the warriors, also in the shape of a square, behind the barbed hedgerow.

It was a simple but highly effective defense against the kind of attack the Old One had sent against the Masai. If the rhinos again smashed through the walls they would impale themselves with their own furious speed on the huge lances. A mere spear was useless against their armored bulk, but the low-set posts would rip open their vitals. And the grey beasts would rip themselves open if they tried to pass the barrier of swords and knives. The Masai warriors standing safely inside their defense could riddle the confused beasts with arrows.

"Your men take heart," the jungle Lord pointed out to Nibaiya. "That's why I was interested in rushing the work, so they would feel secure again. And the best part is that your Old One won't have the least suspicion of the welcome that awaits him inside the walls."

The warrior fidgeted. "They don't realize, as I do," he said gravely, "that you haven't yet made the juju which will be their real protection." He pointed to the moon which now stood high. "It grows late and he could come at any time."

"True!" the White Lord said. "I didn't realize it was so late!"

In a hurried voice, he told Nibaiya to collect for him a ball of wet clay and a number of items extending from spiders to plum pits.

Almost as an afterthought, he added, "And I must have a drop of blood from the fingers of three different white men, taken in a certain way."

Nibaiya's face dropped. "But we only have two." He gave a low wail.

Ki-Gor stroked his jaw thoughtfully. "Well, that'll be all right," he decided, "My own blood can make up the third. You go on and get the other things, while I take the blood."

In the sudden flare of yellow light, the two prisoners blinked at him. They were both bound hand and foot, propped in sitting positions against the wall.

The younger one, a big-framed man, almost as blond as Ki-Gor, with brown eyes and a strong, clean face, suddenly straightened himself.

"You!" he snarled in recognition, and the blood beat into his face. "Get out of here, you traitorous jackal! We certainly don't want to spend the little time we have left in your company."

His companion, a lean, wiry, sun-blackened man perhaps ten years his senior, made no outward display of his feelings, but in his steady gaze Ki-Gor sensed a welling contempt.

"I don't understand," Ki-Gor said, taken aback by this unexpected reception.

"The guard told us you approved Nibaiya's scheme to trade us for Tembu George," the older man said accusingly.

"Yeah!" the other one jumped in. "Stop the acting. You've already been unmasked for what you really are." He spat as though to clear his mouth of a bitter taste. "So this is the great Ki-Gor, a man who'd sell his own kind down the river because he hasn't got the guts to stand up to a bunch of crazed blacks."

"Take it easy," Ki-Gor said gently, realizing the two had had a hard time of it. "You're in a rough spot, but not as bad as you believe."

The blond gave an angry snort. "Not as bad as we believe, huh," he spat. "Listen, who do you think is going to be carried out in those cages?"

Ki-Gor's lips quirked. "I think I'll be carried out in one of them," he stated. "And the other cage will stay right where it is."

The older engineer leaned forward, a baffled expression on his face. "What's that?" he asked. His companion was abruptly silent.

"When the Old One comes tonight, he's just going to get one white man," the White Lord explained quietly. *"I'll be that one.* When the time comes, I'll come to the hut as if I were coming for one of you, but I'll exchange clothes with my angry friend there—" he pointed to the blond engineer—"and get in the cage. Neither the Masai nor the Old One will know the difference until it's too late."

The blond peered at him intently. "Why,

you're out of your head!" he exploded. "That would be plain suicide! No man would be fool enough to throw his life away like that." He rubbed his hand across his mouth, considering Ki-Gor's words.

Ki-Gor regarded him soberly, drumming the while with his fingers against his knife hilt. Then wordlessly, he unsheathed the blade, stepped forward and slashed with quick, deft strokes, the bonds on both men. That gesture was the only argument needed to convince the two amazed men that he meant what he said.

"You'll be more comfortable," he said, "but the guard mustn't know you're free. Stay in the hut and don't cause any trouble, no matter what goes on outside."

THE BIG FELLOW tried to get to his feet, but he'd been tied so long, his legs were numb and he couldn't make it. He straightened them on the ground, grimacing with pain.

"I'm sorry for what I said to you," he apologized.

"Ordinarily," Ki-Gor admitted, "the Masai would do anything I asked. But this is different. They're crazy with superstitious fear. They worship their chieftain and they think he's being tortured in the nether world by evil spirits. To free him, they would pay any price the Old One asked." He shook his head despairingly. "You can't openly order people in that condition to do what you want. You have to lead them back to their senses gradually."

The blond tried again to get up, and this time he succeeded. He rubbed his wrists, worked his feet awkwardly.

"Jack and I have been in some tough spots," he said tensely. "Africa isn't new to us. But we've never come up against anything like this. Like the natives, I'm damned near convinced the devil actually is behind all this"

The older man let himself be helped up. He showed the effects of his ordeal, but his voice was steady as his eyes.

"I'm Jack Miller," he introduced himself, "and this is Bill Owens. We seem to be the cause of all this, even if we don't understand it."

"That's right," said Owens, "and no matter how I sounded a minute ago, neither of us wants you to take the rap for what we've stirred up."

Miller nodded immediate approval. "Smuggle us some weapons and we'll make a break for it. There's no need for you to do more than that."

"Don't misunderstand me," Ki-Gor said. "I don't want to put my head in a noose any more than you do. But there's more involved in this than saving your two lives. For one thing, unless a white man is turned over to the Old One tonight, I believe he'll kill Tembu George. For another, the Masai will go to pieces soon if someone doesn't track this crazed killer down. If I can give them definite proof he's a man and not some dread spirit then I can use them to put an end to his foolishness."

Owens scratched his tousled hair. He plainly disapproved of Ki-Gor's plans.

"You won't do Tembu George or the Masai any good dead," he said flatly. "Those giant dogs..."

"Dogs?" Ki-Gor exclaimed. "What kind? We have no breed in these parts except the wild dingo."

"There's probably a strain of dingo in them," put in the older man. "They're different, though, from any dog I've ever seen. I'd say it was a special breed he's evolved himself, a mixture of large, fierce types."

"Yeah," Owens agreed with Miller. "And they're trained to kill. No wonder the blacks thought they were devils. They'd never encountered anything like them. Frankly, they scared hell out of me."

Miller smiled faintly. "Even worse than those dogs you always tell me about when you get on a binge?" he inquired.

Owens looked embarrassed. "I hate to admit it," he said, as though it were an old joke between them, "but they were worse, and I didn't think I'd ever live to see animals meaner than those I try to impress you with when I'm in my cups."

The older man turned to Ki-Gor in explanation. "Bill ran away to sea when he was a young buck. He tells a wild story about a fire-eating captain who kept a pack of man-eating dogs and a young wife locked up in his cabin." He slapped his friend good naturedly. "Sometimes he gets those dogs as big as Shetland ponies."

Ki-Gor's estimate of the two rose. Men who can still jest when they're facing danger have their full quota of courage.

"To get back to the point," Owens said, "don't just put yourself in the Old One's hands. He'll dump you out of that cage into the middle of his dogs or run a spear through you."

"Maybe," Ki-Gor said softly, "and then maybe not. In any case, it is a thing I must do. The stakes warrant the gamble."

He walked to the door, cracked the skin covering open a bit so he could locate the guard. The black stood in the same place, several yards away by the cages.

Owens strode over to Ki-Gor, reached out with a firm handclasp.

"Our prayers go with you," he said, and there was a boyish sincerity about him. "You've got more stuff than anv man I've ever seen."

"That goes for me too," Miller added. "We'll sit tight like you say."

Ki-Gor withdrew his hand awkwardly from Owen's clasp. He cleared his throat, then failing to find anything to say, turned and pushed out through the door with the torch. Behind him in the darkened hut, the two men stood wordlessly for a long time, regarding the door.

"I always took those wild tales they tell about him with a grain of salt," Miller said at last. "After seeing him, I don't believe the stories do him justice."

Ki-Gor stood beside the cages, talking with the guard. "They're both pretty quiet," he told the black, "but that big fellow might kick up a fuss when we put him in the cage. We'll send him out first." He tapped the bamboo frame he leaned against. We'll use this one for him."

He started off, then hesitated and came back as though a thought had suddenly struck him.

"Maybe I'd better look the cage over, make sure it's all right." His torch had burned almost out while he talked to the black. "Get me a fresh torch," he told the native. "I don't know my way to things very good. I'll watch the prisoners."

All the commands given in the kraal for the past three hours had been given by the White Lord, so the warrior unhesitatingly obeyed the off-hand order. But almost as soon as his back was turned, Ki-Gor dropped to his knees and entered the cage.

By the time the man returned, Ki-Gor was unconcernedly leaning against the bamboo structure. He thanked the warrior, took the torch and appeared to go carefully over the outside of the cage.

"That would hold four like him," he declared. He stuck the torch in the ground. "Now help me put it closer to the hut, so we won't have to lose any time."

Then Ki-Gor hurried to meet the worried Nibaiya and receive the items for the supposed juju. Much to Nibaiya's disappointment, Ki-Gor retired into a hut alone, refusing to let the black observe him make the strong magic which was to unseat the Old One.

"Do not call me until he appears," he cautioned the warrior.

Once inside, the White Lord scooped a hole in the dirt floor, dumped the gourd of materials Nibaiya had given him into it and carefully smoothed the dirt back in place. He kept only the large ball of wet clay and this he worked into the rough figure of a crocodile with its jaws closed over a man.

It was his guess that the Old One would prolong until nearly dawn the agony of waiting for the Masai. And he was right. The first tinge of grey lay in the eastern sky when Nibaiya's frightened voice outside the hut roused him.

"Come quickly, Ki-Gor!" he cried. "The sound of the devil pack draws near. The Old One comes for his prey!"

VI

KI-GOR CLIMBED to the observation tower by the gate with Nibaiya. He wedged the juju figure between the pointed ends of two wall stakes. Then he took Nibaiya's trembling hand, rested it on the clay.

"Take strength," he said, "from this. Already our juju begins to swallow him, to eat away the devils that live within his beasts."

With eyes white and distended, Nibaiya stared at the crocodile. "If it can only be," he murmured. "If it can only be."

New logs had been added to the circle of fire about the kraal, but the light lost itself in writhing patterns of shadows about the edge of the jungle. Though daylight was beginning to probe the far sky, impenetrable night still clutched the base of the great trees, squirming its furry blackness tightly about the underbrush.

Then for the first time Ki-Gor heard the voice of the devilpack. Thin with distance, the eerie cry came down the wind. He listened to that dreadful wailing sound and an involuntary shiver went down his spine. It was the savage, mindless bloodcall of fanged beasts crowding for the kill, and though he had never heard it before, instinct caused him to react as had cave-dwellers in the dawn of time when the wolf-pack swept close.

But the cry had a disastrous effect on Nibaiya. His whole body began to jerk and he clutched the wall for support.

"I can't do it," he said in a paralyzed whisper. "I can't face him and say he can have only one white man." His voice trailed away in a moan.

Ki-Gor's fingers closed hard about the black's arm.

"You will!" he declared harshly. "By

the gods, you will, for if you falter once I swear I'll throw you down to the pack."

The White Lord's voice and slitted eyes reflected the swift upthrust of his wrath. Nibaiya looked on him and saw he was trapped. The two were alone on the raised platform.

Ki-Gor had ordered the rest of the tribesmen not to stir from their assigned places behind the defenses, except for a narrow, winding trail which led through the hedgerow of swords and knives to the observation tower and the gate beside it, Nibaiya had no way to reach his warriors or have them come to him.

"If you fear to put your demand flatly," growled Ki-Gor, "then say that the older man was hurt trying to escape. Say his condition is so bad he cannot be moved yet, and that you fear if you turn him over now and he dies that the Old One will claim the Masai have not lived up to their bargain. Say you will have him nursed back to health in the time necessary for him to bring Tembu George to the kraal as he has promised."

"I'll do as you say," gasped Nibaiya. "But get down out of sight. Please don't let him see you!"

Ki-Gor knelt so his head wouldn't show above the wall. Through an opening between the posts he could watch the trail down which the Old One would come.

"I must warn you," he told the black seriously. "This juju is very powerful. Some strange and unexpected things may happen about the kraal. Be prepared to accept them calmly, because it will be the juju working for the Masai in a way beyond your wisdom."

"Aye," muttered Nibaiya, impressed, and his hand crept over the clay figure for reassurance.

At that moment, the cry of the devil-pack rose loud in their ears and from the dark jungle erupted a squirming grey mass. The huge, savage dogs ran shoulder to shoulder, flooding into the light, racing to the very edge of the blazing fire before they veered away and began to circle the kraal. Ki-Gor judged there were at least two hundred beasts in the pack, though their swift, darting movements and blood-chilling din made it seem there were many times more.

He watched them, fascinated as they raced back and forth about the village. Creatures from a nightmare would have been no more out of place in the Congo than these giant dogs. He thought of the three Masai who had died so near his camp. They had seen these yellow-eyed, gaunt-framed killers, perhaps had narrowly missed death from their fangs when they attacked the kraal, and still those men had been willing to try to reach him to ask help for their people. If they could show such bravery while believing the dogs were evil spirits instead of mere animals, then certainly he should have courage enough to go through with what he planned.

A HUMAN CRY, high and piercing, cut through the deep-throated baying of the now scattered pack. Instantly, every one of those circling beasts fell silent, and when that high voice sounded again, they turned and faded like grey shadows back into the forest.

In the sudden quiet, the moans of the frightened tribesmen drifted up to Ki-Gor. The Old One had gained the effect he desired. The pack was a precisely trained weapon and he used it well.

On the trail, at the wavering, outer edge of the light appeared the master of the pack. He stood immobile in the half-gloom, a tall, gnarled figure in a knee-length white robe. The wild, white froth of hair about his head and the undisciplined mass of his beard gave him a look of incredible age, yet he was ancient as a great tree is ancient, seemingly grown larger, stronger and more contemptuous of the lesser beings about him with the passing years.

His broad, heavy shoulders were stooped, but the long arms revealed by his sleeveless garment were thick and sinewy with muscle. His legs were knotted columns of strength planted hard against the ground. Except for the metallic glint of his eyes in the shifting light, one could see nothing of his face. His thick growth of hair completely swallowed his features.

With his huntsman's eyes, Ki-Gor saw that the Old One stood just out of effective arrow range. For one who claimed to be the Lord of Death, the bearded giant was quite careful. When he spoke, his voice was not the high-pitched tone he had used with the pack, but a deep, resounding bass.

"I have come, O Crawling Beetles Who

Call Yourselves Men," he shouted, "yet I find not the caged white men waiting as I commanded.

"Do you think with this paltry line of fire and your pitiful walls to defy me? Hai! Must I wrench out every one of your rotten souls and plunge it into endless torture before you learn your lesson?"

He paused, his white head thrown back contemptuously so that he looked directly up at Nibaiya. The black began to tremble uncontrollably again, his right leg shivering against Ki-Gor's side.

"Speak!" thundered the Old One. "Speak, or I vow that before the sun rises your kraal will lie in ruins. My wrath runs hot with your cursed insolence."

Sweat dripped from Nibaiya's swaying body onto Ki-Gor's shoulder. The White Lord realized the black would never get his story out without aid. He began to whisper then, putting words into the warrior's mouth. And like a hypnotized man, Nibaiya repeated the story Ki-Gor had planned.

As the Old One listened he seemed to swell and grow taller. He half-raised his gnarled arms, shook them in a frothing excess of anger. Nibaiya had told him that he could have one white man, and one only, at this time. Not until Tembu George was released, could he have the other white, who now lay ill from wounds sustained when he tried to escape.

"You defy me?" thundered the Old One.

He took three furious steps forward. Then he halted and gave another of his high-pitched, piercing commands to the pack. Out of the jungle behind him welled that primeval chorus again and in a solid mass the yellow-eyed killers came sprinting down the dark path into the light.

The river of straining grey forms split apart as it reached the Old One, drove by on either side of him, and then joined once more to rush straight at the kraal.

Ki-Gor himself gave an astonished curse. The madman without a moment's hesitation was sending his beasts against the kraal, disregarding fire and walls alike.

For a few awful moments, Ki-Gor thought he had misjudged his adversary. Then as the dogs reached the circle of flame, he saw them turn as they had before and circle on around the village. The jungle

man drew a long, shuddering breath of relief. This was only more of the Old One's sound effects.

Ki-Gor was certain then there would be no immediate attack. If the Old One had been prepared to crush the Masai, that would have been the time to do it. And Ki-Gor had not wanted an attack yet, for though he felt his defenses capable of giving the Masai the balance of power, he first needed to cut through their fear of the Old One by proving to them as he was now doing that their enemy was not all-powerful.

"Bring out the two white men, you eaters of carrion," raged the Old One above the din of the pack, "or I send my creatures in after you!"

Ki-Gor clutched Nibaiya's leg. "Tell him the trade you have offered is fair and honorable," he prompted, "and that he has no reason for anger if he actually meant his promise about freeing Tembu George."

But though the White Lord was abruptly confident he had taken the Old One's measure, the baying pack and that raging figure on the trail had had a different effect on Nibaiya. The black thought the end had come and that there was no escape. He sagged half-fainting against the wall, making odd whinneying noises of fear.

"We must give way, Ki-Gor," he managed to say. "Look at him! He's going to kill us all."

"You water-bellied dango!" spat Ki-Gor, trying to lash the warrior into action. "He's beaten. Speak up to him!"

"No! No!" wildly protested Nibaiya. "Do what you will to me, but I'll not oppose him."

Ki-Gor swung his knotted fist up from the floor, buried it with sledge-hammer force in the pit of the warrior's belly. It was a terrible blow, carrying all the braced force of the White Lord's powerful shoulders. The black was lifted off his feet, his legs splaying stiffly out in a spasm of anguish.

THE WHITE LORD caught him about the waist with his arms, pinned him close against the wall so he couldn't collapse. Nibaiya was momentarily paralyzed, his mouth gaped open in a strangling attempt to gasp breath into his stunned body. From the ground in the bad light Ki-Gor was gambling that he would look as if he were only violently distraught.

Then mocking Nibaiya's voice, Ki-Gor, still hidden from view, spoke down to the Old One. In the uproar caused by the dogs, the difference in his voice would go unnoticed.

"You may have one white," he shouted in a strong, confident voice, "and no more until you produce Tembu George. Take it or leave it! If you are so faithless as not to intend to release our chieftain, then it is foolish for us to trust you in any matter. We try to treat with you with honor, but if we can't, then turn loose your beasts. We don't fear dying! Our only desire is to save our chieftain."

The Old One was astounded. It was apparent in the sudden way he froze. This was a reaction he had never expected from the Masai. For a full minute, he stood speechless. Ki-Gor watched tensely and knew he had called the old man's bluff. It remained only for his adversary to search out a way to accept the bargain and yet save face.

With a signal, he silenced the pack, but this time he left the animals circling about in plain view as a demonstration of his strength.

"The one who spoke those words shall die!" he declared ominously, "Though he crawl to me on his belly, begging forgiveness, he shall die—at a time which I mark now in my mind. For a few more days I will leave him alive so he may know the full terror of the thing he has done."

Slowly, majestically, he raised his right arm and pointed at Nibaiya. For half a minute he pointed, not moving in a single muscle.

"Aye! For time without end the spirit-devils shall gnaw on your soul. You shall be an example for the Masai to remember always."

He was more cunning than a leopard, thought Ki-Gor, seeing how smoothly the Old One worked around to making it seem to his own advantage to accept the trade which the Masai offered.

"Aye! Since you have chosen to doubt my honor, let the bargain be as you wish. Send out the one white man—the younger one! I shall hold back my hungry devils this time, for I am a just man and I do not wish to make a people suffer for the stupid insolence of a single man."

He stroked his beard, and by the movement of his head and the occasional gleam of his eyes, Ki-Gor could tell he was watching the walls, wondering how many warriors observed him.

"Let us not change the bargain for anything," he continued hoarsely, "for when I return with Tembu George, as was my intent all the time, then shall I"—his finger shot up at Nibaiya again—"strike you dead!" He gave a bellowing laugh, as though vastly amused. "Yes, I like it this way. It is a good joke to see a man hang himself with his own long, waggling tongue!"

Then his voice was abruptly one of angry command.

"Send out the white man, you bleating goat, before I change my mind and crush you all. Quick! I weary of this dallying!"

Ki-Gor let Nibaiya sag down in his arms like a half-filled sack of sand. He was still only partly conscious. The jungle man stretched him full length on the tower floor.

"I'm sorry, my friend," he murmured. "I had to do it."

Then with monkey-like agility, Ki-Gor sped down the ladder, raced along the narrow path between the close-set blades. He had previously selected six of the duller natives to carry the cage and these men waited near the hut where the white men were held. All other natives had been ordered to remain where they were, facing outward toward the walls in case the Old One should try a sudden, sneak attack.

The waiting blacks started to go into the hut when they saw Ki-Gor approaching. He called them back, saying, "I'll put him in the cage. He'll raise the devil if blacks lay hands on him."

He indicated a spot about ten yards from the hut.

"Wait there until I call you. Then pick up the cage and get it outside at a trot."

He started in the door, paused and looked back at the guard.

"Get a torch lighted," he ordered, "so you can lead the way for them and open the gate."

Then the White Lord ducked into the unlighted hut. Owens and Miller tensely awaited him.

"Strip off your shirt and pants," he ordered Owens. "Don't talk, just listen!"

As he dressed hastily in Owens' clothes, he gave the young man the story he was to tell when Nibaiya discovered he was still in the hut.

"Tell him you were carried out in the cage. The Old One took you into the forest, threw open the door and shouted he meant to kill you as he would kill Tembu George.

"Now remember this: He dragged you out of the cage. He snatched out his knife, raised it to stab you. As the knife started to descend, there was a burst of green light and a giant crocodile seemed to materialize out of thin air and smash against the Old One.

"He was knocked off his feet, got up screaming and ran into the jungle. The crocodile turned and looked at you, and suddenly you lost consciousness. When you awoke you were back in the hut and your hands were untied."

KI-GOR fumbled with the last buttons on the shirt. He didn't trouble with the shoes. The cage was tightly woven and in the excitement few details of his dress would be visible.

"And you, Miller," he said tautly, "say you were lying on the floor here and I was standing at the door shortly after Owens was taken out. You saw a burst of eerie green light outside the hut, heard an odd voice say, 'Come, Ki-Gor, I will show you the hidden lair of the Old One'. Then everything went black and when you awoke, I was gone, Owens lay beside you and your bonds had been cut."

"But I don't understand," whispered Owens.

"You don't need to," replied the White Lord, holding out his hands to be tied. "The Masai will know how to interpret your words."

Owens tied him so loosely that he could easily free himself whenever he wished.

"Carry me out quickly, put me in the cage and get back in the hut," the White Lord said. "I'll do the talking." He had stationed the blacks far enough away so they couldn't tell it was Owens and not the White Lord doing the carrying.

Gasping with the strain of lifting the muscled jungle man, Owens did as he was bidden. When he reached the cage, he leaned over, shoved Ki-Gor inside and locked the catch.

As Owens straightened, Ki-Gor called out to the blacks: "Don't stand there like rocks!" he roared. "Get him out of here at a run. If there's the least delay, I'll lock the gates and leave you outside to the devil-beasts."

As though they had been simultaneously jabbed with hot coals, the natives leaped forward and heaved the cage up. Owens was only a dim white form standing in the dark door. The man with the torch sprinted ahead, closely followed by the two men whose duty it was to clear a path through the circle of fire. In a jolting run behind them came the four muscled blacks carrying the cage.

The White Lord huddled on his side, holding his arm close enough to shield his face and yet allow him to see. He tensed anxiously as they neared the warriors stationed behind the steel hedgerow, the four carriers slowing preparatory to threading the precarious path through the knives. The blacks did not suspect that the dimly-seen form in rumpled clothing was Ki-Gor.

The Old One had ordered his pack into the forest and had himself retreated down the path. The terror-stricken bearers had eyes only for the grim figure, giving no heed to the burden they carried. The cage could have been empty at that moment and they wouldn't have known the difference.

They plunged through the break in the fire, so frightened they didn't even feel the burn of the ground on their feet. Anxious to get back within the walls, they started to drop the cage just outside the barrier of flame.

"Bring it here, dangos," the Old One commanded, "before I set the pack on you!"

Finally, he snarled, "Set it down!"

In one common motion, they dropped the cage, whirled and sprinted for the kraal. He had led them beyond view of the walls. They thought death was at their very heels, but they reached the fire and leaped within its confines without a single dog appearing.

When the blacks were out of sight, the Old One shed his pose of frigid dignity. He literally flung himself at the cage, knelt down in the darkness with his face pressed against the side and peered at his catch. Ki-Gor cringed away, keeping his arms over his face.

"Have mercy," he moaned thickly. "Don't kill a helpless man. I've done you no wrong."

"Yes," muttered the Old One, talking to himself, "beg for your stinking life, for all the good it'll do you...bagged like a moth in a net...bagged whole and sound just like I prayed you'd be...at last... at last...."

He went on muttering, his voice sometimes audible, sometimes so low Ki-Gor couldn't understand his words. Obviously, the strange old man labored under a terrible emotional stress brought on by the sight of his prisoner.

The Old One abruptly swung up, pounded the cage with a knotted fist. "Out of hiding, woodenheads!" he cried. "Would you have daylight catch us? Swing this carrion atop the elephant!"

Before Ki-Gor could wonder at his actions, two hands of blacks snaked out of the underbrush. While they tied vine ropes to his cage, the huge grey bulk of an elephant loomed silent out of the dusk, knelt beside the knot of blacks. Swiftly, they maneuvered the cage atop the beast, lashed it in place on the flat wooden platform lashed to its back.

"Take him straight to my cabin," ordered the Old One. "I must see to the work at the lake, so you are fully responsible for him. Let him get away and you answer to me."

Then the elephant's trainer brought the jungle giant to its feet with a low-voiced command, turned it down the trail away from the kraal. Ki-Gor couldn't see the ground, but the rhythmical lurching of his cage told him that the elephant had been urged in the swift, ground-eating shuffle which corresponds to a run in any other animal.

An odd drumming noise started up behind them, gradually moved closer. Ki-Gor was hard-put for a minute to identify the sound and then he realized he was hearing zebra hooves. The blacks had mounted and were following him as a guard. The Old One must value his prisoner highly to take such elaborate precautions.

But why?

Ki-Gor had half-expected an immediate attempt by the greybeard to slay him when the cage was set down on the path. Despite his pretense of fear, he had been prepared to cope with such an attack. But the jungle man's real wish had been to reach the Old One's lair. Now as the grey light of dawn crept over the forest and he saw he was getting his wish, he realized he might never live to see another day break over the green reaches of the Congo.

Escape was still within Ki-Gor's reach. Wedged in a slit length of bamboo beneath him was his knife. He had hidden it there when he had first inspected the cage. He could slip his hands out of the loosely tied bonds, slash the vines which held the bamboo poles in place and be in the trees before anyone could make a move.

But instead of escape, Ki-Gor thought of his friend Tembu George. He was taking the most dangerous, yet by far the most direct way of reaching the chieftain, because it was the best, and probably the only hope of saving the chieftain and ending the Old One's tyranny in one swift blow.

VII

HELENE LAY stomach-down on the vine flooring which she and N'Geeso had woven between two branches. With her chin rested on her arms, she peered over the edge of the platform to the ground twenty-five feet below.

A short distance to her right, N'Geeso sat on a limb, with his back resting against the tree they occupied. He had watched the motionless girl for a long while, guessing her thoughts. Ki-Gor had been gone now for twenty-four hours.

"He will be coming soon," he assured her. "He's a careful man, and if the kraal is destroyed, he will spend much time reading the story which the ground holds."

That is a lie, N'Geeso thought, but perhaps it will sound reasonable to her. Ki-Gor has run into trouble or he would be back by now.

He watched to see her response, and to his disappointment she made only vague sounds of agreement. It would be well to convince her he believed what he said.

"If I know him, he'll be hungry," N'Geeso said, forcing a laugh. "I think we should have food ready."

"He'll be starving," she agreed with apparent conviction. "But he'll want meat, N'Geeso." She sat up, regarded the pygmy thoughtfully. "Look, you try to kill us an antelope, so we can have some good thick steaks or a roast ready for him."

N'Geeso's face lighted. She was taking heart from his words, already planning a feast.

Then abruptly his face grew solemn and he sagged back against the tree. He mustn't leave Helene alone. But she anticipated his objections.

"Now, N'Geeso," she said laughingly, "I'm no baby who will get into trouble the moment you turn your back. I'll sit right here and won't move. You don't have to go far."

"Well..." he considered wishfully.

"There's plenty of game," she pointed out. "You could almost stay within call, for that matter. This isn't Great Ape country and a person on the ground would never discover this platform, so there's no reason in the world for you to worry about me."

He finally gave in to her persuasion. Ki-Gor himself would have agreed it was necessary to hunt, and it would be more dangerous to take her with him than to leave her in the tree. He climbed nimbly down the trunk, checked his blowgun, and set off along an inviting game trail.

When he failed within a short time to find any fresh antelope sign, he turned off the trail, began to work his way in a great circle about the camp. The pygmy wriggled through the thick underbrush like a snake, penetrating with ease thickets which would have held the average white hunter helplessly entangled.

He was crossing a small clearing, approaching one of these thickets, when a sudden crackle and break of twigs sounded dead ahead. An animal hidden in the thicket had been startled into flight. But N'Geeso knew it wasn't he who had startled the creature for it was running towards him.

The wind was against his face, so that his scent couldn't betray him. He leaped back to the cover of the trees, lipping the feathered end of a poison dart, holding his blowgun ready. Only game animals took fright in that manner.

From the underbrush plunged a bushbuck followed closely by two does. Like speeding shadows they darted into the clearing, gaining speed almost the moment they hit the clear area. N'Geeso's mouth was against the blowgun.

Only the sudden jerk of his stomach muscles told that he had puffed the dart on its way. After the dart struck, the buck took four long, reaching jumps. Then as it began the fifth, its head jerked high and a sudden spasm seemed to twist its whole body.

It came down stiff-legged, staggering. With a blind swerve, the buck crashed against a tree at the edge of the clearing and collapsed. The two does whipped on into the brush and were gone.

Satisfied his quarry was down for good, he looked back toward the thicket, wondering what had frightened the deer. Whatever it was, he decided, hadn't attempted to follow the animals. He reached up to take the dart from his lip.

Before his left hand touched his mouth, the brush parted silently and two great, gaunt dogs sidled stiff-legged into the clearing. He sensed instantly that these were the devil-dogs that had puzzled Ki-Gor, the beasts that had slain the Masai. Slowly, making no sudden movement, he inched his left hand down toward the leather pouch at his waist which held the darts.

The strange manner of the animals sent

a chill down his back. Most jungle killers struck with a lightning-quick charge, rattling their prey with a barrage of snarls. These huge-chested dogs bared their cruel fangs but uttered no sound, and instead of charging, they moved to either side of him with rigid slowness.

Their yellow, unblinking eyes told him it wasn't fear of man which dictated their sidling approach. He guessed rather that their maneuver was dictated by contempt of man: they expected him to try to flee and they sought to cut him off from escape before attacking.

And realizing this, he suddenly understood the reason of their lack of fear. He carried neither bow nor spear, which were weapons they knew. They had never seen a blowgun and to their animal minds it was only a stick which he held up in the vain hope of beating them away. They took him to be unarmed, and perhaps because he was small, thought him a child.

N'GEESO closed his fingers over a dart in the pouch, carefully started lifting it towards his lips. At the same time he touched the blowgun against his lips. The practiced puff with which he sent a barb into one of the dogs was scarcely audible.

The animal flinched as the tiny sliver of death punched into its flesh. The pain was hardly more than the bite of a fly. N'Geeso laid the other dart in the cup of his lip, cautiously maneuvered the blowgun and stabbed a poisoned sliver into the second dog.

The second animal seemed to connect the pin-prick with the man. It gave a sudden, angry growl and crouched, the fanged mouth opening wider. Then with a barrage of throat-tearing snarls it came racing at N'Geeso.

The pygmy spun aside, clubbed the beast with his blowgun. His movement and the force of his blow caused the animal to miss in the leap intended to knock him down.

The dog whirled as it struck the ground, crouched for another leap.

Abruptly, its muscles jerked tight over its entire body, so tight they seemed to be tearing apart. It emitted a choked gasp and dropped in its tracks. A second later the other beast toppled over where it stood, having died on its feet without ever making a move toward the pygmy.

Expressionless through the whole encounter, deep concern appeared on N'Geeso's face as soon as both animals were disposed of. He drew his sheathed knife, hurriedly cut a chunk of meat from the buck.

But he had hardly gotten to his feet when what he feared, happened. Three more of the great dogs pushed out of the underbrush, and then at the far end of the clearing four more of them appeared. The whole pack was close about him.

He took the only course open. He dropped the meat, clasped his still bloody knife between his teeth and leaped for the nearest branch of the tree against which the buck had fallen. Catching the limb, he pulled himself up like a chimpanzee, gained his feet and scampered higher in the tree.

N'Geeso looked down at the gathering pack. He was safe so long as he stayed in the tree, and the thought in a small measure eased his mounting worry about Helene. On the high platform she was out of reach of the dogs and she had promised him to stay there. He noticed the dogs appeared tired and footsore. They wouldn't wait too long around the tree, because from experience he knew animals in their condition would grow restless and turn to easier prey.

But even as he consoled himself with the idea that Helene was safe and that he would be able to reach her before long, the White Lord's mate was facing a far more dangerous peril than he.

WHEN for the fifth time within half an hour Vani dropped to one knee to study the ground, Neeba made no effort to conceal her impatience. Nothing would have given her greater pleasure than to crash her spear shaft down across her sister's bare shoulders.

She was utterly sick of Vani and her hateful ways. Yes, Vani would return home—if Neeba came along with her! Vani had forced her to make that long, grinding trek as the price of not turning the pack on Ki-Gor. No sooner would she get Vani home, than she would have to turn around and make the trek back, and for what, for nothing more than to give that cursed witch of a sister the satisfaction of irritating her.

And now when they were nearly home, Vani had to go and discover that canoe pulled up on the river bank and get all excited because she thought it looked like a pygmy craft. Vani knew none of those Masai runners had gotten through to the pygmies, when they hadn't even been able to reach Ki-Gor. It was just another of Vani's rotten tricks to delay her.

"There's no need for us to spend all this time hunting the spoor of a few stupid pygmies," Neeba burst out. "If there are any around, the pack will find them. You gave the dogs the scent they were to follow from those water gourds and other things in the canoe."

"The dogs are only good up to a point," snapped Vani, without looking up.

Neeba stabbed the ground viciously with her spear.

"Bah!" she spat. "It's not Thor. It's just that you love to see the dogs tear a man apart."

Vani laughed mockingly and went on with her searching. When she stood up, she had a pleased look. By the gods, if her suspicions were true, she'd soon have Neeba twisting like a pig on a spear. It was almost too good to believe.

"They're bound to be close by," Vani excitedly declared, "because the dogs keep searching back and forth over this same ground. They've hidden their sign cleverly, but we'll hit a fresh scent soon."

As they trotted down the trail, the great dogs circled and criss-crossed through the brush around them, appearing and disappearing like grey ghosts. The animals gradually moved ahead of the girls because of Vani's frequent pauses to study the ground.

Several minutes ahead of the sisters the dogs reached the clearing where Helene was. True to her promise, she had remained on the tree platform. She saw the grey beasts slide out of the jungle in twos and threes, and knew immediately by the nervous way they cast about that they sensed her nearness. But because she was so far above the ground, her scent was faint and diffused.

Helene flattened on the platform, her blue eyes narrowing. Those beasts! They

must be the kind that had slain the Masai! Her muscles grew achingly tense as she thought of N'Geeso moving alone through the nearby jungle.

She tried to decide what to do. In time, they would discover her. Should she try to slip away and find N'Geeso, keep him from walking into the jaws of the pack? Or would it be better deliberately to attract the dogs' attention and lead them away from the camp? Like Ki-Gor, she could travel through the trees and stay out of the pack's reach.

Before Helene could decide, a dog found N'Geeso's fresh spoor on the ground. Its excited snarls drew its fellows to the scent. The vague smell of the woman-thing was forgotten and the pack swept away in pursuit of the pygmy.

Helene stood up, listening, trying to understand what had set them off. Two minutes dragged by, and hearing no sound, she slowly relaxed.

Unbidden, the thought of the Masai runner's torn remains came to her mind. How horrible it would be to be cornered by that pack. Loneliness pressed in upon her, and she shivered. At that same moment, her straining ears caught a noise below her.

Her eyes widened. Two young girls walked out of the forest. They had a tired, worn look as though they had traveled far and fast. Not having heard of Ki-Gor's experience with Vani and Neeba, Helene had no reason to suspect them. She saw only that they were unusually pretty and not more than eighteen years. Of course, their dress was odd and they carried spears, but they were obviously white and any reticence she might have felt about revealing her presence was dispelled when she heard them speak perfect English.

"Thank heavens, there's a spring," she heard one of them exclaim. "I'm dying of thirst."

As they approached the spring, Helene shook off her surprise. If they had the least suspicion of the savage dog pack's presence, they certainly wouldn't be calmly talking of resting. She must warn them of the danger.

"Hello, below," she called abruptly.

The girls whirled about and moved close together, their bodies taut, their spears firmly grasped.

"Up here," Helene directed, sorry she had startled them. "There's only me. Don't be frightened."

"Eh?" gasped Neeba as her glance found the tree platform. Then in an amazed whisper, she addressed her sister: "That's Ki-Gor's wife—here! How can that be?"

Triumph was in Vani's eyes. "I knew it!" she hissed. "Now who's been wasting their time?"

"Then he must be nearby, too," said Neeba. She paled, thinking of Thor. "Thor will beat us to death."

"Not me, my dear," gloated Vani. "If you will remember, I wanted to kill Ki-Gor. But no, you wouldn't let me. You were so sure you could handle him. Ha! You and your charms. Thor will beat some sense into you."

NEEBA'S LIPS quivered with anger. Ki-Gor did want her, too. If it hadn't been for the shadow of that red-haired wench between them he would have spoken what was in his heart. Suddenly, Neeba's heart skipped a beat. If Helene were out of the way, there would be no doubt about Ki-Gor's welcoming her.

Helene stood quietly on the platform, looking down at the girls. She saw how excitedly they whispered to each other. After all, she thought, an English-speaking woman living in a tree and clad in two brief pieces of leopard skin was enough to startle anyone.

"I wanted to warn you," she explained, "that this whole place was swarming with huge, fierce dogs a few minutes ago. You aren't safe on the ground. They might return any minute."

The twins exchanged an odd look. It dawned on them that Helene didn't know their identity. She took them for friendly, harmless girls.

"I know how savage they are," Helene went on. "They'd kill you on the spot. Climb up here to the platform where you'll be safe."

Vani was hard-put to hide her exultance, but Neeba actually trembled with eagerness. This was almost too easy to be true.

Neeba muttered, "Don't stand there! Let's go up before she gets suspicious." A note of savagery crept into her whisper. "A quick push and we'll be rid of her."

"Oh, no you don't," said Vani. "She goes unharmed to Thor. I've an idea that with that wench as our prisoner, we won't have to worry any more about Ki-Gor causing trouble."

"You devil! I hate you," gritted Neeba, but she knew it would be futile to argue. Vani's plan without doubt was the one Thor would approve. "You'd do anything to spite me."

"You should thank me, dear sister," returned Vani. "Helene is fresh and young and white-skinned. Such a gift may soften Thor's anger when he learns you failed to keep the White Lord at his camp. At least, she will occupy him for a few days, giving you time to be on your way out of trouble."

As always, there was no escaping Vani's cunning web. The fight went out of Neeba. "Very well," she agreed.

Though she was too high above them to hear their low voices, Helene guessed from their expression that they were arguing.

"What's wrong?" she asked, concerned. "Can't you realize you're gambling with your lives every second you stay down there?"

Vani immediately flung back an answer: "It's my sister. She's afraid of heights." Then, hesitantly, as if she didn't like to trouble Helene, she added: "Could—could you come down and help show her how easy the climb really is? Perhaps then if you climbed just ahead of her and me just below, she wouldn't be so frightened."

It was a perfectly reasonable request. Lots of people were afraid of heights. Helene was immediately sympathetic.

"Is that all that's troubling you?" she

said lightly. "Why, of course, I'll help her. Watch and you'll both see how easy it is."

Helene ran along the branch to the tree trunk, descended rapidly and easily to the ground. Vani and Neeba moved to meet her.

"Watch, now," Helene said, standing between the twins, "you catch hold of that vine, fasten your feet in the bank and climb to that crooked limb. Then you go . . ."

Vani's cold, hard tones cut her off. "Save your breath, wooden head! We're not climbing anywhere."

Helene blinked dumbly. Both sister had jammed their spears against her. Their girlish, half-fearful smiles of greeting were gone, replaced by unexpectedly hard and dangerous expressions.

"Are you crazy?" asked Helene. "I'm trying to save your lives. Those dogs will kill us all."

"Don't worry about the dogs," said Vani. "They happen to be ours and we had them searching for you."

They forced her to stand quietly while they bound her wrists.

"Where are Ki-Gor and the pygmy?"demanded Vani.

Mention of her mate and N'Geeso steadied Helene. The sisters' anxiety to learn their whereabouts told her neither man had fallen prey to the pack. But either one of them might return at any moment.

"We lost the pygmy to a leopard two days ago and Ki-Gor has gone back to the pygmy kraal for warriors," she lied. "Surely, you don't think I'd be spending my time on that platform hiding from the pack if Ki-Gor were here? He'd rid the jungle of them and you in short order."

Neeba swallowed Helene's story. Vani was not so easily taken in. She studied her captive with her strangely blank, expressionless eyes. "I think you lie!" she accused.

"Maybe you'll think differently when the pygmies get their hands on you," bluffed Helene. "It took Ki-Gor only a day to find out what was going on here. He is traveling too fast for me to make the trip. Through the trees, he can go as far in a morning as a runner on the ground can go in three days."

"This is serious," worriedly stated Neeba. "Much as I fear to face him, we must go straight to Thor with this news."

It took all Helene's will power to calmly return Vani's unblinking stare. She was greatly afraid Vani would insist on staying to watch for Ki-Gor's return. But finally Vani decided the gamble wasn't worth taking.

"It's safer to go to Thor, all right," she agreed. "He'll quickly wring the truth from her. If she lies, we can always come back and hunt down that hairless ape."

VANI prodded Helene into a trot with her spear. In their hurry, they didn't waste time trying to gather the pack, but left the dogs to follow of their own accord.

Expecting to be taken to a village of some sort, Helene was surprised when they emerged from the jungle the next morning onto a shelf of rock overlooking a lake. Vani had decided they would probably find Thor where the white engineers had tunneled and blasted an opening into the lake.

"I was right," said Vani as they came within sound of rushing water and saw figures moving about like swarming ants. "He's trying to stop the flow of water."

They approached the canal-like depression that had been cut through gravel and solid rock by the engineers and their helpers so that water from the lake could once more flow into the old river bed.

On both sides of the canal, sweating blacks strained to lever huge boulders into growing stacks. Helene saw the huge, gaunt white man who strode about among the natives cursing and shouting orders and knew that he was Thor.

At Vani's call, he hurried toward them with great reaching steps. He looked fierce and uncouth with his robe soiled and his mass of white hair and beard in wild disarray.

Helene could not know that her mate had already encountered this grim old man, was that very moment, in fact, held prisoner at Thor's lair.

When Vani started to speak, Thor impatiently waved her to silence. He exchanged no greeting with his daughters. Instead, his glittering black eyes regarded Helene, arrogantly searching her features and figure, resting a long while on her red hair.

"This can be only one," he decided in a gruff roar of sound, "the woman, Helene, whom the black dangos have described to me so many times." He clucked his tongue. "Good! Then Ki-Gor is slain."

He reached a quick, cruel hand to Helene's shoulder.

"All smooth and pretty, eh? One of those peaches and cream kind?" There was savagery in his voice, hate in his manner.

With a single hand, he twisted Helene off-balance, flung her away from him to the ground. You could see the line of his lips curl through the stained opening of his beard.

"You'll soon learn you're no more than dirt around here!" he barked. "That body will get you no favors from me."

Helene forgot her fear of Thor. Her face paled with anger and she fought against her bonds.

"You dirty, bullying coward!" she flung at him. "We'll see how brave you are when Ki-Gor and his pygmies corner you."

He started toward her as though he meant to kick her into silence, but abruptly he halted. His icy glance darted questioningly at his daughters.

"What's this about Ki-Gor?" he demanded. "Is it possible that you both failed?"

Vani and Neeba shrank away from their glowering father, each trying desperately to justify herself. They stammered out their stories in nervous, broken snatches, each trying to discredit the other. He listened in ominous silence.

They momentarily forgot Helene. Her initial reaction was surprise at learning they had both confronted Ki-Gor at the Silver River camp, one for the purpose of killing him and the other to try to charm him into taking her as a wife. For a second, she was hurt that Ki-Gor had kept this from her, but when she learned the true reason for the girls' actions her only feeling was stunned horror.

Fearing Ki-Gor's interference in his campaign of terror against the Masai, Thor's twisted brain had devised two possible ways disposing of him. The most diabolical scheme, the one that had sent the Old One into roars of laughter when he first considered it, was to have Neeba so charm the White Lord that for a time he would think of nothing else but her.

To the madman, it was perfectly logical that the beautiful, passionate, young Neeba would be able to make an utter fool of any male, let alone one as unsophisticated as Ki-Gor. That plan had wonderful possibilities, for since Thor could control Neeba, he would through her be able to make a pawn of Ki-Gor once the jungle man was thoroughly infatuated. It would be a delicious joke.

But in case this first plan misfired, Thor was careful enough to send Vani along to carry out a second and simpler scheme. She was to kill Ki-Gor if Neeba was unable to handle him.

Fear trickled like acid into Helene's stomach. The trio who held her were worse than their own ravening devil-beasts. And they were the adversaries her beloved mate must sooner or later come up against. How could a man as honorable and normal and straight-forward as Ki-Gor ever triumph over this cruel, mad devil and his she-wolves?

When the girls finished their tale and stood trembling before Thor, he snarled, "I should flay you both and throw you to the pack!" He cursed them in the vilest language.

"I've been too stupid to train anyone else to handle the dogs, so at the moment I must have your bumbling, inefficient help," he went on. "But don't think you're going scot free! I'll pay you back at a more appropriate time."

His fingers convulsed as though they already clutched the whip he'd use on the girls.

"I'll get Ki-Gor for you," Vani haltingly assured him. Then she sought to shift Thor's attention to Helene. "I'm sure Helene is lying about his leaving to get the pygmies. Beat her, Thor, and get the truth out of her!"

Thor glared consideringly at Helene, then shook his head.

"Later," he promised. "Urgent as it is to get rid of Ki-Gor, there's another matter I must deal with first."

He smiled cruelly as he spoke.

"You mean damming the river," asked Neeba innocently.

Once more he exploded into profanity, belaboring the Masai for trying to ruin his lake.

"No, I don't mean the river work," he cried, "though it must be done before the water level falls. That's why I've had to stay here at the lake."

He tugged at his beard, his voice abruptly velvety.

"You see," he explained, "while you worthless two were failing in your task, I caught the man I wanted. He's been caged in my cabin for hours while I've been held here because I can't leave these stupid blacks unsupervised."

"But isn't it more important to track down Ki-Gor?" asked Vani, "than to fool with a prisoner?"

"Nothing," snapped Thor, "is more important than what I intend to do to that man, Owens."

He turned his back on the girls, stared at the working blacks, and the muscles of his face worked impatiently.

"Take over, Neeba," he commanded. "Vani and I will go to the cabin to start work on that devil. I can wait no longer. Later, I'll send Vani down here and you'll come lend a hand with the torture." He saw how Neeba shrank at the suggestion. "Yes, you will!" he snarled. "It won't be only Vani this time who helps me."

He outlined rapidly how the masses of rock were to be raised on either side of the canyon. When enough rock was amassed, he meant to simultaneously dislodge both piles, try to choke the opening through which the water flowed from the lake.

Helene had gotten up. He grabbed her shoulder with bruising strength, his eyes burning with anger.

"We'll take the red-headed hussy," he said, "and put her in a safe place. I'll have time for her later."

Then half-dragging Helene, he set out at a rapid pace along the lake shore.

VIII

THE PATH KI-GOR'S captors took led into the taboo lands, followed a devious, climbing route through ever steeper foothills to come at last to the precipitous western edge of the lake.

With ponderous caution, the elephant carrying him moved up a rocky trail along the face of the cliff until it reached a flat shelf of rock overlooking the lake. Ki-Gor swiftly looked about him, knowing he had reached the Old One's lair.

The half-completed hulk of a boat rested bow outwards on the very edge of the cliff. Wooden pens were scattered about in a disorganized fashion, half of them filled with the devil-dogs and the other half with zebra. The dogs set up a tumult of barking when they saw the new arrivals. The noise brought a score of Bantu slaves.

With much shouting and arguing, they lowered the cage from the elephant's back, peered disinterestedly at its occupant and then carried it into the cave. They took Ki-Gor through the first great chamber of the cave, down a narrow corridor and into a long, low-ceilinged room.

The Old One's personal chamber was cluttered with a weird assortment of seagoing paraphernalia. The ceiling was hung with swinging sea lamps, the walls covered with yellowed ocean charts, the floor laid with planking like a deck. There were coiled ropes, senseless barriers of railing and in the center of the floor on a raised platform a great spoked wheel such as is used to guide sailing vessels. There were even closed portholes set in the rock along one wall.

And completely out of harmony with everything else was the most dominant piece of furniture in the chamber, a massive, throne-like chair which surveyed the room from the top of a series of stone steps.

As time passed and the Old One failed to appear, the White Lord found it increasingly hard to curb his impatience. He dared not free himself and go in search of Tembu George. The whole success of his plan depended on his unexpectedly overpowering the Old One. By force against the old man's slaves, Ki-Gor couldn't hope to win, but if he could take their master prisoner in his own chambers, then he could dictate the orders he wanted issued to the slaves.

Ki-Gor occupied himself during the long wait by using his hidden knife to cut nearly through the vines securing the front of his cage. He worked with furtive speed whenever the guards' backs were turned. When he was satisfied with his preparations, he concealed the knife beneath his shirt.

Finally, he heard the muffled boom of the Old One's voice, the rapid approach of footsteps. "No, don't come in with me now," Ki-Gor heard him say. "I would be alone with him a bit. Lock the wench up and wait until I call you."

Ki-Gor had no chance to guess that the person addressed was Vani and that Helene was the woman to be imprisoned by the savage girl.

Then the Old One stood in the room, his burning eyes on the cage. He made a savage, guttural sound deep in his throat, reached a slow hand to the heavy door, slammed it shut behind him.

"So at last we meet again," he said in a hollow, ominous whisper.

His hands clasped and unclasped nervously at his sides. "I've dreamed of this happening until my brain was on fire," he went on, "but never for a moment did I actually think it would ever be."

He began to walk back and forth along the wall, making no immediate move to approach his prisoner.

"Why have you brought me here?" demanded Ki-Gor in a timorous key. "I don't even know you. Why do you act this way?"

The Old One gave an ugly pretense of a laugh.

"I know you, Bill Owens," he said softly. "But then perhaps I've changed more than you with the years." Suddenly his voice crashed out like thunder, mad and wild, as though every particle of his control had snapped. "Damn your stinking soul, I've had reason enough to change. You did that to me, you and that whimpering, deceitful whelp of a woman."

HE WHIRLED toward the cage, his face purple and contorted. Then he stopped and by the exertion of a tremendous effort reined in his rampaging emotions.

"But don't think the years have been fruitless ones," he cried. "Every day since I last set eyes on you, I've had a full measure of revenge—every day for eighteen years."

In another lightning change of mood, he chortled to himself, thinking of it, and resumed his talking.

"The most wonderful revenge any man ever had," he resumed, gloatingly. "Yes, it's a pleasant little surprise I'm going to break to you in a few minutes. Ah, ha, ha! So very pleasant—for *me!*"

What was the old man talking about? Bill Owens had made no mention of knowing him. Ki-Gor sought to make him reveal the connection he had with Owens.

"I tell you I don't know you," he declared.

"Owens, it's too late for so thin a lie," snarled the gaunt figure. "You'd remember me from my voice alone. Yeah, Captain Thorsten they called me when I ran the fastest schooner on the Gold Coast and no job was too dangerous for me to handle.

Something stirred in Ki-Gor's mind. What was it he wondered, that the name Thorsten tried to rouse from his memory.

"I had quite a name along the coast, didn't I, Owens, when I signed you on. You were a smooth-faced kid looking for adventure, swore you were twenty-one, but I knew you weren't.

"I hired you because you were a kid. I needed a cabin boy like you." His voice grew sarcastic. "Surely, you remember my young wife. You didn't approve of her foster parents selling her to an old man, even though I did pay a high price and actually had to marry her in the bargain. Seventeen she was, with skin like milk, and beauty enough to make any man's breath stop in his throat."

The Old One had gone to the great spoke wheel, and he gripped it with both hands, his body taut, his eyes staring as if into a far distance. He was talking not so much to Ki-Gor as to himself, dredging up the acid thing that ate his vitals.

"She hated me. All the time I was out of the cabin she'd cry. But I didn't care. Whenever I wished it, the whip and the dogs—you remember my dogs, Owens—made her give me love enough for any two men. She was terrified of them." He gripped the wheel so hard his knuckles whitened.

"I liked it that way. Yes, I liked it very much that way."

His thin bluish lips were trembling and the hard, quick rush of his breathing was clearly audible.

"But I feared two things. One was that the little fool would kill herself. The other was that one of those sneaking cutthroats in my crew would steal her, skip ship with her some night in port. They hated me as much as she did, and for a jewel like her, they'd have taken any risk."

Ki-Gor was silent, listening to the ravings of an obvious madman. Then abruptly he recalled Miller's joking reference to a story Owens always told when he was drinking about his days on the sea. He realized with a shock that there was a basis, whether real or fancied, for this old man's hatred of Owens.

"So I hired you, because I thought you'd be harmless," he said, and the savagery began to rise again in his voice. "I thought after I put the fear of God in you with the dogs, a stinking kid like you would never dare touch her. Yeah, you were the one I was going to trust, to leave in earshot of my cabin at all times."

Suddenly he rushed at the cage, hammered its top with his huge knotted fists. His voice rose to a scream.

"And you were the very one who betrayed me—you, a sniveling kid in rompers!"

For an instant, the White Lord feared that his pounding fists would break the nearly severed vines and smash open the cage. The old man, though, raised his arms

and began to beat at his own head.

"You jump ship with her at Port Tonguay, spent two weeks with her in the jungle. I trailed you with my dogs, caught up with her at a native kraal, but you slipped through my fingers.

"I beat her until she couldn't move trying to get the truth out of her, but she swore you hadn't touched her. So I took her back. And she lied—she lied!" In another of his queer mood changes, the old man quieted, moved away from the cage to a weathered sea chest. He dropped his bulk heavily onto the chest.

"As time passed, she tried to make me believe it was my child she was going to have. I almost swallowed her story. I wanted to believe it because I didn't want the men to laugh at me.

"But the night it happened, the night the two girls were born, I looked at them and suddenly realized the truth, that they were your children not mine. And the crew would know it."

"We were at sea when those cursed twins were born. For a week I could think of nothing except how when we touched Capetown in ten days, the gloating crew would carry the story of what had happened to me—to tough Captain Thor—into every bar along the waterfront. They'd be jeering at me in every port on the seven seas."

His foreboding look deepened. He began to rock back and forth, his eyes glittering. Abruptly, he leaned toward Ki-Gor.

"I was too clever for them, though," he shouted. "No one but me, my dogs and those two girls ever saw land. I blew that schooner sky-high one night, watched it go up from a skiff. And I was rid of the whole batch of them, including the girl who thought she had tricked me."

He fingered his beard, a sly look coming into his eyes. His voice dropped to a silken purr.

"Why don't you ask me about your daughters?" he suggested venomously. "Surely, you're wondering why I took them with me."

He laughed shrilly, hysterically. Then the crazed sound chopped off.

"I didn't want them to die, Owens," he declared triumphantly. "They were the instruments of my revenge on you. I brought them, here, taught them that I was their father—and with *loving care* I taught them to be animals, *worse* than animals."

LIKE AN ELECTRIC jolt the truth struck Ki-Gor. Those two girls who had come to his camp were the ones this madman had debased — this lunatic was Thor.

In great detail Thor described to the stunned White Lord the manner in which he had brought up Vani and Neeba, teaching them to be as savage and cruel as his fierce dogs.

"They're cruel, vicious animals, utterly conscienceless, hating even each other," he gloated. "I've crushed every decent human instinct in them and replaced it with evil. And every day for eighteen years I've been able to look at them and taste anew my revenge on you and that faithless wench."

Thor was too pleased with himself to sit still. He got up, dry-washing his hands and chuckling.

"You can imagine how pleased I was when they stole your belongings from your tent near the lake. It was the supreme irony when they brought them to me and I found from your letters and papers that you were Owens. Isn't that good, having your own daughters responsible for your downfall!"

Snickering, he crept closer to the cage, leaned down to peer at Ki-Gor.

"Your own flesh and blood are going to torture you slowly to death before me," he wheezed. And they'll enjoy doing it, because they think you're their father's enemy and because they like to see men suffer."

He opened the chest, took out a heavy whip.

"I used this on the dogs and on your daughters," he said, caressing its oiled length. "It's the one I flayed your beloved with that day I caught her. And now I'm going to use it on you."

He started slowly towards the cage.

"Think, Owens, how much better off you would have been," he gloated hoarsely, "if you'd been killed before I knew who you were."

He laughed and smashed the whip over the cage. Then he ran forward to open the cage door. Ki-Gor knew it was time to act. The White Lord ripped the bonds from his hands and feet, rolled to his knees and plunged at the wall of the cage.

Like a charging bull, he hit the bamboo frame. The nearly severed vines burst completely apart and the whole side ripped free and flung across the room.

Thor gave an astounded roar. He was caught utterly off-guard. A cat suddenly attacked by a trapped mouse could have been no more surprised.

As Ki-Gor splintered through the cage, Thor vaulted backwards to escape his rush. He swung the whip with all his strength, hammered its lead-weighted length across the White Lord's bowed back. He hit with desperate ferocity, hoping to slam Ki-Gor to the floor with the blow.

The whip's heavy bite sounded like a gunshot. Ki-Gor staggered in mid-stride as pain exploded down the long, raw welt torn across his back. Most men would have dropped in their tracks, and, indeed, for a fraction, Ki-Gor's driving legs shivered and gave beneath him.

But there was a brute power in his muscle-corded body forged through long years of violent jungle life. And a flaming will ruled that matchless body. He wavered under the whip's shock, and then spurred by the whistling sing of its uncoiled length whirling high for a second blow, he steadied and the piston-like drive of his legs plunged him in against Thor.

Ki-Gor's shoulder hit the Old One at waist level, lifted him off the floor and slammed him half-across the room. Only a desperate grab at the spoked wheel kept him from falling. Before he could recover, the White Lord was on him again, tearing the whip from his hand and tossing it away.

"You fool," Thor gasped. "I can still break you in two. I've killed a score of men like this, Owens."

Ki-Gor was surprised at the old man's bludgeoning power. His giant frame had grown gaunt and stooped with the years, but he had retained an amazing core of strength. And the manner of his fighting told a confidence born of many victories.

Slowly, the White Lord was forced backwards, bending under the terrible pressure of the death hug. Thor stood chest to chest with him, his unkempt beard and long white hair catching in Ki-Gor's mouth and eyes. The jungle man writhed and struggled, cursing himself silently for underestimating the Old One's ability in a rough and tumble fight.

"This is what I wanted to do to you eighteen years ago," hoarsely panted Thor. "I'd have killed you then. But now I'm only going to injure you. This is too easy a way for you to die."

To speak, it was necessary for him to loosen momentarily his crushing grip. That brief opportunity was the respite Ki-Gor needed. He sucked a great breath into his aching lungs, fought his arms up in a renewed burst of strength and fastened his fingers in the Old One's hair and beard. Back he jerked Thor's head, heaving until he feared the wiry hair would tear out by its roots.

STRAIN as he might, Thor couldn't keep his face from being turned up toward the ceiling, his bearded chin jutting out at an angle, his tortured neck exposed. With his own head, Ki-Gor began to hammer at the vulnerable chin and throat, and with every blow Thor winced more.

The old man's neck muscle couldn't stand the strain. Soon his head had been pulled back so far he was choking. Doggedly, he tried to retain his grip, but it was only a matter of moments before his arms began to loosen.

Then abruptly his grip broke completely and he sagged backwards, his mouth working and eyes bulging. Ki-Gor slid to the side and pulled the old man to his knees. Now that it was too late, Thor tried to call out to the guards, but his weak, strangled voice couldn't penetrate through the stone walls or the massive wooden door.

Ki-Gor flung him on his face and knelt on him. He ripped away a length of Thor's garment, used it to tie the old man's hands behind his back. Thor resisted, but quite feebly. He was strong as he had boasted, but he had retained none of the endurance, the saving second strength of youth, and once he had spent that first violent bolt, he was finished.

After tying Thor, Ki-Gor picked up the whip. He cracked it viciously above the old man's head.

Thor gave a weak scream and scuttled into a corner on his knees.

"I'm going to give you the beating you meant for me," grimly threatened Ki-Gor. His stony features gave no hint he was bluffing. He reached inside his shirt, took out the concealed knife. "First, though, I'm going to split that evil tongue of yours."

The only part of Thor's face that was visible, the weathered patch around his eyes and nose, was a sickly grey. He shrank back against the stone, trembling. He judged others by his own standards, so he believed Ki-Gor's bestial threats implicitly.

"You can't get away with it," he said thickly. "There are guards everywhere outside. They'll cut you to shreds if you harm me. They'll do away with you with more pain and bleeding than any panther killing a water-fowl."

Ki-Gor leered at him. "I know all that," he admitted. "And since I can't hope to leave here alive, I haven't got a thing to lose by killing you."

Thor's shaking hand fumbled at his mouth. The White Lord could almost read the working of that cruel, faithless mind.

"Look, Owens," he said jerkily, "I'll let you go free. I'll forget everything, if you don't harm me." He tried to make his voice sound sincere. "I—I didn't really mean to kill you. I just wanted to scare you up a bit." He swallowed, watching the knife in Ki-Gor's hand. "Now, is that a bargain?"

"No!" declared the White Lord. He shifted the knife to his right hand, taking the whip in his left.

"Wait, Owens," cried Thor. "I've got gold and—and even some diamonds in that chest. You'll be rich. You can have them all."

Ki-Gor shook his head. "I don't trust you," he said simply.

Thor couldn't hide his guilty look, but he redoubled his pleading, terrified by Ki-Gor's slow advance toward him.

"Don't!" he shrieked. "Ask anything you like. You can use me as a shield to get through the cave. I won't trick you."

"Well, maybe I'll chance it," Ki-Gor said. "After all, if I keep my knife at your throat, I can kill you if you try any tricks. I do owe a debt to Tembu George, so I should try to set him free."

"Anything — anything at all," gulped Thor. "Let me call one of the guards and tell him to have the prisoner brought here."

Ki-Gor went to the door, rested his hand on the catch.

"The guard will also bring two swords, two bows and full quivers of arrows," he directed. "Tembu George and I will destroy those dogs in the pens. Order your men to go to the deepest section of the cave and stay there until we're gone. It will mean your life if we see a single person after we leave this room."

Thor wet his lips nervously. "I'll do everything you say," he swiftly granted.

Ki-Gor hesitated a moment longer. It seemed to him the Old One seemed too little disturbed by the news that the dog pack would be destroyed. Those devil beasts were actually the heart of his power, and he would be more upset if he actually thought he was going to lose them.

"I must be ready," resolved the White Lord. "He has some scheme in mind now to thwart me."

Ki-Gor raised the latch gently, then abruptly threw the heavy door wide. He leaped back to the wall near Thor, ordered him to summon one of the guards. The old man stood with his head shoved forward, his broad shoulders made more stooped by the tightness with which Ki-Gor had bound his arms. He breathed gustily, like a beaten old bull driven into a corner by a young adversary.

"Molat," he called harshly. The summoned guard, a squat, brutal-faced Bantu armed with a long sword, came quickly into the room, closing the door after him. His cruel eyes went to his master, and then slowly as he realized something was wrong, he looked at Ki-Gor, saw he held the whip and a knife.

His jaw dropped.

"Yes!" rasped Thor. "I'm his prisoner. Don't stare like a dolt, come closer and listen carefully to what I have to say."

Ki-Gor's level voice commanded the man to stay where he was. Then the White Lord detailed exactly what the guard was to do. When the black looked questioningly at Thor, Ki-Gor snapped, "Tell him it's your will that these things be done!"

The old man glowered, opening and closing his mouth several times as though it were hard to utter the words.

"I . . . order . . . you," he falteringly began, and then his voice suddenly crackled, *"to kill this man!"*

As he spoke, he flung away from the wall and darted for the door. Ki-Gor hadn't tied his legs, so Thor gambled now on putting the black between him and his enemy before the White Lord could stop him.

Ki-Gor could have leaped forward and intercepted the old man, but he would have laid himself open to a deadly sword stroke from the guard in the struggle to subdue Thor. And there was no way to avoid such a struggle, because he couldn't afford to kill Thor. The gaunt leader alive was his only passport to freedom.

Ki-Gor thought with lightning speed. In another moment, the guard would collect his senses, dash at the jungle man with his sword. The White Lord's left hand tightened on the whip, he lunged out far enough from the wall to swing it.

LIKE A SPEEDING missile, he sent the studded end of the whip darting out for Thor's head. The curling length of leather outraced the straining man. With a flat, hard splat it came against him, whirled two lightning coils about his neck.

Like a lassoed steer, Thor hit the end of the rigid tether. His feet shot out from under him as Ki-Gor heaved back on the whip. He spun up from the floor, half-turned in the air and then crashed full-length against the solid planking. He lay limp and stunned where he fell.

The guard gave a shriek of rage and burst at the White Lord. He whirled his sword high. Ki-Gor dropped the whip, leaped backward to the wall. He had one single fleeting chance for life, but the least tremor of his hand, the slightest misjudgment of his eyes meant death for him.

In that moment he moved almost too fast for a person to follow his actions. His right hand came shoulder high, clutching the hunting knife. With the blurred movement of a striking snake, he threw the blade. Then from his crouching position, he threw himself to the side.

The berserk rush of the black was not to be halted. His sword cut down through the space Ki-Gor had just vacated. It spanged against the wall with terrible velocity. Then the charging guard himself drove face on into the stone.

The native reeled back from the impact, turned uncertainly toward Ki-Gor. He raised his sword jerkily, took a stumbling step forward. His movements suddenly lost all direction. He swayed off a few steps into the room and collapsed.

Ki-Gor was on him as soon as he fell, wresting the sword from his grasp. He stepped back, regarded the black with harsh, pitiless eyes. The White Lord's knife was driven up to its hilt in the black's chest. The man had been dying as he hit the wall.

A strangling sound snapped Ki-Gor's attention from the dead guard. He hurried to Thor, tore the whip from the old man's neck. He caught Thor by the front of his white robe, lifted him upright. It was a full minute before the Old One was able to stand.

As Thor caught his breath, he saw the black stretched on the floor and shrank fearfully away from the White Lord. But Ki-Gor drew him close, shook him for all his size as a terrier would a rat. The jungle man pricked the point of his sword against the Old One's belly.

"You'll have no second chance for treachery," he snarled. "Call the other guard, and if you so much as utter a single wrong word, this blade sinks home."

The Old One regarded him with wide-eyed fear. He was actually seeing Ki-Gor clearly for the first time, searching his features with an awed intensity.

"The hair is the same, and the eyes," he mumbled to himself. "He was big, with a promise of growing larger. Time changes a man's features, and yet . . ."

Suspicion came in his face, flaring abruptly. He hadn't seen Owens since he had grown to manhood, and when he had spied him on the project at the lake, he had seen the engineer only from a long distance. His deranged mind had accepted the man in the cage as Owens, and through all the time of his gloating over his prisoner, he was actually crowing over a hated figure in his mind rather than the man in the cage. He had been superimposing over his prisoner the remembered features of a youth.

"You can't be Owens!" he said with abrupt certainty. "Who are you? What trick is this the Masai have played on me?"

But even as he asked the questions, the truth was trickling into his mind. He had heard descriptions of the famed Ki-Gor from many of the blacks he had hired or had captured as slaves. Now as he remembered Helene's capture, he put the facts together.

"You're *Ki-Gor!*" he cried angrily.

"Never mind who I am," Ki-Gor said sharply. "Get that guard in here!"

When the guard had been summoned. Ki-Gor again rattled off his orders. Thor meekly nodded approval the whole time he spoke. The discovery that Ki-Gor was his captor seemed to have taken the last fight out of the tricky old man.

"To be sure everything is done as he orders," he told the black when Ki-Gor finished, "go to my daughter, Vani. Make certain she understands it is Ki-Gor who overpowered me. Say I can trust only her to handle this, because we are trading a life for a life."

As the flustered black left, Thor turned apologetically to Ki-Gor.

"I couldn't risk a mistake," he said. "There won't be a chance for anything to go wrong with Vani's handling it."

There was a cunning gleam in Thor's eyes which Ki-Gor didn't like, yet he had heard exactly what the old man said and he could find nothing untoward in his words.

IX

WHEN the guard returned with Tembu George, the Masai chieftain limped painfully in the door ahead of his escort, his face hard-set, his shoulders squared. Then when he saw Ki-Gor, he stopped in astonished disbelief. He hadn't been told why he was being brought to Thor's room.

His hard mask dissolved and an expression nearer to pain than gladness caught his features. He stood wordlessly, relief and gratitude welling into his eyes. That moment told Ki-Gor how deeply his friend had suffered at the hands of the fiendish Old One.

"You are free," Ki-Gor said, talking to cover his own feelings. He cut Tembu George's bonds, put weapons into his arms. "Your people are unharmed. They only await your return before smashing this madman."

With a near-sob, Tembu George spun towards Thor. "I'll do it now," he said, "slowly and with my bare hands." The Masai leader's back was lined with raw welts from repeated beatings.

Thor screamed and leaped back. "Stop him!" he pleaded. "Remember our bargain!"

Ki-Gor held the Masai chifetain back. "You shall have your revenge, but you must wait for it," he said regretfully. "I've given my word that I wouldn't harm this dango if we were given safe passage out of the cave."

After giving them the weapons Ki-Gor had demanded, the guard disappeared. Ki-Gor shoved Tembu George toward the door.

"I grant it was a bad bargain," he soothed, "but it was the best I could make, since I came alone,"

"Alone!" cried the chieftain in awe. "By the spirit of my grandfather, you are a greater madman than the Old One. Why didn't you tell me? Come, let us get away from here!"

Ki-Gor went in the lead, holding Thor as a shield. Tembu George protected his back. Like stalking leopards they padded down the deserted corridor, expecting treachery at every step. Wall torches thinned the gloom but didn't disperse it. Other than the slight scrape of their feet on the dusty floor, there was no sound.

"You see, all the blacks are gone," muttered Thor. "You've nothing to fear, so be careful with that sword. A bargain is a bargain with me."

But despite Thor's assurances, Ki-Gor kept the point of his blade against the old man. Thor was much too tense himself, thought the jungle man, to be urging them to relax.

"What are you watching for, Thor?" he asked grimly, noting how his prisoner kept twisting his head to peer into every corner.

Thor started. "Nothing—nothing!" he stuttered. "I—I'm just afraid you'll mistake some shadow for a man and kill me."

Shoving Thor along, Ki-Gor went to the dog pens. He pushed the Old One up against the gate, ordered him not to move. Then the jungle man secured his sword in his belt, slid his bow from his shoulder and fitted an arrow to it. He picked out one of the larger snarling killers, took careful aim.

A few yards further down the wall, Tembu George followed suit.

"I wouldn't do that!" said a cold, flat voice behind Ki-Gor.

WITH HIS BOW ready drawn for the kill, the White Lord spun to smash an arrow into the speaker. His eyes were pitiless slits as he turned, for he knew this was a last, desperate try by the Old One's followers to thwart their escape. If he could drop their leader with his arrow and then grab Thor and threaten to kill him, he might stop the attack before it began.

His stabbing glance caught on the figure standing by the ship's hull. His bow strained back an additional inch, the fletching full against his ear. With the automatic skill of a master bowman, he lined the arrow on the breast of the target.

Then in the fraction of a moment before he shot, his eye actually registered the details of the target. Like a graven statue he froze, his arm and back muscles tense and swollen from the pull of the bow. He uttered a hoarse, hurt cry.

And slowly he lowered his bow, leaving the arrow unshot.

"Why didn't you go on and shoot?" taunted the flat voice. "I hoped that you would."

The person Ki-Gor had come so near to slaying was Helene. With a gag about her mouth, she was held rigidly against the outside of the hull by a rope looped about her neck. The rope was held by Vani who crouched behind a stack of rotting timber on the deck above Helene's head.

"Stay back," warned Vani, guessing his intent, "or I'll set the dogs on her."

And with that she gave a cry which brought four of the grey devil-beasts charging from the hold of the craft where they had been hidden with Helene and her when Ki-Gor came out of the cave.

"Before you can stop them all, one will tear her throat out," Vani declared.

The four gaunt dogs bristled and snarled about Helene, awaiting the command which would set them free to tear that soft, curved body to shreds.

Vani's taunting laugh rang out. "The game is up, Ki-Gor," she said. "Surrender or she dies!"

Helene's face was immobile.

Ki-Gor pulled Thor away from Tembu George, lifted him above his head in an angry surge of strength.

"You're forgetting I have your father," he said fiercely. "Free Helene, or I'll smash Thor's life out. I can be as ruthless as you."

Vani's laugh floated across to him.

"Go ahead, Ki-Gor!" she urged. "That's a trade to my advantage. Your young wife for a worn-out, evil old man who hasn't many more years to live anyway. I can do without Thor and his lashings."

Thor writhed in terror, squealing like a stuck pig. He couldn't speak because Ki-Gor held his throat.

Slowly, Ki-Gor lowered Thor, set his feet on the ground. A normal man was no match for that she-beast.

He was beaten.

"So you're giving up," sneered Vani. "Ha! What a joke to think of anyone giving up his life because he can't bear to see this spineless, sniveling ninny of a wench slain."

"I'll throw down my arms," Ki-Gor said, "if Helene and Tembu George are freed."

Vani hesitated. Then slyly she answered, "You drive a hard bargain, but since it's you we really want, I will agree. Both of you give your weapons to Thor. Then I'll turn the woman loose."

"Oh, no," said Ki-Gor. "No more of your lying tricks. Tembu George keeps his arms, and only after he and Helene are safe in the jungle will I surrender."

"I trust you no more than you trust me," snapped Vani.

"Let—me—talk," gasped Thor, half-choked by Ki-Gor's right arm wrenched tight about his throat. "I'll—make—her—do—it."

Ki-Gor learned then the power by which Thor controlled the two sisters. Regaining his voice, the old man wildly cursed Vani, ordered her to accept Ki-Gor's offer immediately or he would set the four dogs on her.

Thor was sole master of the pack. The dogs were raised, trained and fed by him and not until they were full grown did he teach them to submit to the direction of the girls. They submitted only because their master wished it, for their full allegiance remained fastened on Thor. The beasts had no love for the girls and if the old man commanded it, they would as unhesitatingly attack Vani or Neeba as anyone else.

Faced by Thor's angry threat, Vani swiftly accepted Ki-Gor's offer. But by then Tembu George was protesting that he wouldn't leave his friend at the mercy of the crazed pair.

"It will avail me nothing to have you stay," said Ki-Gor. "The greatest favor you can do me is get Helene to safety, and then return at the head of your warriors."

Tembu George's face was tortured. He stared at the White Lord and tears glistened unashamed in his eyes. He said nothing more, for speech was impossible, but all that he felt was in his look.

He went at a limping trot to Helene. Vani had called back the dogs. Tembu George untied Helene's hands, pulled off the gag,

Forced to listen in silence while Vani trapped her husband, Helene was in near hysteria. She cried to him that she wouldn't be the cause of his death.

"If it weren't for me, you'd rid the jungle of these killers right now," she said. "I won't do this to you. I'll kill myself and then you'll be free to fight."

She tried to snatch Tembu George's sword, but he was too quick and tore it from her grasp. She turned, wildly looking for a means of self-destruction. Not fifty feet from whre she stood lay the edge of the cliff.

Thor gave a frightened cry. If Helene died, Ki-Gor would kill him in his tracks. "I swear I won't harm him," he shrieked. "He's to be a hostage." Then shrilly he appealed to Tembu George, "Catch her!"

Helene paid no heed to Thor's hurried promise. With a leap, she started for the cliff, meaning to jump to her death in the lake far below.

TEMBU GEORGE took two long, straining steps, oblivious in that terrible moment of the tearing pain the effort caused him. He knew with his injured leg he could never outrun the fleet Helene, so before she could gain momentum, he dove at her like a football tackler, his long arms slamming about her knees.

The two rolled over and over, with Helene fighting him. "He lies! He lies!" she kept crying about Thor. Then Tembu George pinned her wrists, picked her up in his arms and started down the path to the jungle. He was crying openly like a heartbroken child.

The four dogs with Vani, upset at seeing their intended prey taken away from them, began to bark. Their savage excitement spread to the dogs in the other pens, and like great sounding boards, the cave and the cliff walls echoed and intensified the chilling chorus.

Thor finally roared them to silence. "Helene and the black have had ample time," he said. "I've kept my word. Now keep yours and release me."

Still Ki-Gor held him, saying nothing. As the minutes dragged by, both Vani and the Old One grew increasingly nervous.

"No one will lay a hand on you," assured Thor in a whining voice. "You're to be a hostage, treated like a guest, while I make peace with the Masai."

Listening to that jackal voice, Ki-Gor's lips thinned into a hard, contemptuous line. Abruptly he released Thor. He tossed away his bow and the quiver of arrows. He drew the sword, cut the cloth which bound the Old One's arms.

Thor took a quick step away. Ki-Gor yet retained the sword, his broad fingers gripped tight about the hilt as he seemed to weigh its balance. The triumphant gleam which had flickered up in the old man's eyes died as he saw the way the White Lord held the blade.

"We—we'll go in the cave," he said. "Walk ahead, Vani," he called, "and tell the blacks that Ki-Gor is to be treated with respect." He motioned for the jungle man to precede him. "After all, we are white men, so we may as well make the best of an uncomfortable situation."

Ki-Gor drew a deep, slow breath. He balanced the sword for a last time in his hand, then with a toss, spun it away through the air to stick upright in the ground twenty yards away. He strode past Thor toward the cave, his expressionless face betraying nothing of his feelings.

Before he had gone ten steps, he heard a jarring crash behind him. He spun around to find that the moment his back was turned Thor had darted to the dog-pens and thrown open the gate. The disheveled old man crouched in the opening, the huge, gaunt dogs pressing all about him.

"Now you filthy scum," ranted Thor, "I'll deal with you!"

Ki-Gor's features registered neither surprise nor fear. He regarded the bearded figure calmly.

"I never expect a jackal to act otherwise than a jackal," he said contemptuously.

Thor shook uncontrollably, spraying out wild curses. Several of the dogs tried to pass him, but he kicked them back, delayed a fraction longer the order which would seal the White Lord's death.

"Don't try to console yourself with the idea that you've saved Helene and Tembu," spat the Old One. "You're dying for nothing—nothing—do you hear! As soon as I've finished you, I'll set the pack on their trail and we'll run them to bay before the sun is down."

At his reference to Helene, the White Lord's eyes narrowed and his jaw set hard.

"Hai!" crowed Thor, seeing he had touched a vulnerable spot. "But that's not all! At dawn I mean to teach the Masai a bloody lesson. They, too, will pay for allowing your blundering interference in my affairs. And when I ride back tomorrow, Owens will be with me."

He broke into a cackling laugh.

"You've accomplished nothing, you meddling fool," he shouted. *"You die for nothing!"*

Then Thor stabbed a forefinger at the White Lord, screeched hysterically the order for the grey devil-beasts to attack. And at the same moment behind Ki-Gor rose Vani's hate-filled voice sending in her four dogs to join the kill.

IN A MAD, slavering flood, the pack burst out of the pen, past the screaming, leaping figure of their master. Thor's raging excitement seemed to catapult them instantly into the wildest kill-lust. This was the duty they were bred for, to drag down and kill men, and the victim who stood before them was alone and unarmed.

Like a great cat he whirled away in front of the pack and sped toward the sword he had so recently tossed away. The blade stuck upright in a patch of sand and gravel. For all his flashing speed and power, he could not hold his lead on the huge, gaunt dogs.

With their every straining leap, the pack leaders cut away the gap which separated Ki-Gor from death. Ki-Gor sensed their nearness, saw from the corner of his eye the approach of the first two. Though he felt the effort must burst his heart, he dredged up a last, unused remnant of power, sprinted the final few yards necessary to bring him to the sword.

In full stride, he reached and caught the sword by its hilt. One of the grey beasts lifted in a leap even as his hand closed about the metal. Ki-Gor turned abruptly to the left and the dog flashed past him at shoulder height, missing by inches. A fanged devil lunged in at his legs and he chopped its neck open.

Then he was running for the half-completed ship's hull. He reached it, with the pack at his heels. He hurtled upward, landed on the upper planking. Carried by the momentum of their rush and the press of the animals behind them, many of the dogs were swept into the open hull beneath him.

Ki-Gor turned just as other of the animals launched themselves for the weathered deck on which he stood. Like a flickering beam of light his sword darted in and out among the grey bodies. Then abruptly the blade was red, and grey forms went kicking and sprawling back to earth, literally sliced apart.

As the place for his last stand, Ki-Gor had selected the hull because it gave him a small area to defend and the dogs couldn't get behind him. They had to leap up to the deck as he had done and there was room for only a few at a time to come at him.

Thor raged and screamed when he saw what the White Lord had done. Vani rushed close to the pack, flung her spear at the jungle man. In the bare nick of time, Ki-Gor threw himself to one knee, letting the barbed shaft whir over his head.

That interval in which he was forced down allowed three dogs to reach the deck with him. Vani cried out in glee, thinking he was finished, but Ki-Gor ripped open the first animal to rush him, sprang up and drove the other two beasts tumbling from the deck. Once more he held an advantageous position to fight off attack, and he laid about him with a ferocity which took a swiftly mounting toll of the dogs.

Thor tore at his hair like a man possessed. His precious dogs were being cut to pieces before his eyes by that steel-nerved devil. They would never pull him down from that narrow deck without help. He reeled about, tore open another gate and sent a fresh pack of grey killers into the fray.

Then the Old One scooped up the bow and quiver of arrows which Ki-Gor had dropped. He'd drive that hated figure off the boat! He ran forward, lashing an arrow at the battling jungle man.

When the first arrow twanged into the railing beside him, Ki-Gor leaped back a step. He saw Thor whip another arrow from the quiver and come at him. With all the luck in the world, he couldn't hope to avoid many arrows in his exposed position, and yet if he dropped down on the deck so the old man couldn't easily hit him, he could no longer fight off the dogs.

It was the end, and Ki-Gor knew it. If he leaped to the ground and tried to reach the path to the jungle, the pack would soon overhaul him. He might manage to outrun them to the mouth of the cave, but there was no safety there and on open ground Thor would probably drop him with an arrow. And the cliff at his back offered no avenue of escape for it was a sheer drop hundreds of feet long to the lake.

In that hopeless moment, Ki-Gor's courage didn't desert him. At least, he would cheat the blood-crazed pair of the privilege of killing him. Their frenzied lust to see him go down under the pack would remain unsated. He'd leave them no littered remains to gloatingly show their black slaves.

He turned and ran to the prow of the boat which extended out over the edge of the cliff. In some mad whim of the past, Thor had started his slaves to building the craft with the idea of having a look-out post which would give him the illusion of having a vessel beneath him once more.

Ki-Gor looked down at the distant lake surface. His left hand was on the railing, with his right he still gripped the sword. His whole body was tense, braced for the leap.

Ki-Gor saw that the cliff was cut back at an angle under its rim. And there in a strata of softer rock starting about ten yards below him were rooted several twisted patches of vines.

An arrow burned across his back, furrowing the skin. In a snarling rush, the dogs poured up on the craft and drove toward him. His next act wasn't a reasoned one. It was a desperate, instinctive grasping for life, an act which his brain under any other circumstances would have immediately rejected as hopeless.

He sprang up on the railing, stood to his full height. A lifetime of whirling through the trees had accustomed him to heights, so he remained unshaken by the dizzy void which opened below him. He pitched his sword away, sent it in a gleaming, twisting drop toward the lake.

For the merest fraction of time, he balanced on the narrow foothold. Then he crouched, his muscles bunching. The dogs were almost on him. As they leaped, he dove off the prow and flashed downward through space.

X

NOT UNTIL they actually saw Ki-Gor lift in the dive did Thor and Vani believe he would throw himself to his death. They had expected him to go down fighting, trying in a last frantic, hopeless effort to stave off the pack. And when they saw they were to be cheated of that spectacle they screamed out furiously as though by the sound of their voices they could hold him.

From where they stood, it looked as if Ki-Gor had angled straight down, going deliberately to his death. Actually, however, he had dived inward so that he cut back beneath the rim, skimming close against the undercut cliff face as he aimed for the area where the vines grew. And as soon as he dropped from Thor and Vani's view, the rigid perfection of his dive shattered as he endeavored with frantic contortions to bring his feet forward and fling himself in against the rock.

From long experience in twisting to catch limbs, he was able to manage his body. He came in against the rock in a scraping fall. He caught a patch of vines and they tore free in his hands. Immediately, as he fell, he reached for the next bunch, and though they also ripped loose, his descent was noticeably slowed.

Then he was at the farthest inward point of the undercut area and the incline began to angle outward again. Grappling desperately for handholds among the scattered vines, he kept from being thrown away from the rock face as his feet struck the grade. But the shock buckled his braced legs and he kept skidding.

He was no longer falling free, however, and though he was numbed and breathless, he gradually slowed his descent. Finally, the liana strands held him at one point. He flattened against the sharp grade, lay gasping and spent, his arms trembling.

He had no need to fear discovery. Thor and the girl had not the least suspicion of what he had done. With a kind of awe they stared at the vacant air where he had disappeared, making no immediate move to approach the edge of the cliff. Vani looked queerly at the Old One.

"He could have killed you, Thor," she said thoughtfully, "and yet he threw down his weapons and kept his promise to surrender. Why didn't he lie and double-cross you? And why didn't he squeal with fear or ever beg for mercy like you did when you thought he might kill you? I must think about that, Thor. I must think about the difference between you two."

The Old One seemed uneasy under her probing glance. She was very quiet and intent.

"He was a fool, and now he's dead," he blustered. "He was a yellow coward, you hear, and I never want him mentioned again. He's gone, wiped out, and that's exactly what I wanted."

He hawked loudly. When Vani continued to watch him so oddly, he turned his attention to the dogs crowding about the deck and the cliff's edge, barking and bristling excitedly.

"Silence, you stupid beasts," he roared, and using his bow as a flail, he drove the pack back into the pens, striking out at every dog in reach with unnecessary violence.

"Get Neeba," he snarled at Vani. "We leave at once to catch those other two and then attack the Masai kraal."

Vani nodded, but before leaving, she went to the side of the hull. She leaned over and stared down at the lake. There were no ripples to show where the White Lord had fallen.

The mere act of looking at the place where Ki-Gor had disappeared served to alter Vani's mood. She began to laugh in her ugly, mocking way.

"I must hurry to Neeba," she said. "This will be a wonderful little surprise for her. I want to be sure my darling sister knows every detail of what we did to Ki-Gor."

Still laughing, she hurriedly got two zebra from a pen and went to gloat over Neeba. While she was gone, the White Lord's strength returned and he inched his way to a small shelf of rock where he could huddle in a sitting position.

After a long time, Ki-Gor heard a shriek. "I told you to leave me alone. Curse your rotten soul, I've had enough. Let's see how you like to die." It was Neeba's voice from above.

Vani screamed in terror, and the White Lord surmised that Neeba had snatched up a weapon. He heard Thor's angry voice added to the uproar.

"No more of this brawling," the Old One ordered. "We'll be ready to ride as soon as the men are fed and armed. Since I can't be watching you two every minute, you stay here until I come for you."

To Ki-Gor's surprise, a short time later when he glanced up at the prow of the boat, he saw Neeba leaning there with her face in her arms. She was crying heartbrokenly at the spot from which she thought he had leaped to the lake. For all his modesty, there could be no doubt in his mind that her grief was entirely for him.

As he watched her, hope suddenly kindled in his eyes. He excitedly tugged a small rock free from the cliff, threw it so that it struck the railing beside her. Neeba jumped and turned with an angry face as though she expected that Vani had crept up and tried to hit her.

When she saw no one behind her, she looked puzzled. Ki-Gor was afraid she would walk to the other end of the craft to see if someone were hiding from her. Hastily, he dug out another rock and hit the railing.

This time Neeba saw the direction from which the stone had come. Her glance swept down along the cliff and as Ki-Gor motioned with his hand, she saw him. She gripped the rail with white-faced astonishment. For fear she would cry out when she found her voice, Ki-Gor put his finger to his mouth in a gesture of caution.

His hopes were suddenly dashed. Before he had an opportunity to communicate any message at all to her, Neeba drew back a step, her eyes wide and frightened. She pressed a clenched fist against her lips, and then with a smothered cry, whirled and dashed out of sight on the deck.

Ki-Gor's shoulders slumped, his features going bleak and hopeless. He should have known she wouldn't dare help him. He'd have to jump now. After she told Thor about him, the old man would drive him from the cliff with arrows.

Bitterness welled over him in a consuming flood. He looked down at the lake. There was no escape. He felt the slow, draining lethargy of hopelessness.

Then, he heard his name called softly. Neeba stood above him on the ship's prow. He blinked. She was alone. And what was it she held up for him to see?

Like the lifting beat of an eagle's wings, his heart soared. She held a length of rope. She was risking her own life to help him. She hadn't told Thor!

HURRIEDLY, Neeba knotted one end of the rope around the prow. She tied one of the rocks Ki-Gor had thrown at her to the free end, glanced nervously at the cave, then threw it at the White Lord.

Ki-Gor drew the rope taut, testing the knot Neeba had tied about the prow. He forced himself to look up, trying to keep his thoughts away from the yawning abyss. He couldn't think about the rope breaking or of his strength failing before he reached the hull. He had to make it!

Hand over hand he started up the twisting, swaying rope. His head grew giddy from the sickening swing of the rope. He was a heavy man and the aching pain in his knotted arm and shoulder muscles grew with every upward movement. Sweat beaded his face stained through the tattered remnants of Owens' clothes.

His upward progress grew slower. Tremors caught at his muscles and there was cloudiness before his eyes. His chest was a knot of pain. The rope seemed endless.

He faltered, almost lost the rhythmic swing so vital in that manner of climb. Then his jaw clamped shut, and by sheer force of will he forced a last reserve of strength from his body, shinnied the last three yards to the prow.

He got one exhausted arm over the railing, but that final spurt had taken its toll and he was suddenly too weak to draw himself to safety. Neeba caught at him, and with a desperate heave, helped get him onto the deck. He sprawled out on his side, panting, his eyes half-closed. It was a full minute before he was recovered enough to talk.

Neeba was bent over him. "Oh my darling, you're alive, you're alive!" she kept repeating. Her hands caressed his hair, his cheek.

He pushed himself to a sitting position, still groggy. Neeba hastily shoved him back on the deck.

"Stay flat!" she said frantically. "Any moment Thor or Vani might come from the cave."

The White Lord's senses cleared. He must get away. After the tremendous exertion of the climb, he was in no shape to travel either fast or far on foot. If he could only rest for a bit, his strength would renew itself, but until he was within the Masai kraal with Helene and Tembu George he couldn't afford the luxury of rest. He would need every bit of lead he could get before the pack was loosed from the pens.

And as he thought of the animal pens, he remembered the zebra. That was the answer to his problem.

"I owe my life to you, Neeba," he said gratefully. "You're different from your sister and Thor, different despite everything they've done to form you in their own cruel mold. I'll not forget what you've done for me."

Neeba frowned. "Don't be too generous," she told him seriously. "With another man, how can you know how I would have acted. When Vani told me you were dead, it was as if the sun had fallen from the sky."

"I'm all right now," Ki-Gor assured her. "I'm going to try to take one of Thor's zebra. Why don't you go in the cave, so if anything goes wrong, you won't be suspected of having helped me."

The hot darkness of her eyes regarded him.

"The zebras Vani and I were riding are tied at the end of the deck there. We will use them."

The way she employed "we" left no doubt but what she meant to accompany him. That was a development he hadn't expected.

"I'm glad you'll go with me," Ki-Gor

said frankly. "I was just going to warn you not to ride against the Masai with Thor because this time he and his pack will be slaughtered. It's better that you break with him now." He paused uncertainly, then added, "And there's a white man at the kraal who can give you the kind of life you deserve."

Neeba bit the full redness of her lower lip. She shook her head slowly, tossing her long hair.

"I care nothing about the Masai or that white man," she declared. "I go because I want to be with you."

Ki-Gor raised himself on his elbows, trying to judge her. She had saved his life and he had to be honest with her.

"This is a thing you must know," he said gravely. "There exists but one woman for me—my wife, Helene. Our first duty when we leave here will be to seek her."

Swift anger drove into Neeba's face.

"Think what you're saying," she warned. "I need only cry out to bring Thor and the guards. This is your last chance to choose between Helene and me, because if I can't have you, no one else will."

"You aren't Vani," Ki-Gor answered. "You won't betray me."

She drew away from him, watchful as though she expected him to use force to try to silence her.

"Oh, won't I!" she cried. "If I betray my own father like this, why wouldn't I betray you?"

"But he isn't your father," Ki-Gor said quietly. "He told me that himself. Your true father is the white man I'm taking you to at the Masai kraal, the man Thor means to kill."

And as he told Neeba the ugly story of a madman's vengeance, she sank to the deck beside him as though her legs could no longer hold her. She was utterly dazed for a moment. Then she broke into tears.

"I'm sorry to hurt you," he continued sympathetically, "but it's best you learn you owe no debt to Thor. He's done a terrible wrong to you, and the sooner you realize that, the sooner we can begin to undo his evil work."

Neeba put her hand on Ki-Gor's arm.

"I'm not crying because I'm unhappy," she said unsteadily. "I hate him. I've always hated him. And now I know it was right for me to feel that way."

She wiped her tears with a brown hand. Her eyes were wide and luminous, her face like that of a little girl's.

"I'm glad," she said fervently.

Ki-Gor swung erect, pulled Neeba up beside him. His arm was about her shoulders for a second. "Good girl," he said. "Everything will be all right from now on."

Then they ran to the end of the deck, mounted the two zebra and kicked them into a gallop.

The dogs set up a clamor, but they reached the path and started down before anyone was drawn from the cavern.

They came into the jungle at breakneck speed, straining to get as far from the area as possible before Thor should decide to set out without the suddenly missing Neeba.

HOURS LATER, long after sunset, Ki-Gor and Neeba urged their exhausted ponies up to the Masai kraal. A great cry went up when the warriors saw the White Lord, and a way was swiftly made for him through the circle of fire.

But when he was met inside the kraal surrounded by the crowding blacks and they saw who it was rode with him, an ominous silence fell. Helene, N'Geeso and the two white engineers were trying to push through to reach him, but the tight-packed warriors made it slow going for them.

The White Lord's attention was torn from Helene's excited face by Tembu George's strange action. The Masai stepped up beside Neeba and caught the bridle of her zebra.

"Get down, daughter of the devil," he said coldly. "Ki-Gor has given us a real present in you. But we are kinder to prisoners than are you and your father, even those who have treated us as cruelly as have you. With us, you will die swiftly."

Neeba looked with sudden, terrible suspicion at Ki-Gor.

The White Lord read her thoughts. "Wait!" he cried to Tembu George. "Neeba is not my prisoner. She helped me escape and came of her own accord to join us."

But Tembu George had told the Masai of Thor's daughters, how one of them had tortured him, how they ran with the pack.

"It's another of the Old One's tricks," snarled a black.

"Aye!" roared the crowd. "Kill her! Kill her before she betrays our defenses to the Old One!"

Neeba looked about frantically. "Ki-Gor, it was Vani who directed the pack. Thor wouldn't let me take it out because he found out I wouldn't kill. And I never tortured this man. He takes me for my sister."

The White Lord tried to explain the difference between the two girls.

"Perhaps she wasn't the one who beat me half-to-death," Tembu George said sternly. "But she's Thor's daughter and as such she deserves no mercy."

Owens and N'Geeso had broken through the crowd and hurried to Ki-Gor's side.

"She isn't Thor's daughter, shouted the White Lord. Thor has done her more evil than he has any of you. He told me himself he had slain her mother and had stolen her from her true father because he hated him."

He pointed to the startled Owens.

"There stands her father," Ki-Gor said. "That's why that madman Thor was so anxious to capture Owens. He meant to force the girls to kill their own father."

Tembu George dropped his hand from the bridle.

"Isn't it true," demanded Ki-Gor of Owens, "that you served under a Captain Thorsen and that you took a young woman from him, escaped with her into the jungle?"

Owens went pale. "Great god," he exclaimed. "After all these years, to run into him here! But the dogs—I should have known by the dogs." He looked at Neeba with shocked eyes. "Yes," he admitted. "I did what you say."

He was terribly shaken. He put his hand to his head.

"It's unbelievable to think a human being could do such a thing," he said unsteadily, "but he should have been locked up when I knew him. The whole crew lived in terror of him. He was a monstrous, crazed devil even then."

Owens stared at Neeba, an expression of pain on his face. His eyes were haunted.

"Poor, poor child," he muttered. "Your mother was the lucky one—she died."

Neeba watched him, fearfully at first, and then with a pitiful hunger. With a sudden awkwardness, she slid from her zebra, advanced hesitantly toward Owens. The crowd was quiet, touched by the meaning of the scene.

Owens lifted his arms to the girl, and with a low cry she ran to him, buried her face in his shoulder. He turned, keeping an arm about Neeba and started toward his hut.

The wall of warriors split apart to let them pass.

XI

KI-GOR slid stiffly from the zebra as Helene came to him. Their eyes spoke for them, and only after a long, silent moment did they melt together in a kiss. When Ki-Gor reluctantly released Helene, she whispered seriously to him and immediately he looked around for N'Geeso.

The pygmy hung back, keeping his glance down, seemingly ashamed to confront the White Lord. The faithful little man was miserable because he had allowed Helene to be captured.

"Is this a greeting for a friend?" asked Ki-Gor lightly.

"I'm unworthy to be your friend," mumbled N'Geeso. "I'm carrion from which even the dangos turn."

Ki-Gor reached a broad hand for the pygmy, roughly drew the little man to him.

"Helene has told me how it was," he assured him. "You were without fault."

"But I left her," groaned the pygmy. "If I hadn't gone to hunt, I could have prevented the whole thing."

Ki-Gor laughed. "I didn't expect you to grow to that tree. You had to have food."

N'Geeso peered from under his brows at the White Lord. His friend might be satisfied with him, but he still wasn't satisfied with himself.

Nibaiya was standing close by, anxiously awaiting a chance to talk to Ki-Gor. When he heard the devil-beasts mentioned, he broke into the conversation. He was a different man from the trembling, frightened wreck the jungle lord had last seen.

"Ah, Ki-Gor, greatest of wizards," he said warmly, "I can't wait longer to thank you."

Ki-Gor grinned. "Thank me? I was afraid you wouldn't be too pleased to see me. That was a dirty trick I played in hitting you."

Nibaiya beamed. "That's what I thank you for. To think I was ready to give the Old One everything he asked, instead of putting my faith in the juju you fashioned."

N'Geeso pursed his lips wryly, gave a tuneless, but eloquent whistle.

"Oh, yes," he said, and his tone of voice told Ki-Gor he was himself again, "Nibaiya showed me that juju when I came in with the skins of two dogs. He was very pleased, not with me for killing them, but with the juju for making it possible. He said if it hadn't been for your magic, a hundred darts wouldn't have stopped them."

Nibaiya nodded excited agreement.

"It's still on the wall up there," he declared, "and having seen the magic it wrought in bringing back Owens, whisking you to Thor's den and making the devil beasts into ordinary animals, the Masai are ready to smash the Old One and his evil forces."

Ki-Gor's face remained solemn.

"Good," he told Nibaiya, "because the Old One will try to attack us either tonight or early in the morning."

"I go to alert the warriors," the black said eagerly, and Ki-Gor had no further doubts about the morale of the tribesmen.

Helene cocked her head. "What have you been up to, Ki-Gor? All I've heard since I got here is about what a great wizard you are."

Tembu George and Miller, the older engineer, shouldered in on either side of the White Lord.

"Believe me, he is," said Miller. "He saved Owens and me from certain death. Why, since he worked his magic, the Masai have treated us like honored guests.

"His juju did more than save your lives," said Tembu George. "It saved the Masai." He tapped his knuckles in native fashion against Ki-Gor's chest. "I'll be forever grateful, and I can promise that no matter what comes in the attack, the Masai will fight as they never fought before."

Helene suddenly woke up to Ki-Gor's utter weariness. Now that the excitement of his arrival was over, he had let down. She took him by the arm as a mother would a small boy.

"I'll ask the great wizard to make all of you disappear permanently," she theatened, "if you don't clear out and give him a chance to eat and rest."

He gave her a grateful look and followed her to Tembu George's hut. After eating, he fell into a deep sleep, knowing Helene would keep watch beside him. Not until the first stars began to disappear did she rouse him.

He selected a sword and spear from the Masai leader's personal arms. Outside the hut, he stood for awhile with Helene listening to the noises of the surrounding jungle. All was quiet in the kraal.

"It will be soon now," he said gravely. "Thor is waiting for the Masai to let the circle of fire burn down."

Ki-Gor toured the defenses, telling the blacks it was his belief that the Old One's forces already were gathered outside the walls.

"I'll lead a party out and build up the fires," offered Tembu George. "We can keep them going all day."

Ki-Gor advised against it. "That would tell him we're on guard. By letting the fires go down, it will appear we think there's no danger of attack during the daytime."

Busy with last minute details, Ki-Gor had no time for Neeba or the two white men, but they stayed close to him as though his presence gave them confidence. As the sun inched over the horizon, a growing tenseness pervaded the kraal. But an hour passed and still Thor gave no sign of his presence.

Then suddenly a thunderous mixture of bellows sounded out of the jungle deeps. As though that roar of noise were a signal, the dread blood-cry of the devil pack rolled up in a veritable crescendo of terror. The noise erupted over a broad area to the north of the kraal, swept close with the swiftness of a falling sword stroke.

Nearer and nearer it came, growing more terrible with every second. There emerged for the first time out of the blanket of sound the shattering crash of breaking timber and a queer rolling beat like that of a thousand jungle drums.

"He's stampeded the rhino herd," cried Neeba, "and loosened the dog pack to drive them straight against the walls."

Tembu George exploded with a barrage

of orders. The lines of waiting warriors on the north were strengthened by reinforcements drawn from the other points which would be missed by the initial charge. An arrow, already drawn two thirds back on the bowstring, rested in every Masai bow.

Helene's face was white, but with no show of nervousness, she fitted an arrow in her own bow. Like some fierce little gnome, N'Geeso abruptly materialized beside her, blowpipe in hand.

The black on the lookout tower shrieked a faintly heard warning. The earth leaped and trembled. As though a great hand crashed against the north wall, the whole section shuddered and exploded. In a close-packed wave, the rhino swept out of the jungle and crashed head-on into the wooden barrier.

THE GIANT, armored beasts, gone mad with terror and fury, hurled themselves through the churning debris of wood.

The straight ranks of the Masai splintered. Men cried out without knowing what they did. They turned to flee from the rhinos hurtling charge. Then those monstrous beasts catapulted against the sharpened stakes.

Bellowing, kicking the jungle titans piled senselessly into the death trap. They were through the wall and on the stakes before their dull eyes and crazed brains could register the danger. With express-train speed, they hit the low-set tree-spears, and ripped themselves apart.

It was over with incredible swiftness. Dead and dying rhinos lay everywhere among the bloody disarranged stakes. A few whose charge had been shattered against the impaled hulk of some other rhino, raged up and down, tearing with hooves and horns at their less fortunate fellows. And some of those in the rear of the charge turned aside and crashed off into the jungle.

Only three of all those beasts managed to break through into the kraal, and they were so badly wounded that the Masai spearmen felled them in short order.

Like twin furies, even before the charge was broken, Ki-Gor and Tembu George descended on the confused and disintegrating mass of men who had composed the front guard. They flung the warriors back into ranks, screeched to them that they were fools not to see that victory already lay in their hands. The Masai broke into cheers.

Unlike the stupid rhinos, the dogs in the front ranks saw their danger. It was impossible for them to turn back, or even slow their stride against the pressure of the pack. So they lifted in desperate, straining leaps in the vain hope of clearing the sword barrier, while the animals directly behind them were carried straight into the densely planted weapons.

And in that moment of supreme confusion, Tembu George roared the order for his warriors to fire. Like a deadly hail, the slim, cruel arrows hammered into the pack. In solid ranks the devil-beasts died, ripped open by the sword barrier or cut down by arrows.

The Masai went mad with joy. Yelling and cheering they broke ranks and raced forward. With spears and bows, they cleared a path through the sword barrier, finishing off the animals as they went.

"Kill the Old One!" they shouted.

Ki-Gor roared to them to stand firm, but his voice was lost in the bedlam. "The fools!" he said to Tembu George. "They think the Old One has no warriors to serve him. A sudden charge by Thor's mounted guards could rip them to pieces."

The White Lord realized it was impossible to recall the elated men in time so the only thing he could do was call warriors from other sections of the kraal and throw out an army large enough to frighten off Thor. Only the Masai who had actually withstood the attack had left their assigned posts.

Ki-Gor had but to raise his arm and wave it toward the jungle to bring reinforcements racing. A majority of the Masai had been forced to stand by against a surprise attack from some unexpected quarter, while a small portion of their fellows reaped all the glory. These fresh men were anxious to gather what laurels they could by being in on Thor's capture.

Without waiting for them, Ki-Gor and Tembu George sprinted out to do what they they could to restrain the endangered force. He didn't realize that Neeba, Owens and Miller followed on his heels. Lifted by the excitement, they acted unthinkingly, automatically accepting Ki-Gor's action as an indication that victory had been won.

By the time the White Lord had passed the shattered wall, the tribesmen were fanning out as they raced across the cleared space outside the kraal. The blacks intended to comb the brush for Thor.

With a curse, Ki-Gor saw he was too late to prevent the thing he feared. Out of the torn underbrush spurred a double line of horsemen led by the wild, crazed figures of Thor and Vani. The riders, each with a lowered lance, formed a wedge as they came, with Thor and Vani at the apex.

Ki-Gor wheeled to the left, yelling to the scattered Masai to use their bows and draw together. Following his example, Tembu George turned to the right to do what he could for his surprised men.

But to the White Lord's amazement, Thor made no effort to sweep down the widely dispersed line of warriors. Instead, he drove straight at the kraal, plowing into only those few unfortunate men who happened to be in his path. It was a startling maneuver, for the no more than forty guards he had with him would be massacred once they came in range of the fresh Masai pouring up to the wall.

Realizing the lancers would even miss him, Ki-Gor slapped an arrow into his bow and fired. He toppled the black next to Thor. Other empty saddles rode forward as Tembu George and his men came into action.

Ki-Gor fitted another arrow into the bow, glanced back to see how near the reinforcements were. And then he saw the reason for Thor's suicidal charge. His heart stood still. The white-maned old giant had seen Neeba, Owens and Miller follow a miraculously living Ki-Gor from the kraal. The realization that Ki-Gor somehow had managed to live and had united Neeba with Owens plunged the old man into raving madness. The sight of his hated enemy standing hand in hand with Neeba at the moment when ruin was engulfing him was too much. Ordering his men to kill those two no matter what the cost, he had led them from the forest, knowing but not caring that he took most of them to certain death.

When she saw Thor, Neeba lost her head. She was obsessed with fear of him and guessing his purpose, she turned in panic and fled. But instead of trying to get back to the kraal, she ran parallel to the walls. She was like a berserk animal.

Owens ran after her. Miller was the only one of the three to head back into the kraal. Owens succeeded in catching Neeba, but by the time he did, all hope of their reaching safety was gone.

Ki-Gor leaped forward. Concern for his own safety was forgotten. His one thought was to get to Owens and Neeba, put his own body between them and the madman. If only he could stave off Thor for a few brief seconds more, the Masai from the village would break the attack. Already the tribesmen were pouring through the breached walls and their arrows were cutting down the Old One's guards.

OUT OF FORTY men who started the ride, a bare ten still lived, but Thor and Vani seemed to bear charmed lives. Neeba and Owens were running now toward Ki-Gor. He thought for a fraction that he might reach them in time, but the horsemen coming in a little behind them and from the side moved too fast for him.

A storm of arrows swept the riders as the Masai bowmen tried desperately to stop them. Thor reeled in his saddle. An arrow had found him at last, piercing his left shoulder, but he steadied himself and spurred on. Vani's horse was badly hurt, missing his stride and beginning to lurch.

Only one of the blacks had lived through the barrage. He forged into the lead as his masters faltered. He was no more than ten yards behind the fleeing pair and gaining with every bound. The black aimed the gleaming tip of his lance at Owens' back.

The arrow was still fitted in Ki-Gor's bow. He slid to a stop, threw the bow up and whipped the barb at the black. The arrow outsped the reaching lance, stabbed into the native's chest.

Ki-Gor slapped a second arrow in his bow, meaning to shoot directly between Owens and Neeba to bring Thor down. The pair were hardly five yards from Ki-Gor and it was impossible for the old man to catch them before they reached the White Lord.

But the wild-eyed madman swayed up in his stirrups, launched his lance like a spear even as the White Lord fired. The heavy shaft caught Neeba in the back, plunged completely through her. She fell at

Ki-Gor's feet, giving a single heart-breaking cry as she died.

Thor's hysterical scream of triumph as he threw the weapon was·chopped off when Ki-Gor's arrow ripped into his belly. The bearded giant hunched forward in the grip of agony, but his gnarled legs held him firmly in his seat.

"And now you, Owens!" he roared. "I've still strength enough for you!" He wrenched free the sword at his waist.

Thinking Thor was at his back, the unarmed and exhausted Owens spun in an abrupt, right-angle turn.

Thor tried to slash Ki-Gor with the sword, but before he could twist himself into position for the blow, the jungle man dragged him out of the saddle. The two sprawled hard in the dust, rolling and fighting for possession of the blade.

Ki-Gor pulled away from him, staggered to his feet, holding the sword. The arrow wounds had taken their toll. The old man still breathed, but he was unconscious; he was dying.

The White Lord had taken most of the shock of the fall. He was dazed and breathless. Before he could gather his wits, he heard Owens shout, "Behind you, Ki-Gor!"

He wheeled in time to see Vani leap up and come at him with a sword.

A huge-muscled, ebony warrior leaped past Ki-Gor with an upraised spear, hammered it through Vani. She was dead before she struck the ground. Tembu George had paid her back for her inhuman cruelty to his people.

Ki-Gor looked quickly for Owens, wondering what he could say to the man. He expected to find him sorrowing over Neeba, but to his surprise the engineer knelt beside Thor. As if the nearness of his hated enemy were enough to bring him back from death, the old man's eyes opened and he stared up at the engineer.

"I'm dying, Owens," he whispered, "and you're still alive." He gasped painfully for breath. "But maybe it's better this way after all." Again he paused for the awful rasp of breathing. "You'll have all your life to think of them."

Owens stared at the dying man. "To think of whom?" he asked, puzzled.

"Your daughters, Owens," he croaked.

"You poor, miserable fool," he said slowly. "There was never anything between that mistreated girl and me."

The old man's face screwed with terrible slowness in an expression of pain. He closed his eyes. "Oh, no, no, no!" he gasped. And he writhed violently and was dead.

Owens stood up and took a deep breath. "Yes, that was the truth," he said. "I know you're wondering why I let everyone, even Neeba, think I was her father when you brought her here. Well, for one thing, if I hadn't done it the Masai would have killed her." He glanced away into the distance. "And for another, I couldn't bear to break her heart just then. You saw how she looked at me, how she came to me. I was all the hope she had in the world and I couldn't take that from her."

Helene and N'Geeso came up. As the White Lord stood with his arms around Helene, Nibaiya burst up to him holding the crocodile juju.

"Its magic won for us!" he declared.

Ki-Gor reached out, took the figure and crushed it in his hand. "Nothing but clay," he said. "The magic that won for us was here and here." He pointed to Nibaiya's head and his right arm. "Those are the greatest jujus."

THE GOLDEN CLAWS OF RAA

By JOHN PETER DRUMMOND

Sam Slaker, cobra-eyed merchant in warrior-flesh; Mog, the gorilla with human blood on his dagger-like teeth; Raa, golden queen of the ape legions —these were Ki-Gor's enemies in a battle that only the voodoo of Destiny could decide.

THE woman was dead.

Her small, coffee-colored body lay crumpled in an attitude of prayer, her forehead pressed against the base of a tree, her hands gripping the bark.

Across the pygmy woman's naked back a whip had torn deep, ugly gashes. But the gaping wound between her shoulder blades told that a sudden, vicious spear thrust had ended her torture.

Ki-Gor, White Lord of the Jungle, leaned over the dead pygmy, traced a slow, accusing finger over the inch-wide circle of flesh rubbed raw about the woman's neck.

No spoken word was needed for the Masai warriors clustered about the body to understand Ki-Gor's meaning. That raw circle was the grim mark of a slaver's iron neckband. Chained neck to neck in single file, slaves can be driven like helpless cattle.

The huge, bull-chested Masai chieftain, Tembu George, drew a slow, deep breath, looked from the woman to the warriors about him. He spoke to his men, but his words were a promise to Ki-Gor.

"This small one will be avenged," he rumbled. "This evil done to the people of my blood-brother, N'Geeso, is an evil done to the Masai."

Ki-Gor stood up, his face grown harsh. Even among the tall, powerfully-built Masai, the great-thewed White Lord was a commanding figure. He wore only a leopard-skin breech-clout caught tight about his lean, hard loins. With a toss of his head, he threw his blonde mane of hair back out of smouldering grey eyes. His right hand twisted with restless strength along the shaft of his war spear.

"Aye!" he said with ominous softness. "She will be avenged!" But though a thousand die, this small one will never know her father's hut again." His lips twisted with swift bitterness. "Will the jungle never be rid of these human jackals?"

Tembu George motioned to two of his men. They quietly lifted the corpse, carried it off into the jungle to be covered with stones.

Ten yards away, the White Lord's mate, Helene, watched with troubled eyes as the two Masai carried their pitiful burden from view. After an absence of two moons arbitrating differences between the Kamizuli and the Bambala, the looked-for happiness of their return to their home in the pygmy lands immediately was shattered.

The fact that the woman was being bur-

ied instead of taken to the pygmy kraal told Helene Ki-Gor judged he could overtake the killers.

She ran to the White Lord, saying anxiously, "With only twenty-five Masai, it would be suicide to attack armed slave-traders!"

Her slim fingers caught pleadingly at Ki-Gor's arm. The sun reached through the ceiling of branches above to strike glints of fire from her long, red hair. The lithe, curved beauty of this woman was a legend endlessly related wherever men gathered in the jungle.

Ki-Gor's grey eyes softened. "There are chances one must sometimes take," he said gravely. "It would take a sun to reach the pygmy kraal, another sun to return here with N'Geeso and his warriors."

"And if we give those *aasvoels* two suns lead, we'll never find them," added the deep-voiced Tembu George. "For all we know, N'Geeso may be one of those taken by the raiders!"

"But what if . . .?" began Helene, thinking of what could happen to her mate. Then abruptly she stopped, biting her soft, full underlip. Her fingers tightened on Ki-Gor's muscled forearm. "Of course!" she said. "It's the only thing to do." And her voice was steady, utterly sincere.

WHAT other way could there be for a man such as her mate? That was the thought that stopped her even as the sick gnaw of worry caught her heart. He was the "jungle protector" to the black men, regarded almost as a god by half-a-hundred tribes, beloved and trusted by those who walked the paths of peace and justice, fanatically feared and hated by those who followed the ways of evil and injustice.

"Their spoor is fresh," said Ki-Gor. "Perhaps we can overtake them by nightfall."

Tembu George grinned savagely. "They knew you were busy elsewhere. This raid is some coward's cruel way of getting back at you. No slaver really wants pygmy slaves."

"Wah!" rasped Ki-Gor in agreement. "It's like caging wild birds. They quickly die, and the most brutal master can't make them submit."

The two warriors returned from the bush. Sweat gleamed on their stern faces. They recovered their spears, stood staring down the path. There was no doubting their desire to come to grips as soon as possible with the slavers.

"I'll go ahead by the tree-paths," Ki-Gor told Tembu George, "learn their strength and work out a plan of attack. Their spoor will be easy for you to follow."

He handed the Masai chieftain his spear. His bow and quiver of arrows he could carry on his back without difficulty, but the spear would hamper his movements in the trees.

"Shall I go with you, or with Tembu George?" asked Helene.

Ki-Gor's glance avoided her, his manner grown uneasy.

"Neither," he declared with unnatural curtness. "You will go through the trees to N'Geeso's kraal. Wait for us there."

He anticipated difficulty with Helene. She would want to go with them. It would be awkward having her argue with him before the Masai. Natives did not understand the freedom of tongue and action which the wives of white men possessed.

But Helene had no intention of making her husband lose face before the blacks. She modestly lowered her eyes before her husband, as a proper wife should, but in truth the gesture was more to hide from him their sudden flare of inspiration rather than to indicate submission.

"Your wish is my command, O Husband," she said meekly, using the Masai language rather than English. She backed away as though meaning to go immediately.

Ki-Gor looked startled. Then recovering himself, he gave a relieved sigh.

But after a few steps Helene halted.The angular, heavy-thewed bodies of the blacks behind her provided a striking frame for her provocatively feminine beauty, a beauty displayed rather than concealed by her narrow halter and brief shorts.

Her voice was soft, almost apologetic, as she asked: "And if I find the kraal destroyed by the slavers and the pygmies gone elsewhere, should I remain there, anyway?" Her blue eyes moved hesitantly over the group, somehow evoking in those male minds the picture of her alone, unprotected, in a ruined village.

"That's true!" exclaimed Tembu George. "The raiders may have burned the kraal." Several of his warriors gave grunts of agreement, glanced questioningly at Ki-Gor. With a single mild question Helene had won the sympathy of the Masai.

"Ummm," said Ki-Gor. Whether well founded or not, she had planted a worry in both his and the warriors' minds which would make them keep her with them.

He frowned at her. "All right, go with the Masai," he sighed. "But remember . . ."

"Oh, I promise not to be in the way," Helene declared. "I'll do everything you say."

Ki-Gor, the frown still on his face, started toward an ankle-thick length of liana hanging from a branch. Helene ran to stop him, and raising on tiptoe, brushed his lips with hers. He received the kiss sternly.

Then abruptly he swept her up in his arms, kissed her resoundingly to the delight of the warriors, and holding her feet off the ground, shook her gently.

"Witch!" he said, and his teeth flashed white in a laugh. "Beautiful, cunning witch!"

He put her down, took three running steps and caught the liana. Great, writhing cords of muscle ridged out over his arms and shoulders. With a prodigious bound, he hurled himself upward.

At the very height of his swing, Ki-Gor released the vine, drove free through the air. Up, up, he went in arcing flight, his suddenly relaxed body twisting slowly so that his arms came straight before him.

THEN there was the leaping bulge of muscles across his back as he braced. His momentum was nearly spent. But at the very moment he would have begun to drop, his spread fingers came against a limb. He caught the support, whipped his body under it like a pendulum.

He shot away from the limb, feet-first, angling horizontally across ten yards of open space for another branch. In midleap, he curled into a ball, snapped his legs straight again, and once more his arms were before him in position to grasp the limb.

Though the Masai had witnessed the White Lord's hurtling flight through the tree-routes countless times, always they watched with awed, astonished expressions.

It was a reminder that he was linked as closely to the savage, primeval animal world as he was to the world of men. He had known the animal world first, had started life as fierce and wild as any beast, removed from the society of men, hardly identifying his kinship with them. But he had gradually come to know the natives, and through his unusual physical and mental powers had won their respect.

His gloss of civilization, though deeper since Helene had become his wife, was still barely more than skin-deep. The red-haired American girl, who had been plummeted into his life by the crash of her airplane in the jungle, had wrought many

changes in the White Lord. But he had changed her even more, for finding love and happiness with Ki-Gor, she had abandoned her whole way of existence, changed from a wealthy social butterfly to a fitting mate for the jungle lord.

But now as Ki-Gor ranged alone through the tree-paths in search of the slavers, he became a true jungle denizen again. The changing forest breezes brought him many sounds and scents, and as instinctively as any animal his ears and nose deciphered these subtle messages.

He knew that a lion lay couched in the still Wassa grass beside a waterhole. He knew that for a time a leopard silently kept pace with him off to his right when he dropped low to check on the spoor. He followed by sound the flight of a *klipvard* antelope.

An ever-altering variety of sounds and smells he identified, all helping him know what went on about him, what enemies were near.

But a persistant scent which puzzled and interested him most was the harsh Ingagi smell, the gorilla smell, which lay heavy along the way he travelled.

This was not the country of the Ingagi. The fierce great apes lived further west in a dense, unpopulated section of the jungle. The natives only entered that dark land in armed force, for the murderous strength and almost man-like cunning of the great beasts made them fearful adversaries for hunters armed with only spears and bows.

Three hours after leaving Helene, Ki-Gor caught his first glimpse of the great apes he scented. Moving silently through the leafy heights, he saw four of the huge beasts passing through a clearing on the jungle floor below him.

They went in single file, in a shambling sort of trot, knuckling the ground with their long arms at every step. They kept parallel with the path, turning and circling with it, but not once in the several minutes the White Lord watched them did they ever actually set foot on it. Instead, they chose the much more difficult going of the underbrush.

Another strange thing was their sustained fast pace. The Ingagi is usually an unhurried traveller, stopping often to browse for choice green shoots or overturn a fallen rotted limb in search of grubs.

Ki-Gor, though intrigued, had no time to waste on idle curiosity. Without ever drawing abreast of the apes, he turned off to the right, circled around them and came back to the path. They might not take kindly to the sight of a hairless white ape swinging over them.

But to Ki-Gor's surprise, he no more than got around the first group, when he found himself over six more of the beasts. They behaved in the same manner, keeping well away from the path, yet following its windings exactly. And they were all bull apes, not a single female.

He tried again to avoid discovery, but a sudden downcurrent of air carried his man-scent to the brutes. The creatures abruptly halted, uttering low, rumbling growls while their bloodshot, beady eyes searched for the human who dared come near them.

THE APE that sighted Ki-Gor first gave a roar of rage, thrust up on his hind legs and hammered his chest thunderously with giant, knotted fists. The beast allowed himself only this single, surging outburst of wrath, then he raced to a low-hanging limb, leaped high to grasp it. Within seconds he was swinging and leaping upward through the branches toward the White Lord.

Ki-Gor didn't want trouble, but he was unwilling to engage in a grim game of hide and seek with six raging bull apes. In order to lose them, he would have to swerve far off his course, uselessly wasting both time and energy.

So instead of running, he swung his bow from his back, snatched a long barbed arrow from his quiver and fitted it to the bowstring. He was drawing a bead on the rapidly climbing ape, when the largest of the beasts on the ground broke into furious barks and snarls.

The outburst apparently was directed at the bull going after Ki-Gor, for the shaggy giant immediately stopped climbing. He glared fiercely at the White Lord, baring his fangs. Then slowly, reluctantly, the ugly beast started down toward his fellows.

Ki-Gor lowered his bow, a faint frown coming over his taut features.

He studied with new interest the ape-leader who had called back the bull. The gorilla was fully six feet tall, but his chest and shoulders were of such tremendous breadth that he had an almost squat look.

But the gorilla's most awesome feature was his face. In some past battle, the whole left side of it had been torn open. A hideous, many-tongued scar ran from temple to jaw, lifting the beast's huge lips in a perpetual snarl.

To Ki-Gor's added astonishment, as soon as the tree-climber reached the ground, the six apes wheeled about, set off in single file through the brush without wasting another glance on the jungle man.

With all his knowledge of animals, the White Lord could find no possible explanation of the behavior of the Ingagi. Apes simply didn't act that way. He proceeded more warily than before, and though he avoided further trouble, he passed six more groups before the harsh gorilla scent disappeared, telling him he was ahead of the strange migration.

An hour later, he caught up with the slave caravan and all thought of the apes was thrust from his mind.

Though he kept well away from the cruel procession, he could still hear the steady crack of whips, the sudden agonized screams of tortured men and women. And a few times through breaks in the wall of foliage he kept between himself and the slavers he caught glimpses of the long shuffling lines of shackled prisoners.

From the slow pace of the caravan and the large number of captives who fell and had to be whipped to their feet, Ki-Gor saw that even the most brutal taskmasters wouldn't be able to keep the slaves moving much longer.

The blacks were exhausted, having been driven mercilessly the past two days while the slavers sought to get away from the scene of the attack. Ki-Gor was acquainted with the habits of slave-traders, knew from grim experience that the unfortunate natives in their hands had had little food or water since their capture.

Ki-Gor made a circle, putting him ahead of the caravan. He dropped down into the lower branches, and keeping directly over the trail, began to travel fast. Within thirty minutes, he found what he was searching for, a sizeable river crossing the path.

II

THE SUN was low in the west. The slavers would have to make camp before darkness. Even terrorized men have a point beyond which they can't be driven. The site by the river was the logical place for the caravan to halt.

Ki-Gor studied the area carefully, mapping the terrain in his mind. He dropped to the ground, tested the depth of the stream and trotted up the bank a hundred yards. Then he took to the trees again, coursed about slowly, observing the many small game trails in the neighborhood of the stream crossing Once he stopped to pick several handfuls of brown, strongly scented berries from a vine with pale, whitish leaves. He wrapped these berries in a huge leaf, and returning to the river hid them beneath a rock.

By the time the caravan's advance guard arrived, the White Lord was posted high in a tree in a vantage point which he had carefully camouflaged with vines.

Four armed Bantus came down the trail at a weary, dogged trot. Sweat cut glistening rivulets down their dusty bodies.

They went straight to the stream, drank thirstily for a few minutes. Then after a brief, low-voiced conference, one of their number turned back toward the caravan while the others splashed across the stream to investigate the other bank.

The black who had gone back with news about the campsite returned with a tall, broad-shouldered Arab and ten Bantu warriors. Ki-Gor's eyes glittered from slitted lids as he followed every movement made by the burnoose-clad man.

The man's arrogant stance, his swift, hawk-like movements faintly stirred Ki-Gor's memory. But try as he might, Ki-Gor could not go beyond that slight feeling that he had seen the slaver before. Except for a narrow strip for his eyes, the Arab's face was veiled, and the loose robe hanging to the ground was undistinguishable from the soiled garments worn by uncounted true believers.

The slaver stared about. "It will do!" he snapped in Bantu, managing to sound displeased that the blacks could find him no better place to camp. Then he growled, "Well, don't stand about! Clear out the brush!"

He leaned against a tree, stared into the water while his men worked. He apparently was oblivious of the blacks, but his hands lingered always near the brace of ornate, long-barreled pistols shoved into his girdle.

That single detail was highly significant to Ki-Gor. The Arab didn't trust his own servants. If he was as harsh a master as that, the Bantus would desert like jackals any time the tide of battle went against him.

The slaver didn't rouse until the straggling lines of chained men and women began dragging into the clearing. He shoved away from the tree, stood poised like some evil bird of prey. As though impelled to cruelty by the very sight of their master, the guards strung out along the weary files began to wield their whips, cursing and threatening the prisoners. Ki-Gor noted there were two more Arabs in the caravan, both armed with rifles. The furtive manner in which they kept glancing at the burnoose-clad figure by the stream indicated they feared their leader as much as the Bantus.

The captives were chained in groups of twenty. Studying them, Ki-Gor knew the slavers had moved swiftly over a wide area, making quick strikes against every unguarded kraal they encountered, rather than risking an all-out attack against any single people.

In addition to about eighty pygmy prisoners, they had snared some fifty Obanti, ninety Wasuli, and sixty Watussi. The fact that nearly two-thirds of the captives were young women told Ki-Gor another unsavory truth about the slavers.

Angered and sickened by the spectacle, Ki-Gor was watching the final group driven into the clearing with senseless whippings, when a totally unexpected sight made him start.

Ten paces behind the last of the black captives came a single woman closely guarded by four Bantus. She was a white woman, young and strikingly beautiful. She was blonde and her long, abundant hair streamed free to her waist. So well proportioned was her lithe, curved body that it took a second glance for one to realize how much larger and stronger she was than most women.

STRANGELY, she was clad in a crudely fashioned halter and a wrap-around breechclout of monkey-skin. The firm set of her red mouth, the quick way her grey eyes lashed her guards told of a seething anger. And there was no doubt that the slavers had failed to break her will. She walked firmly, even arrogantly, and her straight-held shoulders betrayed no weariness.

Her hands were tied behind her, and in addition to the steel circlet around her neck, another band of steel had been locked about her naked waist. Two guards held rawhide thongs attached to the neckband, while the other two Bantus held thongs tied to the waistband. By keeping these ropes taut, they forced the girl to walk between them and were easily able to control her.

Although there were whip-welts on practically every one of the black slaves, the blonde girl's honey-colored skin was unmarked. She was the Arab leader's prize. He took no chances of marring that fair, smooth body. If he managed things properly, she could bring him her weight in gold.

The captives were taken to the stream, one group at a time, and briefly allowed to drink. The tall leader stood unmoving until the blacks were finished and the blonde girl was brought up. He stepped close as she knelt to drink, tensely watched her.

When she stood up, the Arab's hand went out to touch her bare shoulder. His hand was on her for no more than a second, but there was a lingering ugliness in the gesture. As the blacks led the girl away, the man followed her with his glance.

"I could rid the jungle of him with a single arrow," thought Ki-Gor.

But he gritted his teeth and lay quiet on the limb until dusk fell. He watched the Bantus build a high thorn wall against animal prowlers on the forest side of the camp, smiled grimly when he saw that they left the river side open. Then he slipped quietly down the tree, wormed away from the camp through the underbrush and made his way back to the trail. He trotted about a mile along the path, then climbed into the fork of a tree and made himself comfortable.

The late moon was rising when he sat up, tested the breeze and listened. After a time, he gave an odd, warbling whistle. Among the myriad night noises that bird-like call would pass unnoticed by any but the Masai.

Tembu George's answering whistle was not long in coming. Ki-Gor dropped to the trail and hurried to meet Helene and his friends. In the faint mist of moonlight sifting through the trees, the Masai were drifting shadows clustered protectingly about Helene.

"We come at last, O Ki-Gor," hoarsely whispered Tembu George, "You've found where the dogs are bedded?"

"Aye," answered Ki-Gor, quickly explaining what he had learned.

"Lead us swiftly, O White Lord!" demanded a Masai warrior. "Yes!" clamored another. "My blood boils."

"You've travelled far," the White Lord reminded them. "Perhaps you should rest and eat."

"We need no rest!" indignantly put in one of the warriors.

"Our blades alone are hungry," declared another hotly.

Ki-Gor smiled thinly in the darkness. The Masai's eagerness was no pose. Battle was the principal end of life, the ultimate fulfillment for these savage warriors. A Masai counted himself as worth ten warriors of any other tribe, and on many occasions Ki-Gor had seen it proved that he was not far wrong in his estimate. Before Ki-Gor had channeled their warlike energies into policing the jungle, the fierce Masai had been the Congo's greatest troublemakers.

"So be it," Ki-Gor said, and in contrast to the warriors' tones his voice was slow, tinged with regret.

Though he knew it must be, he hated leading these men into battle. He had no love of war, only an abiding hatred for it and for those who were its cause. And yet even the dread Masai themselves hailed Ki-Gor as the greatest of warriors.

The darkness was no hindrance to the White Lord in leading the Masai into position. He had photographed the area and its paths in his mind before sunset, and now like a night-prowling animal he led them quietly along tiny game trails, circling the camp and coming out on the bank of the river a hundred yards above the sleeping caravan.

Except for a few quivering pools of quicksilver where the moon fought through breaks in the overhanging branches, the stream ran in eerie blackness.

"There's plenty of driftwood along the bank here," Ki-Gor said. "We'll float down the river and then rush in upon them."

The slavers naturally would expect any trouble to come from the forest side of their camp. The river was broad enough to bar any animal prowlers from coming in behind them.

"But the darkness out there may be swarming with crocodiles," pointed out an alarmed Helene. "You could all be torn to pieces."

That same thought was in every warrior's mind, but not one of them had protested Ki-Gor's orders. Crocodiles abounded in these sluggish, muddy rivers.

"They won't bother us, thanks to a pygmy trick N'Geeso taught me," Ki-Gor assured her.

He leaned down, lifted the rock at his feet, retrieved the berries he had cached earlier. He began distributing a few to each warrior.

"Smash these in your hands and smear the pulp over you," he ordered. "They are M'tika berries. The Long-noses won't come near a man with that smell on him."

THE MASAI dragged dead limbs, remnants of the last flood, into the water. They waded out, hip-deep, three or four men to each piece of driftwood, lining up parallel to the shore. Ki-Gor took Helene with him out to the first group.

"After we leave you," he told her, "stay with the log. In this slow current, you can keep within sight of the camp with very little paddling. You'll be safer in the water than anywhere else."

She stood close against him, trying to see his face. His strong, blunt fingers were very gentle on her arm.

"If anything goes wrong," he said quietly, "you are to drift on downstream. You musn't do anything foolish, because I would rather die a thousand times than think of your being captured by these men."

"Oh, my dear," she murmured unhappily, pressing her cheek against him, "please be careful. Please don't take chances."

He patted her head with awkward gentleness. "The Masai will take care of me. They always do." He turned her away from him, put her arm on the log.

Then he was calling softly to the warriors behind him. Group by group they pushed off into deep water, began drifting down toward the slave caravan. From the forest on their right came a hyena's crazed laughter, twice repeated. There was no sound from the men in the water except their tense, quick breathing.

III

THE SMELL of woodsmoke reached them first. Then like yellow blooms among the black trees they saw the slavers' fires. With nerve-rending slowness, they drifted abreast of the camp.

The exhausted prisoners, still chained together, lay in three long rows along the river bank. Wary guards paced slowly down the aisles between the lines of sleeping natives, watchful of every suspicious movement. The whole area was illuminated by fires.

The Masai needed only to see the high thorn boma extending in a solid, U-shaped wall about the camp to appreciate Ki-Gor's wisdom in choosing to attack from the river side. Just within that wall, armed Bantus stood vigil, kept alert against any danger from the jungle by the presence of one of the Arabs.

Ki-Gor estimated that about twenty-five Bantus, a third of the slavers' whole force, were on guard, while the others slept. When a quick glance failed to locate either the head slaver or his other Arab lieutenant, Ki-Gor knew they were both slumbering in the single tent which had been raised.

The blonde girl was chained to a tree outside the tent. She sat with her back against the trunk, her head dropped forward in sleep. She looked as though the least sound would bring her leaping to her feet.

To offset superior odds, Ki-Gor and his men had only the slender weapon of surprise. They had to hit so hard and fast that they would shatter the men on guard in their first rush. If the guards held them for any time at all, the sleeping Bantus would have a chance to arm and organize.

Ki-Gor felt the muddy bottom come under his feet. He set his strength against the log, drifted it in closer to the bank. He counted the moments, waiting for the Masai to come into position. On shore, one of the Bantus patrolling between the rows of slaves glanced idly at the river. Ki-Gor's heart skipped a beat. But the black went on with his pacing, his bored eyes seeing nothing unusual in a few drifting logs, if the dim hulks registered on his consciousness at all.

Ki-Gor knew he could wait no longer. His men were coming within reach of the firelight. He didn't worry about signalling the Masai. They would be straining their eyes, watching for his white body when he started for shore.

He said nothing to Helene, but she seemed to sense his decision. He knew she turned her face toward him. As he took his hand from the log, he touched her chin, her throat. Then he lifted his spear from the water, where, like the Masai, he had trailed it a few inches beneath the surface so no gleam of its shovel-bladed point wouldn't betray them.

The water was only to his chest now. He stepped around the log and started toward the camp. From the corner of his eye he saw the long, uneven line of shadows surge outward from the driftwood.

There was the faint wash of disturbed water, the glimmer of wet spear points. But so quietly did that desperate band of warriors advance, they were in ankle-deep water before the first Bantu sensed their presence. He was the same guard who had glanced out at the river before.

The man was almost directly in front of Ki-Gor when he suddenly ceased his pacing, spun toward the river. He stood close enough to a fire for the White Lord to see the astonished look which exploded over his face.

The black's eyes bulged, his mouth dropped open. Then he leaped backwards, his features wildly working as he fought to throw off the effects of shock and cry out to his fellows.

But even as the Bantu lunged backwards, the White Lord's right arm whirled high, then drove forward with explosive power. The heavy war spear leaped toward the beach like a ray of dark light.

Full in the face the huge, shovel-bladed weapon caught the native. His ebony features shattered apart, his head cleft completely through. He leaped high like a great frog, somersaulted backwards and fell kicking into the wash of his own blood.

And as the Bantu died, the huge, glistening figures of the Masai gained the bank. They were like great black cats, drifting out of the darkness in long, reaching bounds. It seemed impossible that men could move with such terrible speed, in such chilling silence.

Over the first row of sleeping prisoners they swept, engulfing three startled guards. The Bantus saw them now. Shrill, frightened cries broke out over the camp. The Masai swept over the rousing prisoners in a swift wave and the still-warm bodies of eleven Bantu dead marked the way they passed.

Like a cornered mongrel, the Arab lieutenant made little senseless runs back and forth, yapping confused orders in a thin, hysterical voice. But the hurtling spears of the Masai cut black furrows in the firelight even as he cried his first command. Under the hammer blows of these deadly shafts the bulk of his force melted away within seconds.

In desperation, the Arab flung up his rifle. Yellow fire streaked from its trembling barrel. The blasting echoes *caroomed* out through the jungle. And a Masai running beside Tembu George twisted sideways and fell, his throat torn away.

TEMBU GEORGE'S fury burst out of his throat in roaring madness. He seemed to spurt ahead of his men. His long, broad-bladed knife was a burst of gleaming light as he swung it high. In four incredible, lashing bounds he was on the Arab.

All the brute power in his giant shoulders was in that flickering knife-blow.

The Arab literally exploded into death, his body rent apart with the stunning swiftness of a tree split by lightning. Tembu George whirled away from the thing that had been a man, tearing his knife free as he turned.

He stabbed the red-dripping blade toward the sky and from his lips roared the dread Masai war-cry. Until that moment the attackers had fought in silence. Now in concert the huge chieftain's war-dogs chorused their chilling battle challenge, and wheeling behind their leader, raced toward the Arab tent and the Bantus who had been sleeping about it.

Tembu George knew the demoralizing effect that welling battle-cry would have on the groggy Bantus. It warned the scrambling blacks that the jungle's deadliest warriors were loose in their midst.

The sleep-dazed Bantus in those first minutes could not guess how small was the force opposed to them. They awoke to noise and confusion, the screams of frightened slaves, the clash of steel, the pound of running feet. And their first reaction was naturally that a vast force was flooding out of the jungle to destroy them.

Cat-swift, across the camp came the charging Masai. But yards ahead of them the Bantus saw a figure more dread than even the giant Tembu George. Seconds before the Masai turned toward the tent, Ki-Gor had cut away from his fellows and sprinted for the haven of the two sleeping Arabs.

"Aaaiiieee!! *The White Lord!*" shrieked a dozen blacks. Their master had assured them Ki-Gor was too far from the scene of their raids to interfere.

"Fight for your lives!" shouted a Bantu, bravèr than the rest, and darting forward, he cast his spear at the White Lord.

Ki-Gor veered, dodging like a broken-field runner, and the hasty throw skimmed past him. But the grey-faced Bantu, lashed by desperation, flung at the white man, sword in hand. A Masai spear took him in the belly, flung him sprawling in agony.

The White Lord flashed past the screaming, bucking black. Intent as he was on his objective, he yet noticed that the blonde girl stood wide-legged against the tree, her body taut with excitement, no sign of fear etching her face. Her grey eyes glowed with an electric brilliance as they whirled over the battle scene. Her reaction was certainly not what one would expect of a civilized woman bound helplessly in the midst of a death-struggle between savages.

Ki-Gor meant to call to her a word of hope, of reassurance. But before he could speak, the tent flap was ripped open and the Arab leader burst out. He apparently had been sleeping fully dressed, for he wore his white robes and had even taken time to hood his face. In his hand was a gun, not one of the ornate, long-barrelled pistols he had worn earlier in his belt, but a squat, ugly German Luger.

Coming so suddenly out of the dark interior of the tent, the Arab blinked rapidly, narrowing his eyes against the hurt of the light. That brief moment of blindness saved Ki-Gor's life.

Going at full tilt, the White Lord dove for the man's legs.

He hit him like a football tackler and at the impact the Luger went off in a series of rapid shots. The slugs sprayed harmlessly upward as the Arab careened against his tent, carried by the jungle man's driving weight. As the two of them went down, Ki-Gor caught the gun with one hand, the man's throat with the other.

WITH a mighty wrench, the White Lord tore the Luger from the Arab's grasp, hurled it away. The whole side of the tent collapsed, billowing down over the struggling men. The Arab fought like a maniac, writhing and twisting, gouging and kicking as he sought to free himself from both Ki-Gor and the smothering folds of the tent.

He was a powerful man, and as Ki-Gor quickly learned, an accomplished rough and tumble fighter. He managed to rip the White Lord's merciless fingers from his throat and hammered his knees into the pit of the jungle man's stomach.

Momentarily numbed by the blow, Ki-Gor lost his grip. The Arab plunged upward, throwing off the folds of tent. He didn't try to run. Instead, he turned, balancing himself to deliver a kick which would knock his opponent senseless.

Ki-Gor whirled in against the Arab like a rolling barrel, knocking his legs from under him before he could get set. And when he fell this time, there was no hope of again escaping the jungle man. Ki-Gor was a pouncing leopard, mauling and rocking the man with lightning blows.

The White Lord hit in the manner of the great apes, never knotting his fists, but using the rock-hard lower edge of each hand like a club. Tough and hard as the Arab was, no human could long survive such a beating. With his own blows seeming to have no more effect against Ki-Gor's muscle-padded bulk than rocks against armor plate, the Arab's nerve broke and he squawled for help.

And to the White Lord's surprise, the man in his fright cried out in English instead of Arabic.

"Carl——Carl! Help me! Shoot!" he yelped.

But the lieutenant was in no position to offer him immediate help. Slower to act than his master, he had been caught in the collapse of the tent. He was plunging about like a netted bird, trying to free himself. He heard the tremendous uproar as the Masai ripped into the Bantus, heard his leader's terrified screams, and his resulting panic made him even clumsier than before.

Despite the chief slaver's certainty that Ki-Gor meant to beat him to death, the White Lord had intended from the first to take him alive. Otherwise, he would have buried his knife in him in the opening seconds of the struggle.

The Arab's stiff resistance took Ki-Gor off-guard. Ordinarily, his race, though bitter fighters with sword or gun, had little skill in an out and out slugging match. But, finally, Ki-Gor twisted the man's head back, slammed him twice across the temple, finished him with a pile-driving blow full on the chin.

As the man went rubbery beneath him, Ki-Gor sprang up, intent on reaching the lieutenant before he could bring his gun into play. He would have gotten to him, too, had not a Bantu broken out of the melee of fighting men and come sprinting around the tent chased by a Masai.

In his frantic attempt to escape his pursuer, the Bantu headed straight into Ki-Gor. Too late the Bantu realized he was getting into the reach of another enemy. He tried to veer, slashing with his sword in an effort to keep the White Lord away. But his foot caught on one of the tent pegs and he dove face-first into the ground.

Ki-Gor was on the black before he

stopped skidding, twisting the sword from his hand. Then as easily as he would lift a rag doll, he heaved the native to his feet, and standing behind him, snaked his right arm about the man's face, forced his head back.

The Bantu, with the bones of his neck ready to snap under the pressure, was abruptly motionless, all thought of fight gone. The Masai braked to a stop, disappointment in his fierce features as he realized Ki-Gor didn't mean to kill the native.

But instead of wasting time trying to argue the White Lord out of taking a prisoner, with a snort of disapproval, the Masai whirled and started back for the main battle. At the moment the warrior turned, the Arab lieutenant managed to get free of the tent.

The two men stood face to face, no more than five paces apart. The Masai reacted first. With a wild yell, he leaped for the Arab, swinging his heavy knife like a cleaver.

The Arab threw himself to the side, triggering two pistol shots at point blank range. The warrior was flung half about by the slugs, his whole body shuddering under the impact. His legs started to give at the knees and his knife fell from his fingers.

But gathering the last broken fragments of life in him, the Masai somehow righted himself and took another full step toward the Arab. With his last conscious thought, the warrior tried to fling himself on the robed killer, hamper him long enough to give Ki-Gor a chance to reach them. But the Masai's fantastic courage went for naught. A third shot deliberately aimed this time, tore away the black's forehead.

KI-GOR knew he was trapped. He was farther away from the Arab than the Masai had been. The gun would cut him down before he took two steps. The Bantu he held before him was no protection, for the slaver would gladly sacrifice the black, knowing the same slugs which killed him would also tear out Ki-Gor's life.

As the Masai collapsed, the Arab jerked his attention to the White Lord. But even as he did, Ki-Gor tried a last desperate measure of defense. He caught the Bantu by the throat and the thigh, lifted him bodily overhead and hurled him at the Arab.

All his phenomenal strength was in that throw. A less wary enemy would have been knocked kicking. But in the Arab's case, Ki-Gor only bought himself a few extra moments of life. With a startled lizard's speed, the gunman darted aside, firing as he dodged.

The slug burned past Ki-Gor's arm. Ki-Gor's racing hand caught his knife from its sheath, swung it up with straining speed for a throw. But the White Lord knew as he lifted the knife that it was a futile action, that he could never beat that next shot.

Then suddenly, as though an invisible hand had reached out of the dark heavens to strike him, the gunman gave a queer backward jump, his gun blasting far wide of the jungle man.

The Arab staggered drunkenly, cursing in a voice edged with pain. The hand holding the pistol sank to his side. And unexpectedly, as Ki-Gor raced toward him, the man sat down heavily. His voice trailed off vaguely, and when Ki-Gor got to him, he had dropped over on his side and lay quiet.

The White Lord reached down, took the gun from the Arab's dead fingers, rolled him on his back. Then he saw what had saved his life. An arrow was driven through the center of the man's chest, a small, light arrow tipped with yellow feathers.

Ki-Gor grunted in surprise, glanced narrowly at the dark trees about him. Then as the battle-clamor bore in on him, he dropped his eye abruptly to the head slaver and the Bantu. Neither man showed any signs of life, so the White Lord snatched up the broad-bladed knife which the Masai warrior had dropped and ran toward the main fighting.

He found the Bantus had never recovered from the Masai's initial onslaught. When they reeled back from that charge, they left a score of dead and wounded behind. Now, with machine-like efficiency, the Masai were hemming them against one corner of the thorn wall, attacking with a concerted savagery which kept the Bantus from ever getting off the defense.

The White Lord's sudden appearance beside the giant Tembu George was the final straw needed to break the Bantus' crumbling morale. He had slain their masters and now he came to direct personally their own destruction.

IV

UNDER any other circumstances, natives in their position would have thrown down their arms and surrendered. But having been caught red-handed trafficking in slaves, the Bantus were afraid to surrender. If the Massai didn't kill them immediately, they would be marched to the white man's gallows on the coast.

Therefore, when they realized all was lost, a wild panic burst over them. The one urge in every Bantu's mind was to save his own skin. It happened with amazing swiftness. A black suddenly wheeled from the line of battle, darted for the thorn wall, tore frantically at it with his bare hands.

That started the rout. Instead of closing up the gap behind the deserter, his fellows needed only his example to set them off. Immediately, they were clawing at the thorn all about him, screeching and hitting in an insane effort to be the first to get away.

The Masai swayed in, clubbing the insane Bantus, determined none of them would get away. In that scene, the orderly precision with which Tembu George usually handled his men was impossible. He was helpless, therefore, when fifty yards away he saw four Bantus tear through the mass of struggling men and flee for the river.

He pulled Ki-Gor out of the fray, pointed to the running blacks. "Come! We must stop them!" he exclaimed in alarm. "They'll run head-on into Helene in crossing the river. They'll kill her out of spite!"

Before Ki-Gor could speak, the upset chieftain was sprinting after the Bantus at top speed. Ki-Gor leaped after him, straining every nerve to overtake the big man. He caught up with Tembu George just as they came abreast of the crumpled tent.

He shouted to make himself heard above the din. "Wait!" he cried, putting his hand on the chieftain's shoulder. "They won't find her there."

Tembu George turned on him excitedly. "But they might! They'll kill her, I tell you."

"She's perfectly safe, Tembu George," Ki-Gor assured him.

"You can't be sure."

"No?" the jungle man snapped. "Look at the arrow in that Arab beside the tent."

The tension left the Masai leader's face as he saw the arrow. There was no mistaking it. It was one of a set he made especially for Helene.

Ki-Gor's glance combed the dark branches of the trees about them. "It was well, for once, that she disobeyed me," he said with a grim smile. "She saved my life!"

Tembu George laughed hugely. "And now she is afraid to show herself."

He started back at a run with Ki-Gor to help his men, but saw there was no need for haste. The fight was over. A sudden stillness came to the camp. The last fear-crazed Bantu had been subdued. Not more than seven of the entire number had managed to reach the safety of the dark jungle.

Several of his men came toward him. "What about those who got away?" they asked.

"You've done enough for one day," Tembu George declared. "Morning will be soon enough to worry about them."

Pride shone in his usually stern, unreadable face.

Ki-Gor's eyes touched each man in turn, halting last on Tembu George. "I know now what it is to run with lions," he said and pleasure at the compliment rose strong and quick in the Masai.

The files of men and women who a few minutes before had been doomed to slavery were on their feet, still too dazed to fully comprehend what had occurred.

"Free them," Ki-Gor ordered.

"But lest their chains grow rusty," added Tembu George, "lock the Bantus in their place."

Ki-Gor frowned, but offered no objection. He walked to the head slaver, took a ring of keys from his belt. The slaver was beginning to stir and moan.

"Let's look at this Arab dango," he said angrily, and reaching down, ripped away the folds of cloth covering the man's face.

"Wah!" exclaimed Tembu George in astonishment.

"By all the gods," said the White Lord, and with eyes suddenly grown bleak and cold, he stared at the man's long, narrow face.

It was not a face one would easily forget. Beneath the high, white forehead, close-set eyes hugged a thin, long nose. Except for a few coarse, reddish hairs, the man had no pretense of eyebrows. His mouth was a crooked gash, like a narrow ridge of scar tissue set in a receding chin.

"Sam Slaker!" Ki-Gor gritted. "No wonder he hid his rotten face and body behind Arab robes."

Tembu George chopped the air viciously with his great knife.

"Stand aside," he growled. "One blow and we'll be rid of this evil dog."

Ki-Gor raised a protecting arm.

"No," he said. "He must be returned to prison. This time they'll put a noose about his neck."

"We thought that last time," argued the Masai leader. "Instead, he was sentenced to work his life out in a rock pit. I knew he'd escape. He's too clever for them."

STILL Ki-Gor stood between Tembu George and the slaver. He hated Sam Slaker as much as his friend, but he realized that the formal execution of the blackbirder by the government would carry much more weight with others of his kind than his slaying by a native war party. And it might help convince certain lethargic officials that, as Ki-Gor warned, slavers were again becoming a serious problem in the Congo.

"I want him alive," Ki-Gor declared firmly, without explanation. "Chain him with the Bantus."

For a tense moment, Tembu George didn't move.

Then he shrugged his massive shoulders and stepped back.

"It shall be as you say," he granted. "You do nothing without good reason"—he hesitated—"but I ask you to remember that this dango lives only for the day he can kill you. So long as he breathes, you are in peril. He has the devil's own cunning."

Ki-Gor's grey eyes softened as he realized it was his own safety Tembu George was concerned about. Then abruptly he remembered the white girl.

"Ho!" he exclaimed. "The girl will think us mad, chattering like monkeys and not raising a hand to free her. We are fine rescuers."

He walked with his lithe, easy stride toward her, apologizing for his thick-headedness. He felt even more badly when he saw how tensely she stood, her long legs wide-spaced, her back pressed hard against the tree. The way she was turned, her face was too much in shadow for him to read her expression.

"You're safe now," he said soothingly. "Everything's going to be all right. We'll get you back to your people in quick order."

He raised his right hand to show her he held the key to her iron neckband. The moment he moved his arm, her foot lashed out at him. It was a lightning kick, aimed at his groin.

Purely by luck, he started to turn as she kicked, meaning to go behind her and untie her hands before he unlocked the neckband, so the blow landed on his thigh. As it was, it staggered him.

With a surprised grunt, he caught his balance and jumped out of her reach. The girl immediately pressed against the tree, poised to deliver a kick with either leg if he started at her. She had moved enough so that the firelight touched her features.

Her jaw was gritted, her eyes as watchful and apprehensive as a cornered animal's. He could see the quick, nervous flare of her nostrils as she breathed.

Ki-Gor frowned, unconsciously rubbing the red mark on his leg as he studied her. It hadn't occurred to him before that a brawny half-naked white man leading a band of tall, black warriors might look far from reassuring to the girl. Instead of realizing she was saved, she thought she had exchanged a bad master for a worse one.

"Look," he said, pointing to where the Masai were releasing the jubilant prisoners from their chains. "I've come to free you. I'm Ki-Gor. Surely, you don't think I'm a slaver."

She gave no sign she heard him. If anything, she grew more wary, as though she believed his pointing was only a trick to distract her attention long enough for him to reach her.

"What's wrong with you?" asked the puzzled jungle man. "Can't you understand me? No one is going to harm you."

Tembu George had remained by the tent while his warriors went to free the prisoners, not wishing to divert any of the praise from the fighting men. He used part of Slaker's robe to tie the slaver's hands and feet, before he went to Ki-Gor's side.

"Perhaps mistreatment has shaken her mind," he offered sympathetically.

"It is something strange," agreed the White Lord.

There was a movement in the lower branches of a tree near them. A white figure showed vaguely against the dark foliage. Then Helene dropped lithely to the ground.

"Oh, you men," she said disgustedly, her very tone betraying that she had been eavesdropping on them. "Just look at yourselves and you'll see why no stranger would trust you. Bloody knives in your hands, blood stains all over you, frowning

like you were going to eat the poor thing up."

She came toward the two speechless men, waving her hand for them to stand back. With slow, deliberate actions, she divested herself of her own weapons, dropped them on the ground. She took the key from her husband.

Then talking softly, reassuringly, she approached the girl. The blonde stirred nervously, her nostrils flaring, her eyes bright in the dim light. But, gradually, as Helene advanced she began to relax.

Making no sudden movements, Helen untied the girl's wrists, unlocked the cruel iron band about her neck. From the way the blonde handled her hands, Helene knew they were without feeling from the tight bonds, so she massaged them gently.

THE BLONDE gingerly submitted to her ministrations, but for all Helene's talking, the girl never uttered a word. Most of the time she kept her glance fixed on Ki-Gor, studying minutely the man she sensed was in control of the war party.

When circulation had been restored to her hands, she abruptly pulled them away from Helene. She flexed her fingers, moved her arms, trying them. She seemed to change, confidence coming into her.

She pushed past Helene, and no longer showing any apprehensiveness, walked up to Ki-Gor. Her movements had a cat's smooth, flowing grace. And there was a cat-like intensity to the unblinking gaze with which she scrutinized the White Lord at close range. She appeared unaware of Tembu George's existence, so utterly did she ignore him.

Despite the air of strangeness about her,

word nor expression did she give any evi-

Ki-Gor could not help but be struck with her unusual beauty. She would have brought a fortune to Slaker. Among the dusky-skinned races, a blonde woman was particularly esteemed, and one as fair and young as this would have set any slave mart into an uproar.

He smiled at her. "I'm sorry we startled you," he said. "We'll get you back to your people as soon as we can. Tell me, what is your name and where are you from?"

She watched his lips, tilting her head a little to listen as he spoke. But by neither word nor expression did she give any evidence she understood him.

Instead, she stepped close to him, touched his hair with her hand, dropped her fingers to his shoulder and traced them slowly down his arm. Then she ran the flat of her palm across the rock-like pads of muscle which ridged out across Ki-Gor's broad chest.

There was neither boldness nor affection in the gesture. She seemed to act purely from curiosity, like a child inspecting some strange object.

Ki-Gor's eyes momentarily widened in surprise. She acted as though she had never seen a man before, anyway a white man. And at her touch there rose unbidden to his mind an almost forgotten incident of his youth. He had carelessly fallen asleep on a grassy plot beside a stream, only to be awakened by a velvety touch exploring his bare skin. He found a lioness curiously snuffling his body. He had kept perfectly still, expecting death at any moment, but for some inexplicable reason the cat had padded off into the

jungle once its curiosity was satisfied.

"Helene, I don't believe this girl understands a word we say," he declared.

Helene's answer was drowned out by the blonde's shrill, alarmed cry. Looking past the White Lord, the girl had seen Sam Slaker inching on belly toward a knife dropped by some warrior during the battle. The slaver had regained consciousness and was trying to take advantage of Ki-Gor's preoccupation with the girl to free himself.

Before Ki-Gor could turn, the blonde was racing for Slaker. Hearing her scream, the slaver writhed about into a sitting position just in time to see her literally dive at him. His distorted face, growing swollen and bruised from the beating Ki-Gor had given him, jerked toward the White Lord.

"No! No!" he shrieked. "Keep her away. No!"

And then the hurtling weight of her body chopped off his voice, and you could hear her snarl with the berserk rage of an animal. In her attack there was none of the aimless clawing and flailing with which most women fight.

She rained blows on Slaker much as Ki-Gor had, hitting with deadly strength and accuracy. But where the White Lord's object had been merely to knock the slaver out, it was clear she meant to beat the man to death. Bound as he was, he was absolutely helpless.

He managed once to cry Ki-Gor's name, appealing for help. But the sound of his voice so enraged the girl that she clamped her fingers about his throat. He bucked wildly, making a hideous rattling noise as his breath choked off.

V

NEITHER Ki-Gor nor Tembu George had moved, so spellbound were they by the girl's savagery. But the spectacle shocked Helene into speech.

"Stop her, Ki-Gor!" she shouted. "She's killing him!"

Ki-Gor roused then, reached the blonde in four quick steps. He caught her hands, pried them from Slaker's throat, and it took his full strength to do so. She fought to get back at the slaver, and failing in that, she switched her attack on the White Lord. It finally required the combined efforts of Tembu George and Ki-Gor both to drag her away.

With the same swiftness with which she had attacked Slaker, she suddenly quieted. With smouldering eyes, she glared at the men holding her and at the crowd of blacks which had gathered.

"Wah!" exclaimed Tembu George. "This is no woman from the settlements. By all the gods, she's the spawn of jungle devils."

"She's a strange one, all right," Ki-Gor said, "but I don't blame her for wanting to settle scores with Slaker."

Tembu George shook his head wonderingly.

"What do we do with her?" he asked.

"Let her go," directed the White Lord. "I want her to understand she must leave Slaker alone, but I don't want her to think we're taking his part or are angry with her. Right now, she looks like she thinks we're allies of his and that we might punish her."

He released his grip on the girl, patted her reassuringly on the shoulder. Then he pointed at Slaker, waggled a forbidding finger and repeated the word "no" several times. He was certain she understood his meaning, but there was no sign she agreed to obey.

"Patch Slaker up as well as you can," Ki-Gor told Tembu George. "I wanted to question him, but from his looks, he won't have his senses about him before morning. Meanwhile, I'll see what I can learn about the girl from the Bantus."

But Ki-Gor found that the prisoners knew practically nothing about how Slaker had gotten hold of the girl. Four days before the raid on the pygmy kraal, the slaver had left them in camp and gone ahead with two warriors to scout the area.

When he returned he had the girl with him and was in a high rage because of the trouble he had had in making her walk to the camp. The two warriors weren't with him, and when the Bantus asked about them, he merely snarled that they had been slain capturing the girl and gave no details.

The day had been a strenuous one for Ki-Gor, so he decided to get what sleep he could and leave the solution of the blonde's identity for morning. Before he lay down, however, he stood at a distance and watched her. Twice he saw her leave Helene, stride nervously to the edge of the camp and stare off into the darkness. After a time, she would return, her face thoughtful, sit down beside Helene and resume staring at Slaker. She took no notice of anyone but the slaver, coolly repulsing all friendly overtures.

Perhaps she is worried that the Bantus who escaped will return and try to kill or capture her, thought Ki-Gor. He posted a larger detail of guards than he would have otherwise, thinking the sight of them would relieve her mind.

But because of the way she watched Slaker, he also instructed the guards to keep an eye on her. In her condition, he wouldn't put it by her to get up, once everyone was asleep, and try to finish off the slaver.

Ki-Gor made a last inspection of Slaker, found that Tembu George was taking no chances on his escaping. The battered man was not only tied hand and foot, but also was chained by the neck to a line of Bantu prisoners. Ki-Gor didn't approve of such severe measures, but knowing how the natives hated and feared the slaver, he thought it best not to interfere.

Ki-Gor appropriated for himself and Helene one of the comfortable sleeping mats in Slaker's tent, gave another to the blonde. The night passed without incident, except that several times along toward dawn Ki-Gor was stirred from sleep by the wierd, roaring challenge of a bull ape. There are few more blood-chilling sounds than an angry gorilla's cry, but Ki-Gor wasn't alarmed, because he knew from experience the great tree-people seldom caused trouble unless they were molested.

With the first grey light, the camp began to awaken. Slaker's erstwhile captives were too overjoyed at their miraculous rescue to lie sleeping. Freedom brought renewed vigor to their exhausted bodies, made their hurts seem unimportant.

But as Ki-Gor had noticed, about the first person other than himself to awaken was the blonde. When the gorilla's reverberating roar disturbed him, he saw her sit up suddenly and listen. Daylight found her still sitting there, an air of tenseness about her despite the apparent composure of her face, the utter quietness of her

hands. Without appearing to watch her, he noted the too-quick rise and fall of her full, firm breasts beneath the narrow halter, the constant movement of her eyes along the ramparts of the thorn boma.

Could it be she is afraid, he wondered? Perhaps her apparent bold self-reliance was only a pose. That would be womanlike to face up without flinching to a danger she could see and yet worry herself sick about an imagined threat.

Ki-Gor awakened Helene. "Sit with the girl," he said, "and I'll see what I can find for us in the way of food."

KI-GOR took Helene's light bow and quiver of arrows and left the camp. He moved quietly along the stream, searching out fruit and berry bushes where birds clustered to feed. With his unerring aim, it was only the work of a few minutes before he had enough plump birds for breakfast.

Then he cut the top from a dried gourd, jammed it with blue vastoy pears, a variety of nuts and berries, and kava. Another gourd he filled with cool, clear water which bubbled out of the river bank. When he returned to camp, Helene helped him clean the birds, slice the kava, and cook them over hot coals.

The meal unexpectedly was made more sumptuous when Tembu George sent one of his warriors with a roasted piece of antelope, and a grinning pygmy contributed a large white-fleshed fish which he had speared in the river and broiled to savory tenderness.

Ki-Gor got small gourds for drinking cups and large, dew-wet leaves for plates.

The blonde watched the preparations with a blend of curiosity and suspicion. She held herself aloof as the jungle couple sat down, served her and helped themselves to portions.

"This looks more like a feast than breakfast," laughed Helene.

Ki-Gor smacked his lips appreciatively. "A warrior's meal, as our little friend N'Geeso, would say." He had eaten sparingly the day before, so with an enthusiasm befitting his size, he plunged into the food.

But he had taken no more than a few mouthfuls when Helene, sitting cross-legged beside him, nudged his foot meaningfully with her toe.

The blonde had bolted the berries and fruit but hadn't touched anything else. Ki-Gor knew she must be hungry and he couldn't understand her reluctance to eat. By gestures, he tried to assure her the meal was perfectly all right.

"What's wrong with her?" he asked Helene. "Does she think we might poison her?"

"No," answered Helene, "she acts more like she isn't familiar with cooked food. I begin to think there really is a deep mystery about this girl."

Do what they would, they couldn't get the blonde to taste either the meat or fish. She did sample grudgingly a bit of the crisp, savory kava, but almost immediately she screwed her face up in distaste and would take no more. But when they gave her their portions of fruit, she set to eating with a will.

Ki-Gor waited until she was finished, then set out to learn whether the girl spoke any of the many dialects he knew. Over and over, using a different tongue each time, he asked what her name was. In her odd, unblinking way she watched his mouth, with only her eyes betraying the fact that she had any interest in his actions. Her face remained wooden, revealing nothing.

When he had exhausted his fund of dialects, Ki-Gor sighed hopelessly. "I just don't know," he said. "I was beginning to feel that, perhaps, she was a white girl captured and brought up by some African tribe. There is the feel of the jungle about her, but not a single tongue registered with her."

"I had the same feeling about her," Helene agreed. "We must be wrong, though. I guess she's a European of some kind. If she'd only talk, I might guess at her nationality."

They attempted to elicit talk of any kind from her, even going so far as to pick up various objects, pointing to them and calling their names in an attempt to get her to say something. Except for an occasional quick glance about the camp, she gave them her undivided attention, but not once did she utter a sound.

"Could she be deaf and dumb?" muttered Helene exasperated.

"No," said Ki-Gor definitely. "Maybe she wants us to think so, but you watch, the next time she glances away."

Near his right hand lay a large, flat rock. The instant the blonde's attention was diverted from him, his fingers closed over the rock. With a flick of his powerful wrist muscles, he tossed the stone into the air behind the girl, sending it high enough to hit among the tree branches.

He acted so quickly and silently that she suspected nothing. As she turned her glance back to him, the rock smacked against a limb with a loud report, splintered downward through leaves and twigs.

At the first noise, the blonde shot to her feet with incredible speed, her stolid mask replaced by a strange, wild expression. Her eyes seemed to flame with light and a queer, low cry broke from her lips.

The white stone dropped from the lower branches, hit the ground and rolled with slowly decreasing speed toward her. Taut-drawn as a war-bow, the girl stared for the space of three heart beats at the rock.

Then with narrowed eyes, she turned to face Ki-Gor's amused smile. There was no doubt but that she understood the purpose of his trick. For a bit, it looked as if she might leap at him, but gradually her rigid muscles relaxed and the anger melted from her face.

"Haaiiieee!" chuckled Ki-Gor. "I would say both ears and tongue work very well. Now we will begin again."

THE WHITE LORD pointed to himself. "Ki-Gor! Ki-Gor!" he said. He gestured at his mate, repeated her name three times. Then he pointed at the girl, his face asking a question.

The blonde watched him sullenly. Slowly, her grey eyes smouldering, she touched her breast with her hand.

"Raa!" she said. "Raa!"

"At last!" exclaimed Helene. "She does understand! But what an unusual name."

Before Ki-Gor could go any further, Tembu George called him. The Masai chieftain had assembled representatives from each of the various tribal groups for a council meeting the White Lord had requested. Ki-Gor wanted to learn the details of Sam Slaker's raids, the number of men and women slain on the march, and then he wanted to plan for the return of his charges to their own kraals. Organization was necessary to transport the sick and wounded, and there were many details to be handled such as sending runners ahead, assigning certain men as guards, others to hunt or gather healing herbs.

"I must go," Ki-Gor said, rising, "but keep working with her until I get back. Now that she has melted a little, maybe we can learn something about her."

The council was gathered on the river bank. To reach the circle of blacks, he had to pass Slaker and the Bantu prisoners. They were chained together in a single line guarded by four Masai warriors.

The white man was fastened at the end of the line, chained by the neck to a hulking native next to him. Slaker was too weak to stand, so he slumped in a sitting position, his face swollen and discolored, one eye completely closed. He was a far cry from the arrogant master of the slave caravan Ki-Gor had observed striding into the clearing the evening before. He was completely cowed.

Slaker dropped his head when he saw the White Lord, but Ki-Gor went past him without a word. "Let him squirm, wondering what I'm going to do to him," Ki-Gor thought. "When he's wrought up enough, he'll babble his head off for fear I'm going to give him some of his own medicine."

Ki-Gor sat down with the natives, began to deal calmly and efficiently with the problems before them. He gave his full attention to the council, paying little heed to the camp noises. With so many

men about him, his usual wariness was relaxed.

Thus, when the shattering roar sounded from the middle of the camp, his shock was as complete as was that of the others.

It was a tremendous eruption of sound, which literally engulfed a man, hammering instinctive terror into every nerve and fiber. Deep it was, like a booming roar erupting from some deep cavern, tearing the eardrums with its reverberations, swelling with unbelievable intensity.

Ki-Gor heard it, and for a moment the mindless terror inspired by that fearful blasting challenge held even him motionless. Then his mind conquered sheer animal impulse and he drove to his feet.

"Ingagi! 'Ingagi!" rose the shrill, frightened cry from a score of trembling throats.

Ki-Gor's startled eyes knifed over the camp. Giant hairy forms were plummeting from the trees into the very center of the enclosure. Seemingly insane with rage, the gorillas drummed their monstrous chests and roared defiance as soon as they struck the ground.

And the two persons nearest to them were Helene and the blonde girl!

Never knowing he spoke, he cried Helene's name. Then he was racing toward her, straining with all his magnificent strength to reach her side before one of the ravening bulls should charge down on her. There was real fear in Ki-Gor then, fear for Helene. A score of times he had seen men's bodies hammered to pulp or literally ripped apart by a gorilla's awful attack. He sprinted past a stack of captured Bantu spears and leaned in full stride to snatch one up.

On all sides, blacks were running for safety, a great ring of fleeing natives sweeping outward from the dark cluster of apes. But the two women stood as though paralyzed.

"Run!" screamed the White Lord, but his voice was a tiny splinter of sound against the roaring madness of the gorillas.

He saw how Helene suddenly seemed to awaken, and though he couldn't hear her, he knew by the way her lips worked that she was shrieking. Helene reached for the blonde girl's arm, and leaped away from the apes. She was trying to save the blonde.

But even as his mate acted, a tremendous beast plowed out of the growing horde of gorillas. The bull shoved fully erect, lashed the vast length of his arm overhead and plunged snarling at the two girls.

Ki-Gor saw the animal's hideous face, the whole left side of it permanently distorted by a many-tongued scar which ran from temple to jaw. He saw also that in height, in breadth of shoulders, in sheer bulk, the beast was larger by far than any of his fellows.

This was the gorilla he had seen in the forest the day before, the leader of the first migrating band he had stumbled on.

At the moment he recognized the giant, Ki-Gor saw the blonde girl tear loose from Helene's grip. An agonized curse broke from his lips. In her panic, the girl had lost her head and in jerking away from Helene's guiding hand, she spun squarely in the path of the charging ape.

The huge beast caught her up like a doll and flung her over his shoulder. His triumphant roar blasted up through the din. His head swung about jerkily, surveying the camp. The line of Bantus caught his attention. Being chained, the blacks couldn't flee.

Clutching the girl with one arm, the bull started for the Bantus, apparently choosing to charge a group rather than pursue Helene alone. He scuttled over the ground at great speed, knuckling the earth with his free arm to give himself added balance. Following his lead, all the other apes except one rushed in a solid mass toward the prisoners. That one burst after Helene, his immense fangs bared in hate.

Ki-Gor saw the beast gain on his mate and his legs drove faster. Helene's eyes were wide with fear as she fled. She realized that she ran a losing race. Giving more attention to the monster behind her than to the course she followed, she failed to see the dead limb lying half-hidden in the short grass dead ahead of her.

Her right foot struck the limb. With no chance to catch herself, she went sprawling head first into the grass. The gorilla, when he saw his quarry fall, raised himself in a great leap to clear the branch and reach Helene. He was intent on the girl and paid no heed to the bronzed jungle man who flashed in on him from the left.

Arrow-straight, Ki-Gor catapulted at the hairy giant, the war-spear gripped level before him with both hands. If the beast thought to destroy the girl and still have time to turn and dispose of the man, he misjudged Ki-Gor's lightning speed. The White Lord struck just as the ape leaped the fallen branch and was still in the air.

He hammered the spear into the bull's side, used his driving weight to plunge the shaft half its length through the creature. The shock of the blow and the plunging, upward shove Ki-Gor gave the shaft just before he released it served to pitch the gorilla off-course and make him miss Helene in his spring.

VI

THE APE bellowed in pain, whirled to confront the puny man-thing who had dared attack him. The beast grimaced horribly and in a spasm of pain reached down and clawed the wooden shaft protruding from his side. A bloody froth gushed from his mouth, dripped over the hairy black skin of his chest.

The ape suddenly flung himself at Ki-Gor, but swift as he was, the jungle man was swifter. The White Lord danced away, knife in hand, forcing the beast to whirl and charge again. Continuing these dangerous tactics, Ki-Gor enticed the animal away from Helene.

Blood was flooding from the ape's mouth and wound when the White Lord decided to risk an aggressive move himself. As the animal charged him, he suddenly leaped straight in on the beast instead of dancing out of reach.

He slashed his knife across the ape's right forearm as the creature struck at him and then he leaped away. The gorilla was weakening, growing unsteady as blood gushed from the great tear in its chest. Ki-Gor circled rapidly, keeping always on the side of the injured arm.

Then a second time he leaped in. His knife churned twice into the beast's throat. When he spun away this time, the ape didn't follow. Instead, the monster swayed crazily, his good hand clawing at his severed jugular vein.

Like a toppling tree, the gorilla abruptly collapsed. Without another glance at the beast, Ki-Gor ran to where Helene was dazedly trying to rise. He helped her up, heard her assurance she was only jarred and bruised.

In the interval while the White Lord struggled with the ape, Tembu George managed to gather his Masai and a scattering of other blacks. He rushed these men forward, thinking a shower of spears and arrows would turn the Ingagi away from the Bantus.

As he hoped, many of the Ingagi swung to face the advancing men. Others, more knowing about spears and arrows, shied away and went rampaging through the camp.

But the scarred Ingagi leader and two followers charged into the Bantus. With fists and fangs they laid about them, tearing four blacks apart in the space of seconds. Then they swung toward the end of the terror-stricken line where Sam Slaker was insanely lunging and throwing himself about in an effort to break his chains and run.

One of the three killers staggered and went down under a whistling flight of arrows from Tembu George's men, but the Masai were afraid to shoot at the leader for fear of killing the blonde girl. As the two berserk apes reached Slaker, the unencumbered one reached out and grasped the chain about the neck of the black next to the slaver.

Seemingly with no more effort than if

he were tearing a leaf, the beast jerked the chain and ripped the Bantu's head from his body. Disregarding the blood fountaining over him, the animal fastened his hands more firmly on the blood-wet chain, and with a second tug, snapped its iron links apart.

Slaker, suddenly freed by the breaking of the chain, fell backwards. He tried so desperately to get on his feet and run before the apes should kill him that he literally flailed the ground with his arms and legs. Finally, he shot up, legs pumping, his face wrenched with horror.

But before he had gone six steps, the gorilla leader smashed a club-like arm down on his head and shoulders, knocked him rolling. The other ape bounded to the senseless slaver on all-fours, snarled over the still body. For a moment, it seemed the animal would bury his fangs in Slaker's back.

But just then the scarred leader reared to his full height, gave a thundering road and started running toward the jungle. The animal crouching over Slaker immediately scooped up the slaver in his arms and charged after his fellow.

Ki-Gor, who had left Helene and rushed to help Tembu George, barely had had time to cast his spear when the head bull gave his roar and trampled for cover. The mass of Ingagi facing the Masai wheeled when they heard their leader's cry and went racing after him.

The hairy horde tore through the thorn wall as though it were paper, plunged into the shadowy forest. Behind them in the camp they left six of their kind sprawled dead of arrow and spear wounds.

The crazed screeching of the excited men and women in the enclosure persisted for a few seconds. Then realizing the terror was over, the blacks fell silent. The crash of snapped limbs, the crackle of smashed brush faded as the Ingagi's trampling rush carried them out of hearing.

"May a hundred devils rend my soul," swore Tembu George fervently, "if ever I saw a more fearful sight! What could have happened to drive them so mad with rage that they would attack this many armed men?"

Ki-Gor frowned. "I don't know. It was very strange. But thanks to your quick thinking, our losses were small."

Ki-Gor shifted nervously, his lips set hard. Tembu George studied him knowingly.

"You think of Slaker and the girl," the chieftain quickly said. "You wish to go after them, but you hesitate to ask men to follow you."

With their almost man-like cunning, their insane courage and prodigous strength, no beasts are more dangerous to hunt than gorillas.

Tembu George tapped the knuckles of his left hand against the jungle man's chest. "Gimshai, the Stealer of Souls, has in his mind the exact time and place and way every man will die. He will not be hurried by any decisions we make. We Masai understand that, so lead on!"

Ki-Gor looked sharply at his friend. "Gimshai has never failed to welcome anyone who wanted to hurry matters."

Tembu George appeared not to hear him. In a voice which rang through the camp, he told his warriors that any who wished to do so could accompany him and Ki-Gor in trying to trail the white girl. He didn't even mention the despised Slaker.

The chieftain had hardly spoken when pygmies armed with captured Bantu weapons began hurrying to Ki-Gor.

"Let us be your eyes, O White Lord," said one of them.

And Ki-Gor gratefully accepted the services of the small men as trackers. Better than all others, the pygmies knew the ways of the Ingagi.

Helene anxiously asked Ki-Gor, "Is there really a chance you might save them?"

"Practically none," he unhappily confessed, "but since they were both alive when taken, I feel I must make a search. At least, I can find and bury their bodies."

But Ki-Gor wasn't to have the satisfaction of giving decent burial to the two whites. Once in the jungle, he found that the Ingagi had scattered, and except by following each spoor, which he didn't have men enough to do, there was no way of knowing where the torn bodies lay.

By noon of the next day, after having flushed three wounded apes intensely working back and forth over the jungle following fading spoors, Ki-Gor finally

resigned himself to the fact that his search was hopeless.

AN OLDER soldier would have been cursing the day he had asked for foreign service, but Lt. Philip Arnsdale, assigned only three weeks before straight from military school to His Majesty's Third Fusiliers, only mopped hopelessly at the sweat streaming from his face and tried to hide his nervousness. He felt very alone in the pygmy kraal despite the eight Somali regulars under his command.

This Ki-Gor he was to meet, the lieutenant understood, was quite an extraordinary fellow. Went about unclothed, fighting animals, living like a savage. Arnsdale closed his eyes against the sun, tried to picture Ki-Gor.

He was anxious to get on well with the fellow, because since this was his first solo assignment, a kind of test run given him by his commanding officers, he wanted nothing to mar it. Made him uneasy, though. The man was surely a bit on the balmy side, and the way Arnsdale pictured him, he would be a hulking, hairy-chested type, one of those low-forehead boys with a battered face and an ugly disposition.

The commanding officer in sending him to get the Bantus which Ki-Gor had captured said that the blacks had been taken three weeks previously, but because of the knocking about they had gotten only now were able to travel.

With a start, Arnsdale realized that the pygmy chieftain, N'Geeso, somehow had materialized without a sound beside him. That meant Ki-Gor would appear out of the jungle soon. Curious how these fierce little beggars seemed to know the exact moment anything was to happen, yet they had no more idea of time than the man in the moon. He had come up to the kraal quiet as a mouse yesterday with his men, yet there N'Geeso had been at the gate with a welcome party waiting for him.

Arnsdale turned to the Somali corporal who acted as his interpreter with the pygmies. "Ask N'Geeso," he told the interpreter, "if it would be wise for me to give Ki-Gor anything—you know—a present as I would an important native chieftain."

Except for a faint play of muscles in his cheek, N'Geeso didn't change expression as the interpreter dutifully relayed the message to him.

"One feels too insignificant," declared N'Geeso solemnly to the Somali, "to advise the Lord of Many Guns."

The lieutenant brightened at the phrase "Lord of Many Guns." He must remember that phrase in his letters home.

"But if I may humbly suggest," relayed N'Geeso, "this Ki-Gor is most fond of these objects." His index finger touched two of the buttons on Arnsdale's shirt. "He used them to make bracelets and necklaces. No doubt he would receive a handful of them with great joy."

By N'Geeso's careful estimate, a handful would strip the lieutenant and his eight men of every gleaming button on their blouses.

Before Arnsdale could settle down, he received another shock. Several pygmies jabbered, pointed toward some trees. Staring apprehensively through the gate into the jungle, he saw a running figure appear on a high branch. He caught his breath. It was a man going at full tilt on that narrow, swaying perch.

He forgot his dignity. "Great Scot!" he cried. "He'll fall!"

The man swerved from the branch, dove out into thin air, hurtled at a sharp angle toward the ground. Then just when Arnsdale's face screwed up in horror, the plummeting figure caught a vine, swung twenty yards and dropped free again, only to grasp another vine and skim to earth in a long, safe arc.

This wasn't at all the physical type the lieutenant expected. Despite his massive build, Ki-Gor was a clean-cut, intelligent, even an impressive looking man. But there was no getting around the fact that no normal person would be flinging around trees and living like a savage.

Remembering his position, Arnsdale managed an order to his eight men in a strained voice. The Somali obediently drew themselves up in their idea of attention. They were splendid fighting men, but hardly the European conception of military spit and polish.

The lieutenant had expected this flourish to please Ki-Gor, appeal to his childish nature. But the White Lord seemed not even to notice the salute. Instead, he came straight up to Arnsdale, his ice-grey eyes made a quick appraisal.

Ki-Gor halted, his face devoid of expression, and after a long hesitation, silently extended his hand. The lieutenant could not know that Ki-Gor's sudden woodenness of manner was shyness and reserve. The white man's custom of shaking hands was always awkward to the jungle lord.

"Er——how do you do," gasped Arnsdale.

"Welcome," the White Lord said.

"Great honor, and all that, to meet you," declared Arnsdale unsteadily, with a glance at N'Geeso. "I——I would like to offer you a sort of present."

"Oh?" said Ki-Gor, his brows arching.

"Ah, yes," gulped Arnsdale. "Only take a moment." He turned and muttered to the Somali corporal.

The black looked troubled, but he obediently drew his knife, and starting down the line of soldiers, began cutting the metal buttons from their tunics.

When the corporal was finished, having cut his own and the lieutenant's buttons also, he tumbled them all into Arnsdale's cupped hands. With a strained smile, the lieutenant held the buttons out to Ki-Gor.

"Here," he said. "I'm sorry there aren't more. They aren't much of a gift, but perhaps they will be of use to you."

Ki-Gor fell back a step, his mouth dropped open. The lieutenant followed him, his smile grown more strained as he jerkily encouraged Ki-Gor to take the buttons.

Had the lieutenant had too much sun, wondered Ki-Gor, or had he been foolish enough to drink some of the pygmy beer which N'Geeso pressed on guests? This was the strangest thing he'd ever had happen to him.

Not knowing what else to do, he finally allowed Arnsdale to press the buttons into his hands. He was still holding them foolishly, trying to think of anything in the world to say, when N'Geeso hoarsely invited the two white men to his hut.

THE MOMENT he heard N'Geeso's voice, Ki-Gor's head shot up, suspicion flaring in his eyes. The little chieftain had swiftly turned and started for his hut, entirely too swiftly. Ki-Gor saw how the pygmy leader's shoulders were quaking and heaving.

"N'Geeso!" he snapped accusingly. "I see your handprint in this! Speak up now, you little devil and tell the truth!"

With that, N'Geeso could contain himself no longer. He burst into gales of laughter, and bending double, reeled weakly about, finally falling to the ground in utter collapse.

Ki-Gor gave a violent roar, assailed the pygmy with a storm of native invective. Then chopping off in mid-sentence, he suddenly began to laugh himself, his scowl swept away by delight. He was as convulsed as N'Geeso by the ridiculous prank.

The mass of pygmies quickly took in the situation and also began to laugh, and for a moment, the Somali joined them. Only Arnsdale, who had understood nothing of Ki-Gor's remarks in the pygmy tongue, failed to understand what was going on. He looked about him wildly, thinking over and over to himself that if he ever got home he would never set foot out of England again, no matter if it meant facing a firing squad.

Ki-Gor eventually got hold of himself, and with tears streaming down his face, went over and put both hands on Arnsdale's shoulders in the friendliest fashion.

"That little imp, N'Geeso, made fools of us both," he chuckled.

Arnsdale began to sputter angrily.

"Don't be angry with him," said Ki-Gor. "Apparently, the opportunity to joke me was just too good for him to pass up. He'd sell his soul to make a fool of either me or Tembu George."

"You——you mean he deliberately led me to make an ass of myself?" exclaimed the embarrassed officer.

"I'm afraid so," chuckled the White Lord. "Just what was I supposed to do with your buttons?"

"Why, make bracelets and necklaces out of them," indignantly exploded Arnsdale. "He said you loved them. He made you out a roaring wild man who would be angered beyond words if you didn't get your beloved ornaments."

Ki-Gor's great shoulders shook uncontrollably at the advantage N'Geeso had taken of the green young soldier.

Arnsdale turned to confront his eight Somali. They stiffened to attention, suddenly fearful because they had dared laugh at a white officer. But instead of an angry denunciation, the lieutenant smiled at them.

"It was a wonderful prank on me, Corporal," he said. "I've got lots to learn. Do what you can about getting those buttons back on. And Corporal, when pygmies start giving me advice again, don't be afraid to speak your own mind."

The corporal saluted, his dark eyes beaming approval of his officer. He took the buttons from Ki-Gor, and swinging about, began redistributing them.

VII

WHILE a feast was being prepared, Ki-Gor explained how his friends the Masai had captured the slavers. Arnsdale tried to write the facts down so he could make a full report, but having never heard a gun fired in anger, he grew so engrossed, he kept forgetting to make notes.

"But you make no mention of yourself," he stated, when Ki-Gor finished describing the night attack. "You took part, didn't you?"

"You can mention me in connection with what happened the next morning," directed the White Lord, and he told of the gorilla raid. "Slaker and the blonde girl were lost. The responsibility for their deaths rests on me, not on the Masai. I was in charge of the camp then, and I was unable to save them."

Arnsdale winced. "Horrible way to die," he muttered.

"I don't mind so much about Slaker," Ki-Gor said. "He'd earned an evil death. But I can't forget that girl. She's on my conscience. It was my duty to protect her and I failed."

Arnsdale was quick to try to console him, pointing out how fortunate he was to have suffered as few casualties as he did. Now that he knew why the Bantus had been so long in getting well enough to trek, he was too ashamed to tell Ki-Gor how he had thought the White Lord guilty of mistreating them.

After the noonday feast, Arnsdale made his farewells. The more time he spent with Ki-Gor, the less he was able to reconcile the White Lord's quiet, almost gentle manner with his warlike reputation.

"I'm sorry I can't go part of the way with you," apologized the jungle man. "You'll travel fairly close to where the Masai are waiting for me, but I can't go

until the pygmies finish brewing some poison for us."

"Poison?" said the officer, raising his eyebrows.

"For tipping spears and arrows," explained Ki-Gor. "We're going into gorilla country."

Arnsdale shook his head slowly.

"After what you told me," he fervently declared, "I don't think I'd want any part of such a hunt."

Ki-Gor smiled.

"We're not hunting apes," he said. "My pet elephant, Marmo, wandered off while I was away and a pygmy hunter saw his tracks near the Ingagi territory the other day. The bush is pretty thick in there, so we may be a long time running him down. I want my men to be ready in case the apes cause trouble."

Arnsdale glanced skeptically at the bow strung across Ki-Gor's back.

"What you need is a rifle," he advised, "and a high powered one at that."

"I'll choose the poison," the White Lord told him. "No matter where you hit a gorilla with a poison-tipped arrow, he's finished. But if you miss a vital spot with a rifle, you're finished."

"It works that fast?" asked the lieutenant in surprise.

"It does the way N'Geeso makes it," answered the jungle man.

He saw the question come into the officer's eyes. "Don't ask me what he mixes up," he went on. "I don't know. That's one secret the pygmies won't let out. It's been their protection against big fellows like us for hundreds of years."

Arnsdale glanced at the small figures about him with new respect.

"Jove!" he said. "No wonder the little beggars are so cocky." He stared at the masai with wonder.

N'Geeso came up then, had the Bantus marched up and turned over to the Somali troops. The chieftain spoke rapidly to Ki-Gor, his glance flicking repeatedly to the officer.

"What is it?" asked Arnsdale when the jungle man was slow to translate.

"N'Geeso says there has been at least one ape near his kraal every day for a whole moon," explained Ki-Gor. "He warns you to be careful. He thinks the tree-people have a grudge against the Bantus and are waiting for them to be moved from the kraal."

The lieutenant appeared bewildered. "Eh?" he mumbled.

"He's giving you advice in good faith," Ki-Gor said, warning him to guard his expression. "The natives look on the Ingagi as being considerable more than dumb beasts. I might say, it is rather puzzling for them to stay around the kraal. Wouldn't hurt to be a little careful."

"Uh, yes, yes," said Arnsdale hastily. "Thank him for me."

But his tone betrayed the fact he thought N'Geeso's warning ridiculous. Why, any schoolboy knew a maneuver of that kind was beyond the capabilities of any species of animal.

As he marched away down the trail at the head of his men, he smiled to himself. It was somehow reassuring to find, that for all their supposed knowledge of the jungle, the pygmies were really a naive and simple people. Imagine apes maintaining a month's vigil over a kraal, watching for an opportunity to attack a few Bantu prisoners.

But had he possessed Ki-Gor's animal keen senses, he would have known that even as he smiled, a great hairy figure was crouched in the underbrush not a knife-throw from him, peering with beady eyes at the line of marching men.

Hardly were the men out of sight when the gorilla rose silently, its black, wet nostrils working. A sliver of sunlight reaching down through the branches illuminated its brutish features. The whole left side of the brute's face was distorted into a permanent snarl by a hideous, many-tongued scar. The beast turned with a low, angry growl, and hurried away through the forest.

VIII

HELENE strolled idly down the winding game trail. Until Ki-Gor returned from the pygmy kraal, she had little to occupy her. The Masai, in typical native fashion, were content to eat and sleep away the hours, but time hung heavily on Helene's hands. It was always so when her bronzed mate was absent.

She came to a M'tondo tree, occupied herself like a bored child by prodding its rubbery bulbs with her spear-point to let the white sap drain out. When that task was diligently attended to, she moved on to a bed of Maheena blossoms in a sun-splashed glen.

Helene pored over the clusters of blue, crimson and yellow flowers, trying to make up her mind which blooms she should select for a garland. Finally, she rejected them all, deciding she would wait and find a single orchid for her hair. Without leaving the path, she rejected a score of blooms before selecting a pure white one.

She paused to munch a few berries, debating whether she should turn back to the camp. A vanka lizard darted out of the Wassa grass not four feet from her, snared a green fly with a single dart of its forked tongue. The lizard froze for a few seconds, watching her with its cold, gem-like eyes.

Helene had half-turned to retrace her steps when a blue and orange kingfisher swooped down in its brusque, quick way to perch on a Rapphia palm. The red-haired girl looked at the bird and smiled with sudden inspiration.

She set off along the trail at a trot. The kingfisher had reminded her of a deep, clear pool of water about a mile away. Tembu George would be furious if he knew she had strayed so far from camp, but what better way was there to pass the time than with a cool, refreshing swim.

The fern-splashed banks of the pool lay in shade, but the sun drove its white brilliance into the center of the water, floodlighting the clean gravel of the bottom and the darting shapes of gaudy-colored fish.

Helene gave a contented sigh, leaned her spear against a tree, quickly dropped her bow and quiver of arrows beside it. She had been foolish not to think of the place before. With impatient fingers, she untied her scanty halter, dropped it to the ground. Then, with considerable wriggling, she slid out of the tight leopard-skin shorts.

She took a deep, happy breath as though she had just rid herself of many cloying layers of clothing. As she speculated on where she would plunge into the water, her hands in the immemorial way of women explored the curve of her hips, the smooth flatness of her stomach, the swell of her bosom.

Then taking two quick steps forward, she sprang lightly out over the water, knifed down in a long, slanting dive. For

more than an hour she entertained herself by splashing about in the pool, swimming and floating, diving deep to chase blue and red nuhana fish or retrieve some odd-shaped pebble.

When a pleasant weariness began to permeate her healthy young body, she reluctantly left the water. Her hair had come unbound while she swam, and standing nude on the bank, she ran her fingers through it, fluffing it loosely over her bare shoulders and back. She brushed half-heartedly at the drops of water which clung like jewels to the soft gold of her skin, as she looked about for a place to rest and sunbathe.

She chose a low-hanging limb. She picked up her halter and shorts, and holding them in her teeth, climbed easily the slanting trunk of the tree. She walked out along the broad limb to the point where it was dappled with sunlight filtered through a protective screeen of leaves in the higher branches.

Helene stretched out on her stomach on the warm bark, resting her head on her arms. She relaxed, lulled by the warmth and the faint sway of the limb. She lay so still, two purple and gold virini birds came to rest on a branch a few yards away. While Helene listened to the liquid music of their song, she drifted into sleep.

She awakened with a start, every muscle suddenly tense, her heart racing. There was no mistaking the sound which had lashed her awake. That angry, rumbling burst of noise could come only from a gorilla's throat. And the beast sounded as though he were directly below her.

Helene stifled the instinctive impulse to leap up and flee. She tried desperately to remember Ki-Gor's teachings. Keeping her body motionless, she raised her head with agonizing slowness until she could take in the whole scene about the pool.

THE GORILLA hadn't seen her. She was certain of that, for the brute stood at the edge of the water, looking away from her. He kept shifting and turning, angling his head as though listening intently. He apparently had come swiftly out of the forest, passed directly beneath her.

The ape was clearly wrought up about something, but with a certain measure of relief, Helene realized she wasn't the cause. He hadn't discovered her presence. It was difficult to know what she should do next.

Both courses of action open to her were fraught with danger. The least sound or movement was certain to attract the gorilla's attention, so despite her almost overwhelming urge to flee, Helene would take a long chance if she got up and tried to run back along the limb and lose herself in the forest.

Her only other course was to lie still and gamble that, agitated as he was, the ape would storm off before a vagrant breeze carried her scent to him. The safest plan, she finally decided, was to do as the average defenseless jungle creature would and "play dead."

Her blue eyes never left the bull. Taut-limbed, she endured the creeping seconds, and it seemed she had chosen rightly, for the beast showed no intimation that he suspected a human was within a hundred miles.

But to her disappointment he made no move to leave. Instead, he prowled nervously about the bank, stopping ever so often to listen. Then at last he reared up on his squat, enormously muscled legs, and pounding his chest, sent a shattering roar reverberating out over the trees.

As he finished, he gave a few deep, guttural growls like a man talking to himself, and for the first time wheeled about so Helene could see his face. Her breath caught in her throat. The whole left side of the beast's face was rent by a jagged scar.

The gorilla was the same one who had borne off the blonde girl!

A sick weakness gathered in Helene's stomach. Was she to be the second woman murdered by the vicious beast? It was apparent by the gorilla's looks that he had travelled long and fast. His breath came in quick, hard heaves. His hairy body was matted with burrs and mud.

"He's turned killer," Helene thought.

Then abruptly, the bull threw himself down on the bank, began to noisily gulp water. Lying as he was, there was no chance for him to see Helene.

"I'd be a fool to stay here longer," Helene told herself. "I musn't let this opportunity pass."

Quickly, yet with infinite caution, she raised on hands and knees. The gorilla hesitated in his drinking. Helene froze. The gleam of the sun on her naked body would be certain to attract his eye if he turned.

But after a few explosive snuffles to clear his nostrils of water, the ape returned to sating his thirst. Helene picked up her halter and shorts in her right hand. She was on her feet then, the pulse throbbing in her throat as she turned her back to the beast, started for the tree trunk.

She judged it would take her fifteen steps to reach the trunk. Then she must swing around the bole of the tree, run out along another low branch about ten steps before she could leap to the limb of the nearest tree. Once in that second tree, the dense jungle growth would begin to close around her, hide her from view.

In that moment, Helene was deaf to every sound except the ape's sucking of the water, for so long as that sound continued she was safe. In the same manner, she was momentarily blind to everything except the branch along which she ran. It might mean her life to stumble or to strike against a dry twig.

And being oblivious for that fleeting interval to what went on around her, she didn't discover the line of gorillas threading out of the forest until she had reached the trunk and was starting to swing around it. Her eyes couldn't fail, then, to see the dark, rapidly moving line of beasts.

THE PATH they followed led directly under her tree and the leading animal was almost beneath her. Helen's face went white. Her fingers dug into the bark and her breathing stopped. She squeezed against the trunk, drawing back so for a brief instant at least, she wouldn't be exposed to the view of the whole group.

The lead ape gave a harsh, short bark. The scar-faced gorilla by the pool immediately leaped up and answered with a barrage of guttural sounds. Stunned as she was, the swift hope drove up in Helene that the newcomers would charge the surly beast by the pool. If they fought, there was yet a small chance she might get away while the whole pack's attention was focused on the battle.

As the Ingagi poured past beneath her, the great brute by the pool gave a sudden roar. Helene turned her head, her glance darting to see how many of the newcomers were closing in on him. And as she looked, all hope died within her.

The scarred male was pointing one huge arm directly at her. As he had turned to confront the line of apes, the naked girl had come directly in his line of vision. And to Helene's horror, she saw that instead of attacking him, every one of the newcomers was whirling to search for her.

"It's now or never!" thought Helene, and grasping her clothes in her teeth, she started scrambling up the tree trunk, reaching for the higher branches before she made her break for the forest.

But even as she moved, the scarred brute was roaring again. A vast clamor broke from the throats of the apes as he spoke and they began to rush about in apparent confusion. Helene had barely reached the middle branches, though, when she learned there was a deadly method in their wild scrambling.

The Ingagi fanned out in all directions, some leaping into the trees, some running through the brush, while others gathered around the trunk beneath her. She knew then that her hope of their fighting the scarred ape had been vain from the first. They actually were following his orders to surround her, blocking off every avenue of escape.

The great brute had summoned them to the pool. That had been the purpose of his thunderous calls. That had been the reason for his rapt listening.

Helene suddenly had no place to go except to climb higher. Apes stood guard in the branches of every tree around her. Another loose circle of the creatures ringed her perch on the ground. She cursed the moment when she had selected practically the only tree around the pool which stood so nearly by itself that it could be easily blockaded.

Conquering her first feeling of panic, she realized the apes were making no attempt to move in on her. None were even climbing the tree she was in. They merely held the positions they had taken in the first scramble, warily watching her.

Like a treed animal, she stopped climbing, her head constantly moving as she tried to keep all her tormentors in view. The barking and growling of the Ingagi died away and in the silence she could hear her own quick, labored breathing. It gave her a strange, awful feeling to have those black, glittering eyes staring at her from every side.

She backed against the trunk, raised a hand to take from her mouth the clothing which she had been gripping with her teeth. She held the halter and shorts for a time, and then suddenly looking at them, seemed surprised to find them in her hand. It was as though for the first time she was conscious she was unclothed. Mechanically, Helene donned the two brief garments, keeping her attention fixed on the silent brutes.

She bit her lower lip, looked at the ground far below. That was the better way, down there. Their fangs and brutal, tearing paws would never close on her alive, she resolved. She only needed to step off the branch and it would be all over.

"Oh, Ki-Gor, Ki-Gor," she murmured, and her voice broke.

Abruptly, her jaw hardened and she blinked back the tears which threatened to start in her wide eyes. She waited then, almost calmly poised for the death-fall she planned.

A full minute, and then another, passed before she heard the expected flurry of movement, the burst of snarls from the beasts. That was the signal she awaited. She took a quick, shallow breath and looked down.

IX

NOT UNTIL the next afternoon following Lt. Arnsdale's departure did Ki-Gor get back to the Masai camp. Two things delayed him, the first was the long period required to brew the strong poison he needed; the second, N'Geeso's insistence on returning with the White Lord.

"Tembu George is no more than a helpless child," N'Geeso had scoffed. "It is well to have a man such as myself along in case of trouble."

Ki-Gor had smothered a smile behind his hand. "A rather large child, though," he said.

"Wah!" N'Geeso sniffed, and from his expression no one could have guessed of his great affection for Tembu George. "And what good is size? The more blubber and belly for the mind to push around, the less chance it has to work on important things!"

So N'Geeso came along, blithely disregarding the fact that his company made Ki-Gor's trip many hours longer. When alone, the White Lord could travel the tree paths, but with the small black he had to keep to the winding, difficult ground routes.

As they trotted into the camp, Tembu George rose, mock dismay clouding his face. "I see you, O Ki-Gor," he boomed in the standard native welcome. "But what is that strange creature trailing at your heels? It is too small and ugly to be a monkey."

N'Geeso drew to a stop before the massive Masai chieftain, his glance running disdainfully over the big warrior. He spat in the dust at Tembu George's feet.

"Always the same," he observed to Ki-Gor. "Find a smell-ridden place piled high with gnawed bones and you can be sure it is either a jackal's den or a Masai camp."

He appeared for the first time to notice Tembu George.

"The White Lord begged me to leave my duties," he carelessly confided, "because he needed at least one warrior along on the trek." He squinted at Tembu George's grinning warriors. "After seeing these great-bellied beasts, I can understand his concern. Ho! The Masai women are indeed long-suffering to put up with such sluggish cattle for husbands."

Tembu George grimaced in pain, threw out his hands appealingly to Ki-Gor.

"O, Ki-Gor, my people bear not even the sun a greater love than they hold for you," the big man said. "Knowing this, why must you inflict such cruel punishment on us? Test our friendship by tying us naked across anthills, chain us and let hawks tear at our bellies, but please don't make us endure this demented rooster."

Ki-Gor, who was occupied in looking about the camp for Helene, chuckled and shook his head helplessly at the Masai warriors. He had witnessed a thousand variations of this act. Except in battle, when they fought side by side like twin demons, N'Geeso and Tembu George spent most of their time fanning the flames of their mock feud.

"Watch your tongue, great elephant!" the pygmy snapped, his hand darting to the gleaming blade dangling from a thong at his waist. "Seek not protection in my rule of not slaying inferiors! For a grain of sand, I'd spill your insides out on the earth before you."

"With your clumsy handling of a blade," taunted Tembu George, "it's more likely you'd impale yourself and cry for me to save you." He waved a hand commandingly at his men. "Put all food and belongings under constant guard until our unwelcome visitor is gone."

With a wild sputtering, N'Geeso whirled his long knife free, poised it for instant use.

"No pleading will save you now!" he screeched. "Arm yourself! By all the gods, now I teach you your last lesson."

Tembu George calmly, thoughtfully regarded the prancing, leaping little man. He raised his eyebrows at one of his warriors.

"Moka," he said, "bring me a stick—only a small stick. It would be unfair to use anything else against his unskilled blade."

Ki-Gor cut N'Geeso's tirade short by stepping between the two men.

"Since Tembu George is to die," he laughed, "let me first ask what has become of my mate."

Tembu George was abruptly serious. He pointed to the sky.

"The sun was there when she left for a walk," he said, indicating an interval of about two hours. "She has been restless ever since you left, but this is the longest she has been away. She promised not to go far."

His frown revealed all too clearly, though, that he had begun to worry about her.

"I'll take a few men and hunt for her," Tembu George said casually. Actually, he had been organizing such a search when the White Lord arrived.

Ki-Gor stroked his chin, considering. Helene was like a child when she went out alone, wandering from one bright, new object to another, losing all idea of time. She often roamed much further afield than she planned, but she knew the jungle's dangers and was never really careless.

"She's probably all right," he told Tembu George. "Instead of everybody going out and embarrassing her, I'll just hunt her up by myself. You know how she is about being fussed over."

Tembu George reluctantly agreed that Ki-Gor's idea was best. He pointed out the path Helene had taken. Her spoor was as simple for one man to follow as a dozen, and since she was merely strolling, the fleet-footed jungle lord could easily overtake her.

Ki-Gor took a drink of water, picked his spear out of the pile of Masai weapons and started down the path. Before he had gone a hundred yards, he heard the pad of bare feet behind him. When he looked back, N'Geeso grinned pleasantly at him.

He grunted as though he disapproved. Actually he was pleased by the pygmy's unsolicited company. Ki-Gor set a fast pace, but despite N'Geeso's short legs, he hung effortlessly at the white man's heels. Like all pygmies, he was a swift-moving ghost in the thick bush. The two men had trekked together so much that they seldow had need for words, working a trail with the smooth efficiency of two hunting dogs.

They had trekked for an hour when they passed the sun-swept glen where Helene paused to admire the thick patch of Maheena blossoms. A short way further on they startled a vanka lizard stalking flies which buzzed over some crushed berries she had dropped. Then the path widened, began to follow the bank of a rambling, water-lily choked stream.

To give Ki-Gor's eyes a rest from straining after Helene's spoor, N'Geeso wordlessly took the lead. The White Lord fell back without objection. The pygmy was an expert tracker, and by taking turns, neither would grow weary.

THE TRAIL made an abrupt bend following a turn of the stream. With his attention centered on the ground, N'Geeso didn't see the leopard crouched in the fork of a tree not ten yards ahead when he came around the curve.

But Ki-Gor, running just behind the pygmy caught the strong, warm leopard scent the moment he turned. It was in such situations that his close kinship with the wild became strikingly apparent. His nostrils were keen as any animals, and where N'Geeso, for all his jungle cunning, suspected nothing, that odor was like a jangling alarm to the White Lord.

His eyes, sudden slits of light, flashed over the trail even as the word *leopard* formed in his mind. He saw the tawny blur of movement against the brown bark of the tree.

The yellow-eyed killer had crouched above the trail for more than an hour while the hunger cramps in its belly grew more severe.

Now as N'Geeso reached five strides past the bend, the deadly jungle assassin gave a single slithering movement to gather its strength. Then like molten metal flung from a catapult, it shot in a rippling mass at the pygmy.

Ki-Gor caught the cat's swift, nervous gathering of muscles. *"Devil-cat!"* he screamed in warning, and he was bounding forward, his righ arm whipping in a blur of motion as he cast his spear.

N'Geeso was without means to fend off the unexpected attack. He hadn't brought his spear, choosing to rely on blowgun and darts for protection. And there was no time for him to free his blowgun, fumble a dart from the pouch at his waist, fit it to his lips and puff.

At Ki-Gor's cry, the pygmy looked up, his face blank with surprise as he saw the leopard lunging down upon him. Shock held him immobile for a moment, and then too late, he tried to leap back.

That leap was never begun. More than two hundred pounds of solid bone and muscle slammed into him from the side. The White Lord had cast his spear, and then dropping his left shoulder, crashed against N'Geeso with every bit of driving power he could summon.

Not realizing what had happened, the pygmy chieftain was hammered off his feet, flung whirling through the air to land ten feet out into the stream. Ki-Gor kept his balance as he hit, utilized the recoil from the collision to hurl himself to the furtherest inner edge of the path.

His spear rammed into the leopard's chest just as Ki-Gor struck N'Geeso. The cat screamed with pain, lashing wildly with its claws. It was jolted off-balance, but such was the angle of its leap, that the weight of its body alone would have carried the animal to the spot at which it had aimed.

But thanks to Ki-Gor's lightning quick action the lashing cat struck bare ground. Neither man was within its reach, N'Geeso landing in the water and the White Lord bringing up at the edge of the path.

The leopard reared, screaming and coughing blood. Spinning away from the man in the stream, it came at the White Lord. Luring the beast away from his small friend, Ki-Gor leaped into the bush, bulled his way for a few steps into the mass of vines and bush, then made an abrupt right turn and shoved straight ahead another six steps.

A violent threshing broke out behind him. The leopard, trying to charge after him with four feet of spear protruding from its body, had become enmeshed. The shaft had tangled in the undergrowth, as Ki-Gor hoped, and every movement the cat made helped tear out its life.

Ki-Gor watched the cat grow weaker. Suddenly, seeing his chance, he dove at it, knife in hand. The swift churn of his blade ended the killer's struggles. Without pausing to wipe the knife clean, the jungle man leaped over the beast and ran back to the trail.

N'Geeso stood waist deep in the expanse of water lilies, dazedly shaking his head and wiping wet hands over his face. The unexpected impact of Ki-Gor's driving body had saved the pygmy's life, but it had nearly knocked him senseless.

"Are you hurt?" asked Ki-Gor in concern.

N'Geeso groaned, tried to focus his eyes on the White Lord.

"What happened?" muttered the black.

"I hit you," explained Ki-Gor. "There wasn't anything else to do. You didn't have a chance to escape the leopard."

N'Geeso stiffened. Mention of the cat cleared the fog from his brain.

"It——it's gone?" he asked.

"Dead!" answered the jungle man.

N'Geeso relaxed, rubbed his bruised side. He squinted at Ki-Gor, grumbled, "Wah! I believe the cat got the best of

it. At least, he died quickly. I'll probably linger on for many suns."

"Stop fooling," smilingly ordered Ki-Gor. "Are any bones broken?"

The pygmy grunted miserably. "After all," he said, "what's a crushed chest? And no man needs more than one arm. Only next time, just leave me to the leopard."

Ki-Gor knew then N'Geeso wasn't hurt. If he had suffered anything more than bruises, he wouldn't be taking on so.

"You little fake," laughed the White Lord. "You'll get no sympathy from me. You're not harmed yet, but keep standing in those water lilies and snakes or crocodiles will change that."

"Bah!" N'Geeso scoffed. "Impossible! Have not three wizards foretold that N'Geeso need fear only beer and women?"

But all the same, he began trying to pull his feet from the mud. He wriggled and strained and slowly a queer look came over his face. He looked down at himself. The water had advanced half-way up his chest.

"Ki-Gor!" he cried in alarm. "The mud swallows me."

With surprise the White Lord realized that in the brief time they had talked that the pygmy had sunk deeper. He wasn't upset for there was plenty of time to pull N'Geeso free. He glanced around for something to hold out to the little man. The only thing he saw was the blowgun which had been knocked from N'Geeso's belt in the collision. The gun proved too short, though, when he tried it.

"By all the gods," exploded the pygmy, "don't just stand there! Do something!"

"Don't get excited," Ki-Gor said. "I'll get my spear and have you out of there in no time."

He crossed the path and started into

the underbrush. A low, chilling snarl froze him in his tracks. Two leopards, one of them coal black, the other spotted, stared at him over the body of the animal he had killed.

THE SPOTTED BEAST'S hindquarters were bunched, the muscles of its long body drawn tight as steel cables, one forepaw lifted for the spring. The other cat stood behind it, utterly motionless, its yellow eyes burning into Ki-Gor.

The White Lord's mind raced like the flickering leap of lightning. He had a fighting chance to cope with one leopard. But against the fearful speed and strength of two of the killers he had no hope. There was no time for him to reach the bow slung on his back. The faintest movement would bring them catapulting at him.

Had they not been standing almost on top of him, he could have used his old trick of escaping into the trees. But with the cat a mere six yards away, they could rip him apart before he hardly swung his feet off the ground. He was as much cornered as if he had been backed against the wall.

The knife in his hand, still wet with the blood of the other leopard, seemed puny and useless.

Terror would have exploded in the minds of most men, made them try to turn and run. And death would have brought them down from behind. But Ki-Gor was the jungle's own, and like any beast at bay, he kept his face to the enemy, meaning to fight to his last breath since there was no hope of escape.

Even as the rumbling growls lashed from the leopard's throats, his own lips sheared apart in a snarl of hate. Then, swift as a darting gleam of sunlight, the spotted cat flashed at him. As though triggered by the movement of its fellow, the black leopard sprang a fraction later.

Instead of going to pieces in what he accepted as the last, black moment of his life, Ki-Gor's whole being galvanized in a final, supreme effort. Never before had he achieved such sure and terrible speed.

Exactly as the spotted cat left the ground, the White Lord flung back, crouching. The sun sparked red from his lifted blade. He moved back just far enough to ruin the cat's leap.

Already off the earth, the leopard couldn't lengthen its spring. Yet the man was so close, the hurtling cat instinctively strained out with its forepaws in the hope of reaching him. But Ki-Gor had planned the dangerous maneuver well. The leopard had to touch the ground before reaching him.

The raking claws missed him by inches. And then there was the merest fraction of time in which the jungle killer had to jerk its forelegs to the earth before rearing for the death-blow. That fleeting interval was Ki-Gor's one and only opportunity to strike. Before he could ever find another opening, the black leopard would also be on him.

Too fast for the eye to follow, he was against the spotted beast. His knife outraced the reaching fangs, hammered into the animal's neck. His legs flashed over the leopard's back, locked tight about its belly. He was gripping the creature's neck then with his left hand, hammering and slashing the blade with his right.

He fought in the wildest frenzy, riding the leaping, twisting leopard, expecting any instant to feel the fangs and claws of the black leopard tear out his back. The berserk screams of the cat were deafening. He could see nothing except a whirling blur.

Once he thought he heard shouts, perhaps some frantic warning from N'Geeso, but in that moment of supreme effort, nothing but the leopard actually registered on his consciousness.

The strength went out of his insane mount with startling abruptness. The leopard staggered, bowing its back. Its snarls died as it gave a great bloody cough. Then its legs collapsed.

The White Lord leaped away as the killer fell, his slitted eyes searching for the black devil. The lunging cat had carried him twenty yards down the path by the stream. He was a fearful figure crouched there on the trail, his arms thrown wide, wrath surging over him like the play of flame, the great, blood-streaked drum of his chest swollen with writhing muscles.

For the space of seconds, Ki-Gor stood utterly motionless, staring. A queer, unbelieving look crept over his features. His arms dropped slowly to his sides then, the tense muscles of his body loosening.

"It cannot be!" he said, and again he repeated it.

Stunned, he tore his eyes away, looked at N'Geeso in the stream for confirmation.

"It is true," N'Geeso said. "I saw it happen." And the pygmy was so completely confounded himself that momentarily he had forgotten his own danger.

The black leopard lay dead on the path, its skull crushed to a bloody pulp. And standing wide-legged over the cat was a strikingly beautiful white woman clad in a crudely-fashioned halter and breechclout made of money-skin. She had long blonde hair reaching to her waist. And in her hand she held a long, knobbed club from which fresh blood dripped.

It was Raa!

X

IT WAS the woman taken by the Ingagi, the strange woman Ki-Gor had believed dead these many weeks! And no wound or scar marred her honey-colored skin.

She stood there utterly poised, her grey eyes brilliant with excitement as she surveyed the jungle man's bronzed figure. "Ah!" she declared in an odd, low voice. "Ki-Gor——not——hurt." One could feel her searching for each word, framing her mouth to pronounce it.

The White Lord blinked. Not only had the girl come back from the dead, but now she could speak. Before he could gather his wits, she had turned and disappeared into the underbrush.

Ki-Gor darted forward, thinking she meant to disappear as mysteriously as she had come. "Raa, wait!" he cried. But when he got to where he could see her, he found she was only drawing his spear from the leopard he had killed in the bush.

She walked out on the path with the spear, handed it to him with the merest hint of a smile. She pointed to N'Geeso.

"By all the gods!" exclaimed Ki-Gor. "I had forgotten N'Geeso in my surprise."

He reached the spear shaft out to the pygmy, and then bracing himself, tugged

the little man free of the quicksand, drew him up on the bank. N'Geeso was beside himself with excitement, but not because of his rescue.

"She killed that devil-cat like a tame goat," he babbled. "I was watching you as the spotted one struck."

N'Geeso stabbed a finger at the blonde girl.

"The next thing I knew a black leopard burst out of the bush with her astride it. She killed it with two blows!"

The woman watched N'Geeso curiously. "What——talk——that?" she asked. "Not Ing-less."

"That's pygmy," said Ki-Gor hurriedly. "But tell me, where'd you come from? How is it you're alive and unhurt?" Then he caught himself. "But first let me thank you for saving my life. You took a terrible risk to do it. For a woman——well——I never heard of such courage."

She leaned down, pulled a handful of grass, wiped her knobbed club clean.

"Raa——pay——back!" she said deliberately. She concentrated a moment. "You——save——Raa——once."

What a queer thing to say, thought Ki-Gor.

"Why, you owed me nothing," he objected. "I'm the one to be grateful."

She smiled, waved away his thanks.

"But, please," Ki-Gor pleaded, "tell me how in the world you escaped the apes, how you've managed to keep alive since then. I just can't believe it!"

Then slowly, with many hesitations as she groped for words, she explained.

"Apes not try kill Raa. Make go long walk to where live. All time watch and hit Raa if not like. No can go away. Bad. All time, bad."

"You mean they kept you prisoner?" Ki-Gor exclaimed in amazement.

There were legends of such things among the blacks, of course, but Ki-Gor had been around the great apes all of his life and had never found the least substance to such stories.

She nodded gravely. "Long time Raa watch and wait. Be very good. Then get time to run away. Raa come here."

Ki-Gor puzzled over her words. Then suddenly another thought struck him.

"How does it come you can talk now?" he questioned, "when you didn't seem to understand a word in camp?"

Her red lips curved in a pleased smile.

"Other man teach Raa," she said.

"What other man?" demanded Ki-Gor quickly.

"Su-laa-kur," she answered with difficulty.

Ki-Gor's face hardened. "Sam Slaker!" he cried. "Then they kept that dango alive, too." His mind raced. "Where is he? Did he escape with you?"

She told him "no," that she had fled alone. Slaker was still in the hands of the apes. The jungle man relaxed.

"I should leave him there," muttered Ki-Gor, half to himself. Then he frowned. "But tell me about you. Who are you? What are you?" And the long stored up questions about the strange girl poured from Ki-Gor's lips.

She regarded him hesitantly.

"Not time talk now," she said. "You come! Your woman need!"

"What?" he cried. "Who do you mean?"

"Haa-lane," she pronounced with difficulty. "Apes have her."

Ki-Gor's face went pale. His barrage of questions fell with such violence that the blonde blinked dumbly, confused by the rain of words.

Realizing finally what was happening, he got hold of himself.

RAA explained that Helene had strayed into the apes' feeding area and that they had surprised and captured her. She didn't think Helene had been badly hurt, but she wasn't sure, because Raa had taken advantage of the excitement while the apes were cornering Helene to make her escape. Raa said she had followed the same path along which Helene had come, knowing that Ki-Gor must be near.

"Raa came you," she said, "so can save woman." Her expression was deeply serious. "Raa know way. Raa show you. In night, can save."

A small measure of relief came to Ki-Gor.

With Raa's help, he could at least free Helene within a few hours.

N'Geeso, who had understood enough of their talk not to need an explanation in his language, immediately offered, "I go swiftly to get the Masai!"

Raa looked from the pygmy to Ki-Gor. "What small one say?"

When Ki-Gor explained, she shook her head, pointed toward the late afternoon sun. She declared there would be no need for additional men if they started immediately. At dark, the prisoners were put in a cave and one gorilla left to guard them, while the other apes wandered off to their favorite sleeping spots to nap until moonrise.

She said she could lead Ki-Gor and N'Geeso directly to the cave. They could surprise the ape, easily finish him with their weapons.

But if they waited to get the Masai, she explained, they wouldn't reach the cave until after the moon rose. She pointed out that when the moon was full, as it would be tonight, the whole tribe would be out in force. She added that they could wait until the next night, if Ki-Gor wished, though it was always possible for the tribe to suddenly shift to another area.

But neither Ki-Gor nor N'Geeso could bear the thought of leaving Helene in the beasts' hands throughout the night, let alone through the following day. They immediately decided to forget the Masai and handle the rescue together.

"Good!" approved Raa. "No dan-ger," she assured.

She patted Ki-Gor's spear and smiled faintly. "Kill easy."

Then she turned and set off at a trot along the path. In single file, the two grim-faced men followed her.

HELENE had expected the end to come suddenly. The unnatural immobility, the eerie silence of the great apes couldn't continue long. She was certain, therefore, that the outburst of noise from the apes on the ground signaled the beginning of their rush to kill her.

Like a taut-drawn bow, her lithe, curved body poised for the dive that would smash her life out on the hard earth far below. Better to meet death that way than at the hands of the beasts. Her glance stabbed down, picked the path she would follow, then swept to judge the progress of the climbing apes.

To Helene's amazement, not a single bull was moving up the trunk. The rush of the beasts had been past the tree toward the edge of the jungle.

And there, surrounded by the leaping, bellowing creatures, stood Raa and Sam Slaker, they were flanked by a guard of six burly apes who kept their milling fellows at a distance. From their expressions, they were almost as surprised to see Helene as she was them.

Then over Slaker's thin, ugly face slid a cruel smile. He half-turned to the blonde girl, his lips seeming to move quickly, but in the uproar no sound of his words reached Helene.

Helene was utterly bewildered. She long since had accepted the two as dead, and yet here they were, somehow yet alive, prisoners of the Ingagi. The iron slaver's neckband was still locked about Slaker's neck, a length of broken chain dangling from it. Helene remembered how to kidnap him a gorilla had broken that chain with his bare hands, tearing away in the process the head of the Bantu to whom Slaker had been fastened.

At a roar from their scarred leader, the Ingagi again fell silent.

Slaker's taunting voice broke the quiet, "Well, my dear, so we meet again! How very, very delightful!"

The blonde girl gave Slaker an angry glare. Then she looked up at Helene, beckoned with her hand. "Come!" she said. "Not hurt." She pointed at the apes, repeated, "Not hurt."

The girl was telling her to climb down, that the Ingagi wouldn't kill her.

"What will they do with me?" Helene asked uneasily.

"Nothing," gruffly answered Slaker, "if you don't give them any trouble. They just herd us around like a couple of pet goats and that's all there is to it."

"But—but I don't understand," Helene declared, bewildered.

Slaker spat disinterestedly.

"Who does?" he growled. "If you want to live, come on down and join the happy family. Otherwise, dive on off and break your fool neck. I'm sure I don't care one way or the other."

The blonde beckoned again, frowning as though she couldn't understand Helene's hesitation.

It would be foolish, thought Helene, not to give herself up, when she could see that both Slaker and Raa were unharmed. The idea of being completely at the beasts' mercy frightened her, but she consoled herself that she wouldn't be a captive long, Ki-Gor would find and free her. She might escape within a few hours.

She started slowly down the tree, lowering herself from branch to branch. As though struck with abrupt misgivings, she halted once, looked searchingly at Raa. The blonde smiled and nodded encouragement, and, after a moment, Helene continued to the ground.

She waited uncertainly at the base of the tree, apprehensively watching the hairy giants. They had formed a ragged circle about the trunk while she descended. The scarred leader knuckled forward, glowering. Seeing his fearful face at such close range, her heart almost stopped.

He snuffled her scent, pawed curiously at her halter first and then at her red hair. Then his huge fingers clamped over her shoulder, held her so tightly she winced.

As he caught her, he turned his head, barked gutturally at Raa. To Helene's shock, the blonde girl responded with a swift flow of the same harsh, guttural sounds. *Raa was talking to the brute in his own sub-human language of snarls and grunts.* For a full three minutes, they talked, oblivious of either Helene or Slaker.

But Slaker registered impatience rather than surprise at Raa's actions. "What's he saying," he finally demanded of Raa.

"Bantus coming," she answered. "Mog say these white men." She held up one finger, "And these black men." She held up eight fingers. "Guns!" she added meaningfully.

"Oh, don't worry about a few soldiers," said Slaker scoffingly. "Do what I've told you and they'll never have a chance to use those guns."

She considered his words, her eyes moving thoughtfully over the mass of apes.

"We go," she agreed. She pointed to Helene. "Tie!" she ordered.

"That's right," Slaker said. "Give her half a chance and she'd go skipping through the trees. I'll tie her hands with a long vine and you tell one of these monkeys to hold onto to it all the time."

Helene looked from one to the other in consternation.

"What—what is this?" she asked haltingly.

SLAKER laughed uglily, walked away to get a vine without answering. Helene noticed that a gorilla trailed behind Slaker every step he took. Raa stared at her impassively. Gone was the apparent friendliness the blonde had displayed to lure Helene down from the tree.

Not until after the slaver had tied her wrists did he speak. "It's quite simple, my dear," he said. "Yesterday your husband turned over his Bantu prisoners to a white officer and eight troops. In a short while, though he doesn't know it yet, this white officer will turn the Bantus over to me—uh—or rather to my friends here. We mean to waylay him on the trail. You see, we plan to gather quite a few slaves, and, of course, my Bantus will come in very handy in such work."

Helene heard what he said, but the whole matter was too fantastic for her mind to accept. Surely, this must be some nightmare that she would laugh about when she awakened.

Slaker savored her expression. "Why, I believe you're almost as stupid as your husband, my dear. Can't you understand that our blonde friend rules these apes. She's one of them. They reared her."

"But that can't be true," protested Helene. "You're both their prisoners. I saw them capture you." With her chin, she gestured at the chain Slaker wore. "You wouldn't be wearing that if you were free."

Slaker's eyes grew mean. But he attempted to mask his anger with a false, unpleasant smile. He seemed acutely conscious that Raa was watching him.

"I am merely Raa's faithful servant, her teacher and advisor," he declared. "I am her friend."

Raa grunted disdainfully. "He slave, like you," she said. The least smile curled the corner of her lips. "He slave like try make Raa."

And then the whole incredible picture came clear to Helene. Raa was the ruler of the ape tribe. That explained the Ingagi attack on the camp. They came to rescue her, and she had turned the tables on Slaker, by making him her prisoner.

Helene's face lighted triumphantly. "She's making you serve her," she cried to Slaker. "So the great Sam Slaker has become the mousy servant of a bunch of apes." Helene actually laughed aloud.

The slaver shook with anger, knotting his fists as though to strike Helene. But at a word from Raa, the ape guarding him reached out and grasped the chain dangling from his neck, tugged it just firmly enough to remind him not to cause trouble.

"You'll laugh a different tune before I'm through with you," snarled Slaker. "Maybe I did make a mistake in capturing Raa. I didn't know who she was. But she's learning who her good friend is. I taught her to talk. Now I'm going to teach her to let slaves make life easy for her. Yeah, I'm going to teach her a lot of things, and then we'll see who does tthe laughing."

He was breathing hard. "I promise it won't be Ki-Gor."

Helene disregarded the slaver, turned her attention to the blonde.

"This man is bad, Raa!" she said. "You know that. You mustn't do what he says."

Raa wasn't impressed. "He bring back man-talk to Raa. That good!" She spoke gutturally to an ape standing away from the mass. The brute came forward and Helene saw he was carrying a knobbed club. Raa took it. "He make Raa club," she said. "That good!"

"He did those things just so he could use you," Helene told her. "He's trying now to get you to kill men and you know that's bad."

Slater cursed Helene and began to talk rapidly in his defense.

Raa waved him to silence. "Men kill my people," she said, gesturing to the apes. "Now we able kill men. Men catch my people. Now we catch men."

Helene was shocked.

"Men are your people, not these apes," she said. "You must have memories of your parents, because you just said that Slaker had brought back to your mind the man-talk you'd forgotten. You can't kill your own kind."

Raa stared impassively at Helene. "These my people," she said belligerantly. "They fight for Raa. Now Raa fight for them. Make weak, coward men serve them."

The strained, tense look vanished from Slaker's face. He could be sure of the blonde girl. Helene's words hadn't touched her. Raa was as much a wild animal as any of her apes, as dangerous and devoid of feeling—and as simple, if one knew how to handle her.

"You mustn't listen to Slaker, pleaded Helene. "You know you can't trust him. Look at what he tried to do to you. He'll bring ruin and death to you and the apes."

"Raa strong," said the blonde, balancing the club significantly. "He slave Raa. Do bad, he die." In her naive self-confidence, she was contemptuous of Slaker's ability to harm her.

Helene bit her lip, distressed because she couldn't break through the girl's childish ego. How could she make her see the truth?

"I don't mean he'll beat your head in with a club or choke you to death," she tried to explain. "He'll talk you into destroying yourself. Like killing these soldiers. If you do that, men will hate you as they do Slaker and they'll hunt you down and kill your whole tribe. You can't win against their numbers and their weapons!"

Raa's smile was amused, superior. Taking his cue from the blonde, Slaker laughed, not meaning to overlook this opportunity to flatter Raa and torture Helene.

"You underestimate us, my dear," he said tauntingly. "We've worked it out very carefully, and by dropping so nicely into our hands, you've saved us the trouble of kidnapping you."

He dry-washed his hands, his close-set eyes gloating.

"Before anyone suspects a thing," he continued, "Ki-Gor, Tembu George, N'Geeso and a few other trouble-makers will walk oh-so-innocently into a trap for which you are the bait. And Raa, who your stupid husband and his friends will never suspect of being an enemy, will be the one to tell them the pitiful story of how you are held prisoner by savage apes. She will lead them into our hands!"

He triumphantly threw up his hands, highly pleased with his own cunning in devising such an excellent plan.

"And once we hold the jungle's key leaders," he gloated, "we hold a whip-hand on the blacks. We'll move swift and fast after that. Ah, it's amazing what a really clever person can do if he sets his mind to a thing. And my dear friend,

Ki-Gor, what a pleasant surprise this will be to him."

FEAR touched a cold finger to Helene's heart. "Raa!" she cried. "Surely you wouldn't harm the man who saved you from this mad dango? Ki-Gor helped you, yet here you are plotting against him."

"Raa's people save her," snapped the blonde. "Not need or want Ki-Gor's help. One man all same another. All weak, coward, bad." She grunted in disgust, spun on her heel and walked off. "We go!" she said.

The Ingagi hurriedly cleared a path for her, then fell into file behind, except for the scarred ape. He shoved up to the head of the line, pushed ahead of her. She patted his hurly shoulder affectionately as he took the lead.

Two hours later, a horror-stricken Helene, after being gagged by Slaker, was forced to watch helplessly while the gorillas swarmed out of ambush to overwhelm Lt. Arnsdale and his eight native troops. It happened with such suddenness that the troops had no chance to defend themselves.

Great hairy forms swinging on vine ropes smashed down from trees on the blacks. Other apes charged out of thick brush on either side of the trail. Five Somali literally were torn apart in the first rush. The other three were wounded and knocked senseless after firing a few wild shots.

Lt. Arnsdale, the young officer who had never fired a shot in anger, proved in those few tumultous moments of battle that, as N'Geeso had predicted, he had the makings of a real fighting man.

He was the novice, yet his gun was the first to speak. He triggered three shots into the brute swinging down on him. The animal roared with pain, turned loose of the vine to soon and missed its leap. An ape sprang on a Somali within a yard of the lieutenant, fastened his fangs in the man's throat. Arnsdale shoved his pistol against the back of the ape's skull, fired twice.

The white officer spun, his face paper-white, but his gun steady. The thought of flight seemed not to occur to him, though he must have believed death was certain. He blasted his last shot into one of three beasts charging in on him.

Helene shuddered and turned away as she saw him go down. But to her surprise, a minute later the scarred ape, still surley with battle, brought the white man up and threw him on the ground before Raa. Arnsdale was unconscious, but before the attack Raa had given orders not to slay him. White hostages, she was learning, were far more valuable than natives.

The Bantus, hysterical with fear, tried to stampede when the attack started. The charging apes bowled them over almost as they did the Somali, roughly collaring them. By the time Slaker appeared to quiet the Bantus, two of them were dead and several unconscious.

As soon as the battle was over, Slaker began picking up the soldier's guns. At a word from Raa, Mog went down, knocked them out of his arms. Then the giant brute began methodically breaking and twisting the rifles.

Slaker appealed to Raa to stop Mog. "We need them," he pleaded. "Guns mean power. We can handle the blacks with them."

Raa wordlessly waited until the scarred ape had destroyed the final rifle. Then she calmly turned her back on Slaker. Only the slaver and his men knew how to handle those deadly firesticks, and naive though Raa was, she wasn't fool enough to entrust such power to them.

The blonde assessed her losses. Arnsdale had killed one gorilla, badly wounded another. Two others were hurt, but not seriously.

"You won fairly easy this time," Helene said angrily as her gag was removed. "But enjoy yourself while you can, because from now on the days of you and your apes are numbered. Next time you may be one of those to die."

A faint, derisive smile curled Raa's lips. Any unspoken doubts the blonde had about Slaker's evil plans were swept away by this first swift triumph.

"Raa go now get Ki-Gor," she said. "You see who die."

And leaving Mog to direct the Ingagi trek back to their home area, the strange jungle girl sped away to backtrack Helene's trail. Slaker had impressed her with the importance of capturing the White Lord.

RAA set a swift pace, too swift to permit such conversation. But though Ki-Gor and N'Gesso were puzzled about the girl, they didn't mistrust her. After all, she had slain a leopard to save Ki-Gor, and now risking her life to help them free Helene.

Dusk was blotting out the jungle when Raa halted beside a tiny spring. Ki-Gor could sense a growing nervousness in the girl.

"We are nearly there?" he asked.

She replied, "Soon."

"You're very brave, he said, "to do this."

"Raa not forget you save her from bad ones," she panted.

She dropped to one knee by the spring, drank slowly and sparingly. When she was finished, she stood back as though to give the two men room.

"Drink!" she urged. "Cool. Good."

The hot, thirsty men needed no urging. Ki-Gor let N'Geeso drink first. Then as the small black scrambled up, the White Lord dropped his spear on the ground, dropped on all-fours and lowered his face to the water.

As Ki-Gor took his initial swallow, he heard a thud behind him, followed by a gasp and the sudden thump of something heavy hitting the ground. He whirled, straining to get to his feet, sensing some sudden danger.

Raa's club caught him just back of the ear as he spun up. He lay crumpled on his face.

"Weak, stupid fools!" she gritted. How easy it had been. And these were two the whole jungle was supposed to fear.

Raa stepped back, raised her face to the dark sky. A weird, bestial cry burst from her lips. Twice more in the next ten minutes she repeated the cry. Then, out of the night, her brutish followers came to crowd curiously around the unconscious men. Ki-Gor and N'Gesso didn't stir when the apes lifted them.

When Ki-Gor regained his senses, he was lying on a broad, heavy wooden table in a dark room. Moonlight streamed in a narrow column through a barred window beside him, sifted through a score of breaks in the roof above.

He blinked dully at the two shadowy figures standing by him. They were Helene and Lt. Arnsdale, but for a moment he couldn't understand why they should be there together, or, for that matter, why he was there himself. He stirred weakly, tried to raise himself.

Helene's hand pressed him back. "Don't try to get up yet, darling," she said, and it came to him vaguely that she had been crying.

Then abruptly he remembered. He had had a single fleeting glimpse of the knobbed club hurtling at him, with Raa's contorted face behind it.

"Raa!" he snarled, and despite his swirling senses, despite Helene's restraining hand, he plunged up. "She did it! But why? She was helping. "He broke off. "N'Gesso?" he demanded. "What about N'Geeso?"

From a corner of the room, a shaky voice answered, "I am alive. Think you a woman could succeed where a hundred men have failed?"

Ki-Gor gave a relieved grunt, raised a cautious hand to his throbbing head. "What trickery is this, Helene?" he demanded. "My mind reels so, I can make no sense of it."

But when Helene, with Arnsdale's help, had finished the incredible story, Ki-Gor's brain had been shocked into chill clarity.

"But the idea of using apes for slave raids, isn't all," Arnsdale told him, "We learned something else!"

"It was still daylight when they put us in here," explained the lieutenant. "Though most everything is in ruin, we found a lot of letters and papers in some cabinets and trunks. We wondered why we were put here, why the house looked like the owner had just gotten up one day and walked out."

Arnsdale's voice was trembling with excitement.

"We found this was a Dr. August Montgomery's place, a kind of experimental station. Seems he was carrying on some complicated study of gorillas. His wife and five year old daughter were with him. The way we figure it, Raa is that daughter."

"Yes!" broke in Helene. "Her name was Roberta. Some sudden tragedy must have happened, a native raid or an outbreak of the gorillas he kept for study—there's a big row of steel cages outside. Anyway, everyone except the child must have been wiped out suddenly."

Though a bit unsteady on his legs, N'Gesso had come up to listen. Ki-Gor pursed his lips, and in the moonlight you could see his eyes narrow in thought.

"It could happen, I suppose," he said slowly." Some of the very young apes were probably treated like pets. Left alone, the child would turn to them for companionship. And there would have been food enough stored here to keep her alive until the older apes took her in or she learned to forage herself.

His musing was interrupted by the practical-minded N'Gesso.

"One would rather speak of escape," sourly advised, "instead of how that she-devil was spawned. My knife, blowgun, darts, all are gone."

Helene moved closer to Ki-Gor.

"Slaker had your weapons taken," she said angrily, "and he was the one who wanted us put in here. The door is bolted, the windows barred and there are apes on guard all around the walls."

Though he felt terrible, Ki-Gor prowled and probed over the room for an hour, trying to find or think of some way out of their predicament. But his efforts were useless.

"We may as well sleep," he said finally.

"Sleep?" declared the astounded Arnsdale. "Who could sleep at a time like this?"

"We're safe until morning at least," said the White Lord matter-of-factly. "Raa was careful to capture, not kill us. She may change her mind tomorrow, and if so, we'll need our strength and wits."

HE STRETCHED out on the table. Without a word, Helene climbed up beside him, nestled her head in the crook of his arm. It seemed to Arnsdale that the White Lord fell asleep almost immediately. And like a nervous child, calmed by the presence of a parent, Helene dropped off a short while later.

The lieutenant turned to look for N'Geeso. The pygmy was sprawled on the floor, his arms thrown wide, snoring softly. Arnsdale was both distressed and disappointed. He had expected swift deeds, some miracle of high adventure from Ki-Gor, yet here the supposed jungle hero slept away the hours like a dullard unable to realize they might be his last ones.

"Jove!" he thought. "I've overestimated them all. They've just given up like whipped dogs."

Ki-Gor lounged by the window, looking idly out the window. His complete immobility exasperated the lieutenant. Neither his face not his manner showed any sign of worry, and from Arnsdale's viewpoint, there was certainly little sense, or for that matter coherence, in the few remarks the White Lord did make.

"That scarred ape is pretty much the boss after Raa, isn't he?" Ki-Gor asked Helene.

"Yes," answered Helene. "They all jump when he growls. She's the queen, but he's definitely the prime minister. Why?"

The jungle man shrugged. "Nothing. I was just thinking how odd it was for them to follow a female. The strongest bull usually leads the tribe."

Helene watched him, frowning thoughtfully. He kept staring out the window and after a time she returned to her conversation with N'Gesso. It was a full five minutes later before Ki-Gor spoke again.

"That poison pellet you have hidden on you, N'Gesso," he said idly, "is it from the new supply you mixed yesterday?"

"Poison hidden on me!" indignantly exclaimed the pygmy. "You know they searched me, took everything. Why, the idea!"

Ki-Gor smiled faintly. "I know a few things, Little Lion. You and everyone of your cutthroats carry a hidden pellet. For yourselves, if the wrong persons capture you. And sometimes for an unsuspecting enemy's food, after you've lulled him by putting aside your weapons."

N'Geeso grunted, glared swiftly at Helene and Arnsdale.

"It's new," he muttered.

More minutes passed while Ki-Gor gazed at the green world outside the barred window. Then he turned around and walked over to Arnsdale.

"Could I see that ring you wear?" he asked Arnsdale.

The lieutenant sighed, disgustedly thrust

his hand out. What a time to be looking at a ring, he thought. To his surprise, instead of bending to see it, Ki-Gor reached and slipped it from his finger.

"It's merely a good luck ring my girl gave me," he said testily. "Has little value other than for sentiment. That rat-faced feighter would have taken it, otherwise."

Ki-Gor inspected it closely, even testing with his fingernail the tightness of the four metal prongs which held the stone setting in the ring.

"I can use it," Ki-Gor said, after trying it on his little finger.

The lieutenant choked back a caustic question as to what possible use a worthless ring would be. After all, he considered, what difference did it make. The jungle man was too childish to argue with if he thought he could bribe one of the Bantus with the ring. Arnsdale wearily nodded he could have it.

To his dismay, he saw that Ki-Gor immediately pried the prongs open and took out the stone. Before he could protest, the White Lord called N'Geeso to produce the poison pellet. The poison was thick like resin, and using a splinter of wood, Ki-Gor carefully covered each of the prongs with it, smeared the remainder on the mounting. When he was finished, he dropped the ring into his empty knife scabbard.

A disturbance outside interrupted them. The door flung open and a group of apes led by Mog, pressed into the room. Slaker appeared in the doorway behind the beasts. His little, rat-like eyes darted to Ki-Gor, ignoring the others.

"I'm about ready to begin on you, smart boy," he grated venomously. "I'm gonna make you wish you'd never been born. Sam Slaker's gonna have his inning now, and what an inning it'll be." The pale scar of his mouth broke apart in a wolfish grin.

XI

KI-GOR gave no sign he knew the laver was in the room. The White Lord's whole attention was centered on Mog. He walked slowly three paces past the ape, looking him up and down. A thorough-going change had altered the jungle man, transforming his very features.

Arnsdale studied him queerly, an odd sensation pricking his skin. There was something suddenly menacing about Ki-Gor. He seemed to have grown larger, and beneath his bronzed skin the great muscles had come alive, swelling into writhing prominence.

In his slow, stiff-legged walk, in the taut set of his body was an animal belligerance. "That's it!" realized Arnsdale. "I've seen dogs bristle that way when they were about to fight." And he was certain of his interpretation when Ki-Gor's lips sheared abruptly back over his white teeth and a deep, rumbling snarl ripped from his throat.

Mog had stood motionless, only his red-rimmed, glittering eyes alive, as he watched the White Lord parade before him. But though not a muscle on his giant frame moved, so abnormally quiet was he, the stiff short hairs along his neck rose stiffly. One could feel, rather than see, an electric tension build up in the bull.

Brutish though he was, Mog recognized and did not like the insulting challenge offered by this hairless man-thing. He was Mog, the Feared One! Never in his life had he given ground before any animal.

He had mauled every bull in the tribe into submission. He had fought Kra, the Leopard, and won. He had broken Tar, the Lion, in his great hands like a rotten stick. When he roared his anger, all jungle creatures fled from his path, for they knew and feared him.

Raa had said not to slay this Hairless One, but Raa did not know of this insult. Mog heard how quiet the other bulls had become. They sensed, too, that this strange man-thing was challenging Mog alone, challenging him as another bull-ape would do. And they waited for their leader to crush the Hairless One as he did all who dared oppose him.

Mog's anger grew, building up until when Ki-Gor snarled, the giant brute's control snapped. He gave a thunderous roar, and shoving fully erect, pounded the vast expanse of his chest with knotted fists.

"No, Ki-Gor!" screamed Helene. "He's going to charge!"

Slaker, realizing too late what Ki-Gor

had precipitated, cried shrilly, "You fool! He'll tear you to bits!" And then as the thought struck him that Ki-Gor was deliberately committing suicide to escape torture, Slaker cursed vilely.

Neither Arnsdale nor N'Geeso spoke, the officer because he was too bewildered, N'Geeso because, guessing Ki-Gor's purpose, he was too awed by the jungle man's nerve to think of his own safety.

But before Mog could charge, Raa burst through the door and leaped in front of him. She spoke rapidly to the ape, patting and smoothing him, and gradually she edged him out of the door. He went with her, but his angry growls told that his anger was far from being quenched.

As soon as she got Mog away, Raa returned. "You——do——that!" she rasped at Slaker, apparently believing he had tried to goad Mog into killing the prisoners. Then, her lips curled with contempt, she smashed him in the face with her hand. He staggered back, cowering before her.

She gave a guttural command to the apes and immediately the beasts seized the prisoners, began roughly dragging them from the house. Raa stalked ahead of them, leading the way past rotted, collapsing buildings to what had been a broad, open field.

In the center of this field were gathered nearly a hundred Ingagi, both bulls and she's. Raa sat down on a raised mound of dirt and the prisoners were brought before her. Mog came out of the crowd, walking stiff-legged, and stood by the mound. His red little eyes glittered at Ki-Gor.

"Suu-laa-kur!" summoned Raa. The slaver, who had been sulking in the background because he feared the girl's wrath, hesitantly came forward. "Talk them," she commanded. "Say what Raa do."

The hangdog air dropped from the slaver. He saw she wasn't angry at him. She meant to go ahead with the plan he so cunningly had sold her on. He wet his pale lips with his tongue.

"Raa and I are going to call on the pygmies," he began silkily. "And do you know why? Well, we're going to make a nice, fair bargain with them. We're going to tell them that if they capture two hundred strong, young slaves for us we'll give them back their precious N'Geeso, Ki-Gor and Tembu George."

His lips slid back over yellowed teeth in a cruel grin. "No comment?" he said in mock surprise.

"N'Geeso spat in the dust, looked away disinterestedly.

"So you've decided your hairy brothers aren't such wonderful slave-gatherers after all," taunted Helene.

"It isn't that, my dear," said Slater hatefully. "Pygmies are no good as slaves themselves, but they can catch slaves. We'll save the apes for other jobs, things like going in and finishing off the little devils when they've weakened themselves enough warring on other tribes."

The loud trumpeting of an elephant sounded from the jungle off to Ki-Gor's left. As the sound ended, the sharp clear crack of breaking branches could be clearly heard. An elephant herd was on the move, foraging for tender leaves and shoots as it moved unhurriedly through the forest.

The apes stirred restively, muttering among themselves. They didn't like the elephants being so close.

SLAKER turned to Raa. "Tell them it's the same herd," he said impatiently, "that's been tramping back and forth around here for days. The elephants mean them no harm. Great Scot, they throw a fit every time they hear an elephant.

Following his instructions, Raa quieted the Ingagi. What Slaker said was true. The tuskers never sought trouble. It had to be forced on them.

"You're the smart boy, Ki-Gor," the slaver resumed. "What do you think of our plan? A great man like you should be worth two hundred slaves by himself."

Ki-Gor looked at him with distaste.

"You're a fool as well as a coward," he said evenly, "if you think the pygmies would believe your promise to free us. And as to Tembu George—well—I think he'll have his own ideas on this prisoner's business."

The elephant herd had come considerably nearer. As he talked, one part of Ki-Gor's mind followed the beasts, gauging their distance and their number.

"Tembu George is no brighter than

you," sneered Slaker. "We're going to take him with the same trick." He explained that Raa had left two apes the night before at the spring. "Whenever he gets that far, the apes will hurry here and tell Raa. She'll go into her act and lead the lambs into a foolproof ambush of certain death."

That was why so many Ingagi were assembled. Raa was going to throw the whole tribe against the Masai. Though Ki-Gor gave no outward sign, worry gathered in him.

"And as to the pygmies, they'll do our bidding, all right," continued Slaker. His face had grown more evil, and hate was a hot madness in his eyes. "You see we're going to show them two realistic examples of what will happen to N'Geeso, Tembu George, and you if they don't get the slaves and quick."

He turned and pointed across the open field toward three fresh mounds of dirt.

"There are three holes dug," he explained. "We're going to put Helen and this baby-faced soldier in two of them, bury them up to the neck. And then on a zebra I taught her to ride, Raa is going to give a demonstration of her skill with a club." He glanced around. "You follow me?"

He chuckled gleefully. That had made them all sit up and take notice, even that damnable Ki-Gor. Their faces were shocked, unbelieving.

"To make it sporting," he gibed, "she'll ride at a gallop. That may make her miss quite a few times. Going fast like that it isn't easy to crush a skull."

He babbled on, complimenting himself on thinking up the fiendish idea. N'Geeso would be put in the third hole, he explained, to get an idea of what was in store for him if his people failed to become slaves.

"But when we dump Helene and the soldier's bodies before them," declared Slaker, "they won't fail you. I think, though, you may want to send them a little order, just as a guarantee, after you've seen this work."

"Does he mean that?" Arnsdale asked wildly.

"Yes, he meant it," Helene answered, white-faced but in complete control of herself. "He's an insane killer and Raa is no more than an animal."

In that moment, Ki-Gor knew the greatest agony of his life. Gripped by three massive brutes, he was held helpless as a child. Helene was to be brutally slain before his eyes and he could do nothing to prevent it. He felt his own sanity reeling as Raa barked the order for the three prisoners to be buried.

The ape-guards lifted the victims, started at a run toward the freshly-dug holes.

"Get zee-bra," the blonde told Slaker, and he hurried away toward one of the tumble-down buildings, she strolled over to supervise the placing of the prisoners.

There was a rend of breaking wood, and a small dead tree at the edge of the field toppled over. A grey bulk appeared in the opening where the tree had been. Lazily, the elephant ambled onto the field, and with no more than a glance at the apes, turned westward.

OTHER huge beasts appeared behind the first elephant, until the whole herd of twelve, three of them young ones, was grazing a leisurely path to the west along the edge of the field. Mog snarled at this intrusion and the apes holding Ki-Gor bristled angrily though the unconcerned elephants were fully two hundred yards distant and moving further away with every step.

But Ki-Gor had grown more rigid than his captors. He recognized the vast beast leading the herd as his own half-wild pet, Marmo. Though the great bull ordinarily remained near Ki-Gor's camp, he had grown restive in the long absence of his master and had sought companionship with his own kind.

A desperate idea exploded in the White Lord's mind. If only he could attract Marmo, he might have a fighting chance to help Helene. He shouted with all his might, *"Marmo! To Me!"* startling the apes holding him.

The giant bull's trunk hesitated on its way to pluck a mouthful of grass, the tremendous ears shifted. Ki-Gor cried his name again and the bull slowed, turning his head. The apes had no inkling of what their prisoner was attempting, but they shoved him roughly, not liking his actions.

Raa spun and stared hard at the jungle

man, but she didn't suspect his motives any more than the brutes. Despite the treatment given him, Ki-Gor kept crying to Marmo, and gradually the elephant swung about. The giant would come forward a few yards, then stop as though puzzled, peer about nervously until Ki-Gor called again.

The strong Ingagi smell smothered Ki-Gor's scent, and the tusker couldn't understand why his master's familiar tones summoned him, when he could neither smell nor see the White Lord. But by fits and starts, the giant came on until he was within an easy spear throw of the apes.

The Ingagi grew terribly disturbed. Females knuckled about locating their young, while the bulls, thinking they were threatened by the elephant, grew belligerent. One ape released his hold on Ki-Gor, lumbered about, bellowing.

Slaker arrived at a gallop on Raa's zebra. From a distance, he had heard Ki-Gor's cries, seen the huge elephant draw closer. He understood instantly what the jungle man was about.

"Can't you see he's calling that blasted monster?" he burst out at Raa.

Her brow creased in surprise. To her an elephant was a creature to be given wide berth. It hadn't occurred to her that Ki-Gor could call a beast out of a wild herd. With a swift, wrathful command, she told one of Ki-Gor's guards to clap a paw over the jungle man's mouth.

Deeply concerned, she appealed to Slaker for some way to drive off the tusker. She explained that the apes were growing so angry they might try to attack the elephant and many would be slain.

Slaker pointed to where club-wielding gorillas guarded his Bantus. The suspicious Raa took no more chances with the blacks than she did with Slaker.

"Free my men and let them use those clubs," he demanded. "That devil is just tame enough not to hurt men, yet he's wild enough not to trust strangers. We'll get rid of him!"

As soon as Raa complied with his wishes, Slaker leaped off the zebra, rushed his men between the apes and Marmo. No longer hearing Ki-Gor's voice, the tusker had halted and was eyeing the angry mass of apes in puzzlement.

Marmo was confused. The men sounded angry and shook weapons at him. Was this some kind of trap? Had he only thought he heard Ki-Gor? Marmo trumpeted again, but he was only bluffing. Marmo was too wise to risk wounds from a white man's fire stick for no better reason than to display his power.

If Ki-Gor came to him and commanded that he scatter the men, then he would trample them into the earth, show them what Marmo's awful fury would accomplish.

With anguish, the helpless White Lord guessed what went on in Marmo's brain. He saw the great beast shift uncertainly, then turn and retreat fifty yards across the field. But as soon as Marmo got a safe distance from the men, he stopped and looked back, waiting to see if Ki-Gor would call once more.

The ape-guard on his right clasped one paw about Ki-Gor's upper arm, held the other over his mouth. As the ape shifted his weight so he could better follow what was going on in the field the White Lord's fingers brushed his empty knife-scabbard.

"But it isn't empty!" he remembered.

Slowly, so the fumbling of his fingers wouldn't attract attention, he drew the sheath up, tilted it until Arnsdale's good luck ring slid into his palm.

He maneuvered the ring until he could grasp it between the thumb and forefinger. Then cautiously, he pressed the pin-like prongs of the ring against the ape-guard's hip. He held his breath, pushed the ring hard enough to pierce the brute's thick skin.

The ape flinched, instinctively jerked his paw away from Ki-Gor's mouth to slap at what he thought was some stinging insect. The instant his mouth was uncovered, Ki-Gor was shouting to Marmo, knowing his voice would halt the elephant's retreat.

THE APE ROARED with fury, swung its club-like hand up for a blow that would batter his tricky prisoner senseless. But that blow never landed. The brute's arm faltered in mid-air, his huge lips jerking and twitching. He staggered, his roar abruptly changed into a queer agonized croaking.

His chest leaped and heaved like huge bellows trying to force air through a clogged pipe. Then his finger slid from Ki-

Gor's upper right arm and the beast toppled backwards.

Ki-Gor's other guard stared thunder-struck at his fellow. He barked excitedly at the sprawled figure. He shoved the jungle man out of his path, bent over the dead animal as his slow mind tried to probe this mystery.

Though the bull retained his grip on the prisoner's left shoulder, Ki-Gor's right hand was free. The White Lord stabbed the pronged ring into the guard's arm with a swift movement. The ape started, turned his head so quickly that he caught Ki-Gor's movement.

He glared suspiciously, straightened with slow menace. He reached out and pushed Ki-Gor angrily in the face. He snarled, slapped hard again. Suddenly, an agonized look contorted his face, and seconds later he was dead.

Marmo had swung about at the White Lord's call, and there was a more dangerous note in his trumpeting this time when he faced the line of Bantus. If only Ki-Gor could get to him, he might yet scatter the Ingagi long enough to save his wife and friends. But what chance did the jungle man have to reach the elephant?

Apes were all about him, blocking every avenue of escape. The nearest beast was the huge Mog who had turned in time to see the second ape-guard fall. Raa, too, momentarily speechless with surprise, was staring at the jungle man. In another instant, the blonde girl's lashing voice would send the whole tribe leaping in on Ki-Gor.

For any other man it would have been the end. But with his knowledge of the wild, Ki-Gor had one last thin thread of hope, a thread so slender that only extreme desperation could have driven even him to grasp it. It was a strategem for which he had laid the groundwork when Slaker and Mog first came to take him from the room.

Ki-Gor had deliberately goaded Mog to battle fury in the room. He had challenged the ape leader as another bull would do. He had done it because he realized that it was Mog's brawn that actually ruled the tribe. Perhaps Mog was one of the pets Raa had grown up with. In any case, he was the weapon she used to keep the Ingagi in line.

And if Ki-Gor could trick Mog into accepting individual battle and could defeat him, then by ape standards the jungle man would have won for himself the scarred ape's place and standing in the tribe. After all, it was not a far step from accepting Raa as one of their own kind to accepting the White Lord. But the main trick was to make Mog and the tribe look on him as a challenger seeking to supplant the scarred ape in the tribe, rather than a man fighting for his life.

That plan had been in Ki-Gor's mind when he left the room. That was why he had prepared the poisoned ring, because without the deadly pygmy poison he couldn't hope to defeat Mog. But the way Slaker had guided matters Ki-Gor never had an opportunity to put his plan in action.

Now when he had to fight Mog or die under the rush of the whole tribe, the ring already had been used twice and the further effectiveness of its poison was doubtful. Ki-Gor knew how terrible was the gamble he took, but his only other alternative was worse.

Ki-Gor slid the ring on the little finger of his right hand. He swelled his chest to its fullest expansion, battered it with his open palms, and with perfect mimicry, roared the challenge of an angry ape.

He took three quick steps toward Mog, stopped to repeat the roaring and chest beating. Mog bristled, a cavernous rumble rolling from his throat. Ki-Gor turned and strode arrogantly back to the two dead apes. He put his foot on one of them, giving the wierd, chilling gorilla cry.

Mog could not mistake his purpose. The Hairless One was boasting that he had slain the two guards and that he would slay Mog as easily. Like searing volcanic flame, rage burst up in the scarred ape. He watched Ki-Gor make another short rush toward him snarling and scowling.

Raa was shouting then for the tribe to swarm at the White Lord. But she was too late. With a single shattering scream, Mog rooted them where they stood. Twice had this puny man-thing dared affront him. Twice had this two-legged white grub faced him with an arrogance no other jungle denizen would have the courage to assume.

Now, no power on earth would keep Mog from taking the Hairless One in his great arms and crush him to a pulp. Forgotten in the red swirl of his anger were Raa and her vaguely understood scheme of holding men in bondage. Forgotten were the elephant and Slaker and the mysterious ease with which the man-thing had killed the two guards. Mog bellowed his wrath to the tribe, signalling his intention of personally destroying this challenger. And then, snarling steadily, he edged forward, wanting to get close enough to take Ki-Gor with a single rush.

But as the hideous giant knuckled forward, the White Lord suddenly streaked in, smashing his right fist against the scarred cheek and spun away. Mog shook the ground with his roars. He was outraged that the man should be the first to attack, but he wasn't hurt. A score of such blows landing simultaneously wouldn't have shaken his muscled bulk.

He raised to his full height, his tremendous arms outstretched. His beady red-streaked eyes watched his quary for a moment. Then abruptly he charged.

But Ki-Gor had known how Mog would react and he was ready. As the bull thundered down on him he waited until the last possible second, then ducked low, avoided the giant paw that hammered at him. As he slid under the upraised arm, he raked the ring across the brute's belly and side.

But before the jungle man could get set again, Mog had spun and was rushing at him. Ki-Gor summoned every bit of his speed, tried once more to avoid the clubbing arms and dive past the beast. The raging gorilla wasn't to be caught by the same trick twice.

Mog whirled with him, handling his immense weight with cat-like quickness and balance. And as he whirled, the bull connected a round house blow with Ki-Gor's shoulder. It was his forearm, not the granite like mass of his paw that connected.

The White Lord was torn from his feet, sent twisting ten feet through the air, his whole left side paralyzed by the blast of pain. He fell hard, rolling to a stop on his stomach. Mog thundered toward him gone utterly berserk.

Ki-Gor fought to get up, knowing death rushed upon him. But for once in his life his magnificent body couldn't respond to his commands. His nerves and muscles needed time to recover from the awful power of that blow. Yet there was no time.

More by sheer will than strength Ki-Gor scrambled his way to his knees. He knew he could never make it. There was no chance to escape the beast, and Mog's scream of triumph showed he realized, too his victim couldn't get away.

XII

BUT KI-GOR, dazed as he was, meant to die trying. He gathered his numb, quivering muscles, and then abruptly, like a startled frog, he threw himself sideways at the charging ape's ankles. He barely flung beneath the reaching paw, but he hit his target squarely.

The gorilla's feet shot from under him. His vast bulk, going at full tilt, suddenly reversed its whole position, with his heels going high and his head whipping toward the ground. He drove face first into the earth, striking with the force of a falling tree.

Despite the terrible fall, Mog was on his feet almost as soon as the White Lord. Though he was slightly shaken, the brute's greatest annoyance came from the dirt he had plowed into his eyes and mouth. Spitting and roaring, he pawed at his eyes, his squat, stump-thick legs already braced for another rush.

The watching apes were silent. It was obvious to them the end was near. Though by their standards the battle had hardly begun, they saw the White Lord was plainly unsteady on his legs, his lungs laboring to pump oxygen into a body shaken by the two collisions. Mog would get him on his next lunge.

To their amazement, however, it was Ki-Gor who drove forward first. Any expectation they had of seeing him actually make a fight quickly faded. The jungle man swung a disappointingly ineffectual over hand-blow at Mog's face, missing by fully two feet, and then jumped back.

What the Ingagi didn't know was that Ki-Gor had slid his ring from his finger, darted forward just as Mog bellowed. Not enough poison was left on the pointed prongs to harm the bull when Ki-Gor hit or scratched him, but a glance had told the jungle man that there was still some of the death-dealing resin caked on the actual mounting. He had taken advantage of Mog's momentary blindness to cast the entire ring into the beast's mouth, throwing it hard enough to lodge it in his throat for an instant.

Mog choked, struggling to dislodge the ring. With a tremendous cough, he raked it from his throat, caught it with his tongue and furiously spat it out. Then he raged forward at the jungle man, running erect, his long arms extended to net his prey.

Ki-Gor tried to dodge him, weaving and back-pedaling desperately, but like a steel clamp one great paw slammed closed over his shoulder. With that single hand, Mog lifted the White Lord and jerked him against his chest. The ape lashed his other arm about Ki-Gor's back, and applying bone-breaking pressure, he bared his fangs and bent to tear out the jungle man's throat.

Ki-Gor squirmed and fought, but against such brute power he was utterly helpless. He saw the cruel mouth open wide for the death bite. And then as the hideous head bent for his throat, a violent spasm wrenched Mog's face.

Ki-Gor felt the arms about him jerk wildly and suddenly the crushing pressure about him was gone. The ape was sagging against him, making odd croaking noises in his throat. The poison had taken effect.

Ki-Gor braced himself against the beast, began battering with his hands and uttering blood-curdling snarls. When the full weight of the gorilla came against him, he couldn't support it, so he caught the hairy body and made it seem he was throwing Mog.

He went down with the dead ape, continuing his play-acting by mauling and choking until it should seem that he had slain Mog with his bare hands.

Then he sprang away from the still form, hammered his chest and roared a victory cry. He swung slowly about, glancing at the astounded Ingagi. Raa was staring at him, dumb-founded by his swift and utterly unexpected victory.

Ki-Gor stalked beligerantly a few paces back and forth past the body, and then growling, he walked directly toward the massed apes. To his well-hidden relief, the wall of hairy bodies split apart before him. He sidled at a snail's pace, growling and turning his head as though searching for some bull who thought like Mog to challenge his might.

Then he was past the apes, his heart racing with the strain of the bluff he had successfully carried out. He put his hands to his mouth and called Marmo. A muttering broke out among the Ingagi behind him. Ki-Gor paid it no heed. He leaped forward, sprinted toward the elephant.

Slaker and his Bantus lay between the White Lord and Marmo, but the tusker recognized his master and trumpeting excitedly, he started to meet him. The slaver and his men tried furiously to turn the grey giant, but Marmo was certain now of his master's wishes and he plunged directly at the blacks.

ARMED with no more than clubs, the Bantus scattered out of his path, despite Slaker's profane efforts to hold them. Once the elephant got past, the slaver turned his attention to Raa, shouting for her to send the Ingagi at Ki-Gor from the front while he and the Bantus attacked from the rear.

Judging by what he would have done in his place, Slaker thought the White Lord was merely trying to save his own skin. Not until Marmo swung the jungle man onto his head and then raced directly toward where the prisoners were buried did the slaver realize what Ki-Gor intended.

"Kill them!" shrieked the running slaver to Raa. "Don't let him reach them! You kill them, while the apes get Ki-Gor!"

But Raa needed no instructions. When the first shock of seeing a man slay Mog had passed, she went insane with rage and grief. She was more intelligent than her followers, and one look at the body had told her that Ki-Gor had won by some evil man's trickery.

She pointed to the White Lord on the elephant, told the apes that he would use the huge beast to slay them all unless they dragged him from his perch.

And roused by the lash of her fury, the tribe surged out across the grass to intercept Ki-Gor. Raa waited only long enough to get them started, then she grabbed up her club and leaped astride the zebra.

Ki-Gor saw her mount the animal, knew

she meant to gallop down on Helene and the two helpless men, batter in their skulls before he could intercept her. But the zebra was half-wild, and frightened by the noise, it bucked, throwing Raa.

The blonde twisted cat-like and landed on her feet, still holding the halter. She fought the zebra savagely and finally mounted it again. The fall, though, had given Ki-Gor the time he needed to smash through the Ingagi, beat off the beasts that tried to clamber up the elephant.

Raa used her heels to spur the zebra into a gallop, straining to outrun the White Lord. She would have beat him to the prisoners by seconds had she been a better rider. But in her anxiety, she failed to control the zebra properly.

Ki-Gor rode Marmo in at an angle, meaning to block off from Helene. An experienced horsewoman would have swerved abruptly, cutting behind the running elephant and reached her objective. The blonde girl turned the other way, trying to outrun and cross in front of Marmo.

The White Lord simply veered the huge tusker suddenly, smashed into Raa. The zebra crashed down with its rider. They both fell directly in Marmo's path and the elephant's great feet pounded over them. As Ki-Gor glanced back at the bloody pulp pounded into the ground, his face tightened, but he could feel no real remorse.

In maneuvering to stop Raa, Ki-Gor had given the pursuing Ingagi time to draw near. He had to drive them off long enough for him to dig out Helene and the two men. He headed Marmo toward the apes, then slid from the elephant's back. Marmo was aroused now and ready to do battle with or without Ki-Gor's direction, so he could rely on the mammoth beast to scatter the gorillas.

The earth was soft about the taut-faced prisoners, and by clearing their shoulders, Ki-Gor was able to pull them out of the holes. As he freed Arnsdale, the last one, Ki-Gor heard Slaker exhorting his Bantus to close in.

The White Lord looked for Marmo, saw there was no chance to use the elephant either to battle or outrun the Bantus. The tusker had the Ingagi in headlong flight across the field and was taking a bloody toll of the slower bulls. In his battle frenzy, Marmo was definitely beyond recall.

Ki-Gor had known Slaker would come in from the field to try to stop their escape, but he had counted on having Marmo's help. Even had he, N'Geeso and Arnsdale been armed, they would have been unable to fight the slaver's force. The odds were too great.

There was no choice but to make a run for the forest. They sprinted toward the path along which Raa had brought them as prisoners the previous day. But the four were worn by their cruel experience, and the Bantus steadily moved up behind them.

If Slaker's men had had spears, they would have cut them down a hundred yards from the trees. As it was, the blacks and their savage leader were no more than twenty paces back when Ki-Gor's little group entered the jungle. Like a pack closing in, the Bantus gave cry.

"My—strength's—gone," gasped Helene. "Can't—run—more."

"You must!" commanded Ki-Gor, though in his heart he knew it was useless.

N'GEESO didn't speak, but his face was grey with effort. Arnsdale was beginning to lurch drunkenly, every breath a quick, pained sob. Twice Ki-Gor's steadying hand had kept the young officer from falling.

The White Lord knew but one way to buy Helene and his friends a little more time. He lagged back, careful not to let them guess his intention. He was the game Slaker wanted most. By suddenly turning and charging into the club-wielding blacks, he could delay them for a time—for as long as he lived.

Ki-Gor gritted his teeth, steeled himself to turn. Then a fierce, wild clamor erupted all about him. Massive ebony figures yelling like devils burst out of the underbrush and engulfed the startled Bantus. With spear and sword, Tembu George and his Masai charged into the men they mistakenly had shown mercy to once before, and it was clear the same mistake was not to be repeated again.

When he heard the Masai war-cry, Slaker, leaped off the path, hoping to hide in the underbrush. The sight of the Masai chieftain, Tembu George, racing down on him was enough to turn Slaker, send him fleeing back onto the path.

In his fright, the slaver got turned around so that he burst out of the bush almost on top of Ki-Gor instead of returning to his men. He screamed in fear when he saw the White Lord, lashed out awkwardly with his club. Ki-Gor ducked the clumsy blow, plowed his right hand into the slaver's belly.

Slaker doubled over, and as he did, the White Lord locked his fingers around the hated man's neck just above the iron slave collar. His fingers bit deep, choking off the shriek which rose in the slaver's throat. In another minute the crazed, cowardly killer was dead, and Ki-Gor, still holding him by the neck, lifted his body as he would a dango's carcass and threw him off the trail.

When Ki-Gor looked around, the Masai had finished their work, and Tembu George was hurrying to him, sorrowfully apologizing for not having reached them before.

"You came in time," Ki-Gor said, putting his hand on the Masai chieftain's shoulder. "Had you come earlier, you'd have walked into an ambush." He explained about Raa and the apes. "Two bulls were supposed to notify Raa of your approach, but you must have slipped past them, because they never did show up."

Tembu George smiled thinly.

"Those two Ingagi lie dead by the spring," he declared. "We saw them watching us, and thanks to N'Geeso's poison on our arrows, we killed them. We meant to slay every one we saw, because after reading the spoor around the spring, we thought the tree-people had slain both you and N'Geeso."

Arnsdale, slightly awed by the tall, granite-faced Masai, edged his way up to the White Lord. He waited, his face troubled, until Tembu George finished talking.

"About that ring, Ki-Gor..." he began hesitantly.

Ki-Gor frowned, "Oh, yes," he said, "That was your good luck ring!" All I know for us to do is go back and get it."

"No, no!" exclaimed Arnsdale, missing the twinkle in the jungle man's eyes. "You misunderstand me. I want to tell you I'm sorry for acting rude when you asked to use it. I'll probably lose my commission for failing so miserably to carry out my orders, but because of you I've lived through a whole, exciting lifetime today. I believe it will be worth the disgrace."

Kindliness was in Ki-Gor's smile as he looked down at Arnsdale's serious face.

"You won't lose any commission, I promise you," he said. "You've acquitted yourself with honor and I mean to go to the coast with you to tell your commanding officer that very fact. Actually, you'll have an impressive report to make."

"Jove!" said Arnsdale, as he watched Ki-Gor walk away. "What an amazing fellow."

There was a low, merry laugh beside him. Helene had heard the words he had unconsciously spoken aloud.

"You're right," she said, "he really is an amazing fellow. I'm quite proud of him."

THE GRANDDADDY OF ALL PULP CONVENTIONS!
PULPCON
2009
JULY 31 – AUG 2
RAMADA PLAZA HOTEL &
CONFERENCE CENTER
Columbus, Ohio
VISIT PULPCON.COM
FOR DETAILS & UPDATES
THOUSANDS OF
PULP MAGAZINES
FEATURING
AUTHORS SUCH AS
RAYMOND CHANDLER
CARROLL JOHN DALY
NORBERT DAVIS
STEVE FISHER
ERLE STANLEY GARDNER
FRANK GRUBER
DASHIELL HAMMETT
HORACE McCOY
FREDERICK NEBEL
ROGER TORREY
RAOUL WHITFIELD
CORNELL WOOLRICH
DIME DETECTIVE MAGAZINE
DETECTIVE FICTION WEEKLY
BLACK MASK
THE GLASS KEY
New & Improved!
NOW FEATURING MORE PAPER COLLECTIBLES
SUCH AS MOVIE POSTERS, BIG LITTLE BOOKS,
LIMITED EDITION HARDCOVERS AND SERIES BOOK
B-MOVIES AND SERIALS, OLD-TIME RADIO SHOWS
COLLECTIBLE PAPERBACKS & MORE!

READ
ATLAS SHRUGGED
BY AYN RAND

Made in the USA